What Happened Next

Jon Colt

Prologue

'Name?'

'Winters, sir. Malcolm Winters.'

'Watch your step off the bus there, Mr Winters.'

'Thank you, I will.'

'My name is Officer Cambridge. I'll be your greeter today. Apologies if you can't hear me through the mask. It does tend to muffle.'

'I can hear ya.'

'Did you have a pleasant journey?'

'Wasn't too bad. About three hours too long, though.'

'Yeah, they built this place out in the sticks for a reason. Double-yew... Double-yew... Ah, Winters. Yep, you're on the list. Let me just tick your name off here. Oh. Says here you've got a record. Anything we need to worry about?'

'I did three months in jail twenty-odd years ago.'

'Hmm, I see. What did you do?'

'Broke a kid's jaw at college.'

'Would you say you're still violent?'

'No. Mostly not.'

'Right. I'll write *no risk*. Now, where do you hail from?'

'Masterson.'

'Masterson. I've heard of it. Is that here, in New Hampshire?'

'Yes sir, it is.'

'Well, then you're in the right place. Welcome to the New Hampshire Distanced Living Center, Mr. Winters.'

'It's a lot bigger than I thought it'd be. Figured you'd be putting us away in chicken coops.'

'Yeah, it's sizable. A thousand homes, a library, a hospital, a schooling hall, a function hall, a chapel, a farm, and a fishing lake. The result of six months of intensive construction from some of the finest firms the state has to offer. Mad rush to get it finished, given the circumstances.'

'How tall is that perimeter wall?'

'Twenty meters. Tall enough to keep everybody inside, that's for sure. Electric wire around the top, too. Now, if you've got this far, I imagine you're pretty set in your decision.'

'I am.'

'But I have to read you this notice from the United States Crisis Authority, all the same.'

'Go right ahead.'

'Dear Avoidant, once you pass through the gates behind me, you will never be permitted to come back out. You will live out the rest of your days inside the New Hampshire DLC, and you will be buried in the allotted cemetery on the far east side. Contact with the outside world is strictly prohibited. Do you understand?'

'I understand.'

'And you've already surrendered your cell phone? And

there are no electronic communication devices in your luggage?'

'Correct. They combed through my bags before they let me on the bus.'

'Alright then, Mr. Winters. Now, that one was from the government. This one is from me. This really is your one and only chance to remain in the general population. To have the freedom to get on a plane. To go to the beach. To spend Christmas with your loved ones. To my right, there is a tent. Inside the tent, there is a registered nurse. Should you wish, she will administer a dose of the Lavitika vaccination. It's completely painless. You may then board a shuttle bus, and it will return you to your home – to your family and friends, and you will not need to enter the DLC. Now, please consider this very carefully. Do you wish to receive the vaccination?'

'Over my dead body, sir.'

'Alright. Then please pass through those gates, Mr. Winters. You'll find a desk just on the other side. The officers there will assign you a chalet. Have a pleasant future, Mr. Winters.'

'Thank you.'

'Next!'

Chapter 1
An Ordinary Sunday in Masterson

The day the world started to end, it was hot outside. When the sun came up over Masterson that fateful Sunday, nobody could have foreseen the carnage that was about to unfold. Before lunchtime, half the citizens of that sleepy New Hampshire town would be dead.

It was a little after nine, and it was already getting warm out. Dick Carnaby on The Weather Roundup said it would hit a hundred degrees by midday. But nothing seemed out of place in Masterson. It looked like a typical Sunday morning. Sprinklers showered down on luscious green lawns. Songbirds fluttered from one tree to the next. The paperboy peddled through the streets, tossing the Sunday Gazette onto porches. And perhaps most traditionally of all, Milo Winters and his dad were out on the driveway, washing the car - a chore they tackled together every weekend.

Milo's mom had insisted that they both wear their thick-brimmed hats. The ones they used to take fishing, back before Milo became a brooding teenager. But while Milo could give fishing the cold shoulder, he couldn't say no to washing the car with his dad – it was the only condition of his weekly allowance, which he'd been saving up for the latest Goblin Avenger game.

Besides, it wasn't a particularly hard chore. He just had to stand on the driveway and hold the bucket up every time his dad came over to re-dunk his sponge. Bucket holder, as his dad called it, had been Milo's job every Sunday morning since he was too young to remember. He was thirteen that hot, awful day, so he was well-practiced by then.

Milo was scrawny and pale and had an untidy mop of mousy-blonde hair. He wore an oversized white t-shirt, with black lounge pants.

In contrast to his son, Dallas Winters was tall and well-built – the result of many an evening spent with the lifting bench in the garage. His hair was dark, and he wore it in a crew cut. He had an all-year-round tan even though he spent most of his time in the office, and he wore ugly, tinted glasses that went brown in the sun.

'Binko, play The Berries,' Dallas said as he dunked his sponge into Milo's bucket.

The smart speaker he'd set down on the lawn started to play. The Berries were a little-known and even-littler-appreciated barbershop band from the sixties. Dallas had become obsessed with them after hearing them on Throwback Hour on Radio Six. Now he played them on loop: while driving round town in the Mamba, while mowing the backyard, while working out, even while washing the car on a Sunday morning.

Milo watched his dad run the sponge over the car's hood. The suds turned crusty white the second they touched the Mamba's skin, and vapor drifted softly upwards into the hot morning air.

That car was his most treasured possession. It was a

classic red sportster (Volcanic Red, if Dallas was to correct you) from the late seventies. He'd gotten it five years back when it came up for auction at Riley's Motor House, down on Benvale Street.

He knew he shouldn't have bought it, but when his dad died, it triggered something in him, and he felt like life was too short not to treat yourself once in a while. So he went down to the bank and withdrew half his retirement pot (even though he was still a good thirty years off retiring).

'I'll have three long decades to build it back up,' he told his wife, but she wasn't the biggest fan of that reasoning.

That was all ancient history now, though. Milo's mom had gotten over it, in the end. She even admitted it was a nice car. She might mention the whole debacle, though, once in a while if Dallas ever questioned some lavish online purchase of hers. *Remember the time you spent half your retirement fund on that fucking car?* He'd bite his tongue pretty quickly.

The Berries suddenly cut off, and a news reporter began broadcasting, 'More casualties are being brought into emergency rooms across the states, with as yet undiagnosed symptoms. The strained services are urging you to...'

'Binko, play The Berries!' Dallas demanded.

The blue LED wheel on the front of the smart speaker started to spin, and then his favorite barbershop quartet rang out across the garden again.

'Smart speaker, my ass.'

A breeze tickled down the street, and Milo heard something flap around in the gutter. He set the bucket down and went to take a closer look.

It was a mask, from the virus, caught in the storm drain. All beat-up and sun-faded. It'd been a long time since he'd seen one. Two years, probably. The Winters used to have a different color for each family member for when they went out to the mall. They hung on nails, by the front door.

His little sister Sally was born just before the lockdown and was too young to wear one, but their mom would pull her blanket up over her nose in the buggy.

Milo was glad to be rid of masks. They made his face hot and sticky, and the elastic cut into his ears. If he ever had to wear one for more than a couple of hours, he'd be guaranteed a fresh zit or two on his chin or just above his lip.

Everyone over the age of twelve got their Lavitika vaccinations down at the school. Milo and his classmates couldn't use the gymnasium for months because there was a queue snaking through it all day. Sheriff Callow had to set up camp on-site because protestors kept trying to burn it down. Before they were sent away, of course.

The virus went away after that. The vaccine had done its job. No more masks. No more video call quizzes with Grandma and Grandpa every Thursday evening. No more staying out of the spare room where the consoles were set up because his dad's makeshift office had taken over.

Things had gone back to normal. It was easy to go about your day without remembering the virus – unless you drove down Hughes Drive, of course. There's a big memorial plinth there, next to the library, with all the names chipped into the marble. Or unless a battered old face mask blew into your life.

'Milo, where's my bucket holder?' Dallas called over his shoulder. He was standing there, clueless, with a bone-dry sponge.

I daydream for a few seconds, and the whole operation falls apart, Milo thought.

He picked up the bucket again and took it over to his dad so he could sink his sponge in.

The fire alarm started going off inside the house. The boys on the driveway weren't too concerned. It had become a typical sound on a Sunday morning. Mrs. Winters would often load up the griddle with bacon and then get distracted by Sally.

Milo watched as his mom threw open the window and wafted out the smoke with an oven mitt. He could hear the sound of the bacon sizzling in the pan.

'Smells good, hon,' Dallas shouted across the lawn. He turned to Milo and whispered, 'Smells like that time we let Uncle Malc put gasoline on the barbecue.'

Milo smiled.

His dad worked the sponge into the ridge, along the bottom of the windshield. When he peered back into the bucket, he saw there was nothing left but some black swill at the bottom, so he dropped the sponge inside.

'Right, time to hose her down.'

Dallas went to the back of the driveway and started to unreel the hose. When he reached the Mamba, he suddenly stopped to clutch at his stomach. The nozzle clattered onto the concrete and came off. Water spewed out from the open hose end.

'Are you ok?' Milo set the bucket down and stepped towards him.

His dad was hunched over, holding his belly with one hand and his knee with the other, breathing deeply.

'Shall I get mom?'

His dad didn't reply. He just sucked in a breath through clenched teeth.

'I'll get mom.'

'No, no. Don't worry your mother!' he shouted. 'It's just

gas, I think. It was hurting last night. It'll pass in a sec.' He straightened up, took a few more slow, controlled breaths, and then forced a smile. 'All good!'

'You sure?'

'Yeah, yeah. Come on. Let's get this finished up. Breakfast will be ready soon.'

His dad fixed the nozzle back onto the hose and rinsed away whatever suds hadn't burnt off in the sun.

'Go and get the rags, kiddo!'

Milo fetched the box of rags from the garage. Every time his mom wore a hole in a kitchen towel, it would end up deposited in the rag box. Every Sunday Milo and his dad would use them to buff the car dry to prevent any nasty streak marks.

The air was suddenly filled with the ringing of a bike bell and the screeching of brakes.

Mrs. Sampson and her children came to a halt on the road, next to them. The three of them were straddling a bike each and touched their feet down to steady themselves.

The Sampson family lived a few doors down. They used to barbecue together all the time, before Uncle Malc offended them.

Mrs. Sampson rode at the front. She was a petite woman, with a blond bob. The basket fixed to her handlebar cradled two over-stuffed grocery bags that were starting to tear in the corners.

Behind her rode her daughter, Becca. She was a pale girl, with a dyed black fringe, purple lipstick, heavy eyeliner, and a choker clasped around her neck. She wore black from head to toe – from the leather jacket down to the fishnet stockings that fed into her boots. She was a year older than Milo.

Milo blushed uneasily as she fixed her deadly gaze on him, with her arms folded firmly across her chest.

Given a choice, Becca would be at home, in her room, with the blinds closed, and Courting Armageddon blaring out of her Binko. But her father had been puking his guts up all morning, and the stench had crept into every room in the house. For once she was happy to be out, in the open air.

Brody rode at the back of the Sampson convoy. He was nine. Fairly heavyset. Pale like his sister, with short brown hair, and watchful green eyes. He was very quiet. But very clever, mechanically speaking. He was always building some contraption or another. '*He has a touch of the autism,*' Mrs. Sampson announced to everyone during one barbecue.

There was a special assembly about autism at Milo's school one morning, on behalf of Brody, not long after the doctors diagnosed him. His name wasn't mentioned, but all the kids knew who it regarded. They all turned their heads and sniggered at him as he stared blankly at the stage.

'You two will have to stop by and do mine next,' laughed Mrs. Sampson as she rested on her bike at the roadside, with both children parked behind her.

If Milo had a dollar every time someone had said that to them over the years, he'd have his own Mamba by now. It seemed the mandatory thing to say when seeing somebody washing a car.

'Put Dan to work! It's a nice enough morning,' Dallas said, with a smile.

'Oh, he ain't feeling too well,' Mrs. Sampson said. 'We just went to the shop to get him some meds, didn't we?'

Brody didn't react. Becca nodded lightly – her hateful scowl still fixed on Milo.

'Poor Dan,' Dallas said. 'What's up with him? Have you called Doctor Singh?'

'Can't get through to the doc. Dan's been in bed two days now. Puking a lot. Started with bad stomach cramps.'

Milo looked at his dad.

'Probably a bug going round,' Dallas told her. 'Tell him I send him my best.'

'Will do!'

Milo's dad shifted his gaze to Brody, who was staring back at him, expressionless.

'How's it going, Brody?' he asked.

Brody didn't say anything.

'Oh, he's just fine,' Mrs. Sampson said.

'Built anything cool lately?'

Again, Brody didn't reply. He just stared. Becca smirked.

'Another slingshot,' his mom said, disapprovingly.

'Ah. I still haven't fixed my fence from the last one,' Dallas half-laughed.

At one of the barbecues the families used to enjoy together, Brody had pulled his latest contraption from his backpack. It was a wooden box, about the size of a shoebox, with a hole in one end, a lever on the top, and a small trigger on the bottom. He then plucked a small rock out of the flowerbed. He fed it into the hole, pulled back the lever, aimed it at the fence, and then pulled the trigger. It blasted a hole through the wooden slats, a foot wide.

'Yee-haw! This mute little dipshit is good for something after all!' Uncle Malc had shouted, so excited he spilled beer all down himself. The Sampsons went home, both embarrassed and insulted, and they hadn't arranged another meet-up since.

'Anyway,' Mrs. Sampson said, as she stood by the road-side, 'we better get these meds back home.'

She cycled away, and her children followed.

A short while after, a pale boy came along the street, dragging his feet. He had long, black, oily hair that had been slicked back with a comb. His eyes were milky blue, with wild black pupils. A bright pink scar ran from his left nostril, down through his upper lip. He wore a battered black leather jacket – even on the hottest of days. Under it, a white t-shirt was tucked into his jeans.

His name was Richard Lachance. But at school he insisted that everybody call him Rex. And at school you did what Rex said.

Milo froze as he locked eyes with him and watched him slowly breeze by, the way a gazelle watches a passing lion.

Every school has that one sadistic prick who thrives on terrorizing others. In Masterson High, Rex was that prick.

Last year Milo had suffered his first serious run-in with Rex. He'd been shoved in the corridor before, sure, but Rex and his two buddies did that to everyone. One gray Thursday morning, though, things ramped up a gear.

'Breakfast is on the table!' Milo's mom called through the window.

Dallas finished buffing the hood and then threw his rag onto the driveway. Milo moved his gaze away from Rex, who was further along the street now, and threw down his rag, too. They looked the car over and then headed inside.

Chapter 2
Life Rafts on a Great Black Lake

Sally sat in her high chair at the table. She had mousy-blonde hair, like her brother, and a few small freckles dotted her cheeks.

A bowl of small, cut-up cubes of bacon and hash brown sat on the tray in front of her. The bowl had suckers underneath to stop her throwing it across the room. She swung her chubby legs happily as she stuffed the breakfast cubes into her mouth.

Dallas set the smart speaker down on the kitchen counter and then went to sit next to Sally.

'Wash your hands first, both of you!' Milo's mom said.

Jill Winters was a short woman, with curly blonde hair. She had a stubby little nose. Her summery dress was over-sized and loose, and it danced as she circled the table, filling a round of glasses with OJ from the carton.

Milo rolled his eyes and then lathered up his hands with soap at the sink. His dad did the same. They toweled them dry and then came over to the table. Milo drew up his usual chair. His dad kissed Sally on the forehead and then drew up his.

What Happened Next

The plates each had three rashers of well-done bacon, hash browns, two pancakes, and a small mound of scrambled eggs. They started to eat.

'I saw him go by,' Jill said.

'Who?' Dallas asked as he tucked in.

'That *Rex*. The demon boy that burnt our son.'

'He went by?' Dallas lifted his eyebrows. 'I would've kicked his ass.'

'Yes, well, his uncle did that. Very publicly.'

'Good,' Dallas grunted. He folded a pancake in half and bit into it.

As Milo sat, running his fork through his eggs but not bringing any to his lips, he thought back to his confrontation with Rex the year before.

* * *

It was third period, and Milo found himself sitting in Mrs. Gleeson's algebra class while she etched equations onto the whiteboard. He'd drunk a liter of Turtle Cola at lunch, and his bladder was starting to sting.

'Toilet break, Mrs. Gleeson?'

'Make it quick, Mr. Winters,' she said; her eyes not leaving the board.

Milo burst into the first floor toilets. He was already peeing onto the urinal cakes when he realized he wasn't alone in the room.

A silvery canopy of smoke hung just below the bar lights overhead. He turned to see one of the stall doors come open, and out came Rex and his two friends, Dean and Brandon. Whenever you saw Rex, you could safely bet that Dean and Brandon weren't too far away.

Dean was tall. He had a shaved head, large ears, and a

lazy eye. All the kids at Masterson High called him 'the inbred', just never to his face.

Brandon was the stockiest of the three. He had two chins, and his shirt didn't quite cover his stomach. His hair was always plastered in gel, forming a crown of twisted, little spikes.

They'd been passing around a Gunslinger cigarette. Now it sat perched between Rex's lips. The three of them quickly surrounded Milo, circling him like chuckling hyenas.

'Winters, that is one tiny dick,' Rex said, as he clasped a hand on Milo's shoulder and peered over it, at the pink appendage.

Milo stopped peeing immediately. The last of the urine gurgled out of the trough. He quickly tucked it back into his pants, tugged up the zipper, and made to leave. But he couldn't leave. Rex's two friends had already formed a wall, and they towered above him, mean-faced and ugly.

'Where you going, Winters? To rat on us for smoking?' asked Dean.

'Nuh-no, just need to get back to class,' Milo said.

The three boys laughed.

'Little nerd, ain't he, boys?' Brandon said.

'I think we need to make him man up a bit,' Rex suggested.

'I think that's a great idea,' Dean agreed.

Milo tried to leave a second time, but they blocked his way again.

'Look, I'm not gonna say anything to anyone,' he said. 'Honest. Just let me go.'

'Unbutton his shirt, boys,' Rex said.

Dean and Brandon looked at each other, a little puzzled, but they did as they were told. They always did.

They grabbed an arm each to steady Milo and then ripped his shirt open, exposing his bare, pasty chest.

'What are you doing?' Milo asked as he struggled. But he couldn't pull his arms free. The boys were too big and too strong.

Rex took the last scrag-end of cigarette between his finger and thumb and brought its amber tip into Milo's flesh. It hissed as it bore through the skin, and a nasty, white plume of vapor shot up into the air.

Milo screamed, and tears poured down his cheeks. The boys let him fall to his knees.

'Don't think we manned him up any,' Rex said, with a grin.

He flicked the ashy butt into Milo's hair, and then the three of them left. The door clunked shut behind them, and then the room was filled only with the sound of gentle whimpering.

Milo didn't say a word to anyone after he left the bathroom, with his shirt hanging open, and blood trickling from the hole in his chest. He didn't even collect his bag or his books from Mrs. Gleeson's room. He walked straight out of the school gates, sobbing and sniffling.

When he got home, he was hoping to slip upstairs to his room without being seen. But instead, he found his mom kneeling in the hallway in front of Sally, zipping up her little coat.

Jill looked up from the zipper to see him standing in the doorway, with his shirt sides drooping down, and his bloody chest on show.

Five minutes later, she was shouting *Who did it?* for the twentieth time. He was perched on the edge of the sofa now, trembling, with a bag of ice clutched to his chest. His mom paced the room, phone in her hand.

'It... it... it doesn't matter,' he stammered.

'Where the fuck is the receptionist?' Chirpy waiting music piped out of the phone, on loudspeaker. 'You better tell me who did this. I'm going to find out.'

Milo shook his head. 'It doesn't go away. It just gets worse. If you call him out on it, if he gets in trouble, it'll just get worse for me. Don't you understand?'

'Nobody gets away with this, My. You'll never see him again, I promise. I'm gonna get him expelled. Just tell me his name.'

Milo sighed. 'Lachance.'

'Lachance? Is he related to Vinny Lachance? With those awful ads on the TV?'

Milo shrugged. 'I don't know. I heard he lives with his uncle.'

'Hello? Mrs. Winters?' the receptionist's voice came over the line.

'Yes, I'm here.'

'Oh, good. We're glad you called. Milo has skipped a class. He told Mrs. Gleeson he was going to the toilet; then, he was seen marching right out of school.'

'Are you fucking kidding me?'

'Mom!'

* * *

An hour later, Milo sat in the small waiting room outside Principal Langley's office, with his fingers laced together, and his head hanging low over his lap. He could hear his mom shouting at the principal through the frosted glass door opposite.

Beside him Rex sat, sprawled back, with his head resting against the paneled wall behind his chair.

'You're so fucking dead, Winters,' Rex said, quietly enough so that the secretary sitting in the corner of the room couldn't hear.

Milo said nothing. He was too busy picturing the horrors he'd face daily from that day forward, at the hands of Rex and his two buddies. Cigarette burns were nothing, compared to what was in store for him. He was certain of that.

'Can I go take a piss?' Rex asked the secretary. 'I'm bursting.'

'Language!' she snapped. 'And no. The principal will be ready for you soon. Once he's spoken with your uncle.'

'My uncle?' Rex sat forward. '*He's* coming in?'

Heavy footsteps thundered down the corridor outside. They grew louder and closer until, eventually, the door flung open, and a man in a pink suit charged through it.

He was about fifty. He was caked in fake tan and wore a bad wig that had slipped while he was running from the car.

Milo *did* recognize him from TV. He didn't know who his mom was talking about earlier. He only knew him by the name '*The RV King*'. His ads would pop up on StreamTube while he and his dad watched old clips from Junkyard Rescue.

He'd spring out of the doorways of the RVs on his lot, shouting out ridiculously low prices, and would always sign off with, *For royal deals on recreational vehicles, come and see the RV King!*

Rex seemed to shrink in his seat the second he saw his uncle.

'What the fuck have you done now?' the man asked.

Rex said nothing. He just stared at the floor, wide-eyed.

The principal's secretary stood up. 'Mr. Lachance?' she asked.

The man hadn't seen her sitting there, tucked away in the corner.

'Oh, hello, dear. Sorry. I was running late. I got a call at work and raced over here.' He caught a glimpse of his reflection in the glass and straightened his wig. 'Am I too late to see the principal?'

'No, not at all. Just knock on the door,' the secretary said. 'He's expecting you.'

The man tapped his knuckles on the frosted glass.

Jill stopped shouting momentarily. The principal called through the door, 'Come in!'

The man in the pink suit stepped inside and closed the door behind him. There were some low, muffled voices. And then some loud, excitable voices. And then the door swung open again so fast that its handle punched a hole into the wooden paneling that lined the wall.

'Cigarette burns?' the man shouted, as he came at Rex. 'What the fuck is wrong with you?'

Rex quickly got to his feet. His eyes were full of fear. His mouth hung ajar.

Milo never thought he'd see Rex look that way. He always assumed Rex was the kind of guy that wasn't scared of anybody. Yet here he was, shaking like a shitting dog. The most surprising thing to Milo, though, was that he didn't enjoy seeing Rex like this.

'Mr. Lachance!' the principal hollered behind him. 'Please! Let's deal with this correctly! Step back into my office. Please!'

But Mr. Lachance couldn't hear him. He was focused only on his nephew, who he lumbered towards, heavy-footed; eyes mad and locked on target.

Rex stepped backwards. His uncle came at him, still. He stepped backwards further and crossed the small waiting room until his back pressed up against the door. But the door hadn't fully caught on its latch, and Rex stumbled backwards, out into the hallway. He fell onto his ass and looked up in terror as his uncle continued to advance towards him.

The end-of-period bell rang. Within seconds, the door to Mrs. Sanderson's room came open, and her geography class filed into the corridor; all talking and laughing as they hoisted their bags up over their shoulders. But they soon fell silent when they came across the sight of Rex cowering on the floor while his uncle stepped towards him.

'Your father died before he could beat the sick out of you,' he said, as he unbuckled his belt and slipped it out of the loops in his suit trousers, 'but by God, am I gonna do it for him.'

He wrapped the soft end of the belt around his hand and grasped it tight. The golden buckle dangled free, and it glimmered under the corridor's bright lights.

Rex started to crawl backwards. 'Please,' he whimpered, breathlessly, almost too softly to be heard.

Another classful of students joined the traffic jam in the corridor. Mr. McGuerry's class wandered along shortly after that. Soon, there were over a hundred confused, young faces watching the scene unfold.

'Mr. Lachance!' the principal pleaded. 'Please, Mr. Lachance! Step back into my office!'

But Mr. Lachance ignored him, still. His nephew had been dumped on him eight years ago, after his brother had run a pickup truck into a tree after too many whiskeys down at Club Hellfire. Every other week since, he'd been called into the principal's office about one thing or another.

Each year the severity grew worse. It started off with simple bullying. Then it was selling cigarettes. Punching holes in the library wall. Flushing someone's head down the toilet. Taking pictures up girls' skirts. Bringing a knife into school. Poisoning the school gerbil with antifreeze. And now, burning another student's flesh with a cigarette.

If this didn't end *right now*, Rex would be the next high school shooter. Mr. Lachance was sure of it. He'd had dreams about it, in fact. He saw Rex stalking the hallways, opening every door and emptying a clip into each room. That's why he'd moved all the guns out of the house and hid them somewhere he knew Rex wouldn't find them.

Mr. Lachance brought the belt up over his shoulder and stared down at his nephew for a few moments. He could feel the crowd around him. He could hear the whispering. But this needed to happen – audience or no audience.

Rex was drenched in sweat, and his skin was somehow paler than usual. He was as white as writing paper.

'Please,' he whimpered again.

But his voice didn't carry over the chattering and chuckling of the crowd that had formed around them. He raised his hands in mercy as he sat shaking on the floor.

The belt tore through the air. A hissing, black blur. The sharp corner of the buckle tore across Rex's palm. The boy screamed and snapped his hand back in. He held it tightly with his other hand, examined it, and then looked back up at his uncle, with tears streaming down his face.

That'll be it, Rex thought. *One nasty stroke, in front of my classmates, to embarrass me. Now the old fuck will lay off, feed his belt back into his trousers, and head off back to his lot.*

Rex was surprised to see the belt raise up again, over his uncle's shoulder, ready for another stroke.

He looked around at the faces that circled him. He hoped to see some terror or some sympathy, or some allies coming forward in protest. But instead, he saw smiles and laughter. And smartphones held at arm's length, snapping photos as he trembled on the floor.

The belt came down fast and hard. This time, it hit his shoulder. It felt like a bullet had nipped across the bone. But before Rex could shout out in pain, the belt had cycled back over his uncle's shoulder and had come crashing down again. This time into his thigh.

Up went the belt again. It came down like a quick, black viper, into the boy's tummy. And then up. And then down. It became one frantic, unstoppable helicopter blade of leather and metal, eating into flesh and bone each time it came around.

Rex flailed and screamed on the floor, with his arms folded across his chest. The buckle nipped at him with each rotation, leaving him riddled in bright pink marks, oozing blood.

The final blow tore through Rex's top lip. It came apart like tissue paper. Like the cleft lip of the boy he used to taunt. Blood showered down onto his shirt.

And then it came – a long gush of yellow fluid from his crotch. It bled through his trouser leg and pooled out onto the terrazzo.

The corridor erupted into a thundering chorus of laughter. More smartphones slipped out of pockets and bags and started flashing.

Mr. Lachance looked down at his nephew, disgusted. He unwrapped the belt from his hand, which had turned white, and he took it with him as he trundled down the corridor. The crowd parted to let him through.

Rex didn't make any attempt to stand up. He just lay on his back, trembling and crying, in a puddle of his own urine, covered in stinging, red marks, while blood poured from his shredded lip.

Then Tasha Levinski, the pretty leader of the school's bitchy little gaggle of stick-thin cheerleaders, stepped forward. She pulled her phone out, put it right up into Rex's sobbing face, and started live-streaming on Facejam, with a big, shit-eating grin.

* * *

'Did he say anything to you when he went by?' Jill asked.

Milo snapped out of the memory and looked up at his mom. She was staring back at him over the breakfast table on that hot Sunday morning. He forked some egg into his mouth, at last.

'No. Just passed by.'

'He'll be outside the Sampsons' again, no doubt.'

'Why's that?' Dallas asked.

'Well, I didn't know anything about it, but Violet, down at the grocery store, told me. He's obsessed with the girl.'

Dallas looked up from his plate. 'Becca?'

'Yeah. Obsessed. She wants nothing to do with him, but he doesn't get the hint. They've had phone calls in the middle of the night. Letters posted through the door. Stands out there for hours. Dan goes out to scare him off, but he just comes back again. They've had Sheriff Callow talk to him a bunch of times.'

'Boy's got a screw loose,' Dallas said. 'Well, I mean, clearly. Who burns another boy with a cigarette? What the uncle did to him, he had it coming. And if I ever need an RV, I'll be getting it from the King, I'll tell you that much.'

'Can we stop talking about him?' Milo asked.

Feeling a little guilty, Jill quickly tried to change the conversation.

'I saw Jo go by on the bikes,' she said. 'I was thinking - we haven't taken ours out in a while. Seems like a nice day for it.'

'Sure. I'll dig them out of the garage.' Dallas slurped egg off his fork.

'We can go and see if that ice cream truck still parks up by Donerson Park,' Jill said.

'Park!' Sally screamed happily. She always got a lemonade popsicle and had to fight off the wasps.

Dallas set his cutlery down. His stomach gurgled. He necked his orange juice and then went to the sink to fill the glass with water. He swallowed that down, too.

'You alright, hon?' Jill asked.

'Yeah, just thirsty. It's hotter than I thought out.'

He turned and saw Milo staring at him, with a face full of concern.

'I'm fine, really!' his dad reassured him. Then, as if suddenly remembering, he patted his back pocket. 'Hon, seen my wallet?'

'Jacket, maybe?'

He went down the hall and rummaged through the pockets of his jacket, which hung on the pegs by the door. When he came back, he was clutching a five-dollar note.

'Here you go, kiddo,' he said, as he handed it to Milo. 'The weekly wage.'

Milo took it and slipped it into his pocket. But his look of concern didn't go away. He observed his dad closely as he sat back at the table.

'What was it you were saving up for again, My?' his mom asked.

'Goblin Avenger 4. Everyone at school already got it.'

'Didn't we get you that for Christmas?' Dallas asked.

'That was Goblin Avenger 3.5.'

'Three point five?' his mom asked.

'Yeah, it's like three, but with some bonus stuff.'

'More goblins,' Dallas said, with a smile.

'Gollin!' Sally added.

'Well, you'll appreciate it all the more by earning it,' his mom said.

Dallas sank back into his seat, holding his stomach.

'Still feeling rough?' Jill asked him. 'Maybe we should call Doctor Singh.'

Her husband looked at her and forced a smile. 'I'm fine. I'll *be* fine. Please, just eat.'

'Maybe you've got what Mr. Sampson has got,' Milo said. 'Didn't Binko say people were getting sick?'

Dallas' face was wet, as though he'd just climbed out of the pool. Beads of sweat speckled his cheeks and forehead. His stomach gurgled again.

He opened his mouth as if he were about to speak. Only no words came out.

'Hon?' Jill asked, leaning forward.

Her husband's eyes widened suddenly, and his face contorted in agony, as if a dagger had plunged deep into his back. His pupils began to dart between the loved ones surrounding him at the table. Then a jet of thick, black blood shot through his lips and hit his daughter in the face. It pooled into the tray of her high chair.

Dallas' fingers clutched the table like crooked talons. He took a long, desperate breath, puked up more dark, congealed blood onto the breakfast table, and then slumped back unconscious in his chair.

Sally broke into a howling scream that pierced the

room. She was black with blood. All Milo could see were the whites of her eyes and the pinks of her tonsils.

Jill's chair clattered to the floor. She was standing over her husband in a heartbeat, clasping his cheeks and listening for breath from his mouth. Blood drooled in long strings from his lips, down onto his shirt.

'Dallas?' she screamed. 'Dallas? Oh, god. Talk to me. Talk to me, baby. Dallas? *Dallas?*'

Milo looked down at his plate. Flakes of bacon floated in the blood like life rafts on a great black lake.

'Call an ambulance!' his mom shouted.

Milo could hardly hear her. He couldn't take his eyes off that plate.

'Call a fucking ambulance!'

Chapter 3
The Unwanted Guest

Becca let her bike clatter onto the grass in the backyard, then she followed her mother and brother up the steps to the side-door, which led through into their kitchen.

Jo put the grocery bags from her bike's basket on the counter and called, 'Dan, we're home!'

No reply from upstairs.

The smell of vomit still hung heavy in every room.

Becca ran up the stairs. When she reached the landing, something metallic clanged underfoot, and she almost fell backwards. She grabbed hold of the bannister to steady herself, and once she'd straightened up, she looked down to see what she'd tripped on.

It was a model of a van, made from pieces of scrap metal. Bolts stuck out of the sides crudely, and there were untidy gaps between some of the panels.

'Brody, don't leave your projects at the top of the stairs!' she shouted. 'I nearly broke my neck.'

She went into her room and slammed the door behind her.

Thick purple curtains blocked out the sunlight, but it was still uncomfortably warm in the room. A salt lamp in the corner painted everything inside in a dim, pink glow.

The walls were lined with posters of her favorite band, Courting Armageddon. She'd seen them live five times and had tickets to their concert in October, too. Her mom and dad had gotten them for her birthday last month.

Becca took her leather jacket off and hung it on the back of her door. Then she unhooked the choker around her neck and put it back in place on the hooks above her dressing table. She sat on the stool at the table and pulled her boots off. They were leather too, and her feet had been baking inside them. Her toes, painted in chipping, black polish, poked out through holes in her fishnets.

She caught sight of herself in the mirror. Her black fringe was messy from the bike ride, so she quickly tugged it back into place.

At the back of her dressing table, beneath a dragon ornament, sat a stack of letters from Rex. They were all tucked back inside their original envelopes. There were over thirty now. At his most prolific point, she received three in one week. Sheriff Callow told her to throw them away, but she'd kept them anyway.

'What triggered it all?' the sheriff had asked while he sat in their lounge, sipping coffee.

Rex's obsession with Becca started the day the RV King came to Masterson High.

* * *

Becca sat at the back of Mrs. Sanderson's geography class. The old, tall, slim teacher, with the bob of silver hair, had just concluded a lesson on Mount Vesuvius. Up on the electronic board was a drawing of Pompeii covered in lava, the rooftops all ablaze.

The end-of-period bell rang, and all the students scooped their books and pens into their bags. They crowded by the door and started to filter slowly out into the corridor.

As Becca hoisted her bag up onto her shoulder, she heard some commotion outside.

'It's Rex,' someone whispered.

'Is that...? Is that the RV King? Off TV?' someone else asked, excitedly.

Becca pushed her way through and joined the crowd that had lined the corridor and had circled around Rex, who lay trembling on the floor, with his uncle towering above him.

'What's going on?' someone next to her whispered.

Then the belt started swinging. And while the kids all around her laughed and cheered, Becca stayed deadly quiet. She winced with each blow. And she stared glumly down at Rex as he writhed on the ground in agony.

The RV King stomped off, having split open his nephew's lip.

Then Becca watched as Tasha Levinski stepped out from her gang of pretty little cheerleaders, giggling. She dug her manicured nails into her bag and pulled out her phone. It was the latest model, of course, the Phoenix 15, which her plastic surgeon daddy had bought her, no doubt. Becca still had a Phoenix 10, and she was sure the company had started to make it run slower on purpose, to force an upgrade.

With a few taps of her nails on the screen, Facejam opened up, and Tasha crouched down and pointed the camera into Rex's sobbing face, sniggering as she did it.

He looked up at her from the floor with pained, teary

eyes – blood oozing from his mouth – and he said nothing. Nobody said anything as the boy's suffering started casting live to all of Tasha's sixty-five thousand followers. The live view count quickly climbed, and comments started shooting up the screen. *Ha, ha! What a mess! Who's that freak?*

'That's enough!' Becca said as she stepped forward.

Tasha had once stuck a note on Brody's back that said *'Retard'*. Everyone had laughed at him all day long. When Becca found out who'd done it, she marched right up to her in the changing rooms and slapped her sideways. Her daddy had threatened to take Dan and Jo to the cleaners, but thankfully, it went away after the principal brought up the 'hate crime' against Brody.

'What's it to you, Sampson?' Tasha asked as she craned her neck to look up at her.

'It's sick!' Becca said.

'This your boyfriend now? I can see that! Mr. Freak and Mrs. Freak.'

Becca slapped the phone out of her hand. It bounced off down the corridor.

'What the fuck are you doing?' Tasha asked. She stood up. A couple of her cheerleader friends stepped out of the crowd.

Milo quickly slid in front of Becca to shield her, but the cheerleaders didn't look the least bit threatened by him. Then, to his relief, Principal Langley rushed over. 'To your next lessons!' he shouted. 'Lessons! Now!'

Tasha picked up her phone and walked off into the dispersing crowd.

'You okay?' Milo asked Becca.

She nodded. 'I'm fine.'

'My!' Jill called through the bustling corridor. 'We're going home!'

Milo walked over to join her, and they disappeared into the mass of people, leaving Becca standing with Principal Langley. They both stared down at Rex.

Rex murmured on the floor. A big bubble of blood blew out from his mouth and popped. His eyes fixed on Becca.

'Let's get him up,' the principal said.

He and Becca both crouched down, scooped their arms under Rex's, and lifted him to his feet. Rex locked eyes with her as she helped walk him into the reception room beside the principal's office. They sat him down in the waiting room chairs.

'Don't just sit there!' the principal barked at the receptionist. 'Get the first aid kit. And call the janitor to clean up that mess.'

Becca looked down at Rex, and Rex glared up at her, with an admiration he had never felt before.

'Back to class, Sampson!' the principal said. And she went.

* * *

At first Rex only approached her at school. She'd tell him, 'I'm not interested. I was just being nice.' But he persisted. So, eventually, she had to tell Principal Langley. And as soon as he threatened to get Rex's uncle on the phone, the harassment at school stopped.

Then he started messaging her on every app under the sun. She blocked him on all of them, one by one. Then he bullied her cell number out of one of her friends. So she blocked his number. Then he got the Sampsons' landline number from the phone book and took to calling the house at all hours, day or night.

What Happened Next

'You've got to stop calling!' Jo screamed down the phone at 3 a.m. one morning. 'She doesn't want you!'

After that he started sending the letters. And when those were ignored, he began following her home or simply standing outside on the path for hours on end. Dan went out multiple times to shove him and threaten him, but he'd always come back.

In the end, Jo and Dan went in to see Principal Langley themselves. But the principal told them, 'If it's happening off school grounds, it's out of my jurisdiction. You'll have to call the Sheriff.'

So that's what they did. But the RV King was Sheriff Callow's main donor. So he'd simply drive the boy home and tell him not to do it again.

* * *

Becca sat at her dressing table, staring absently at the stack of letters. Suddenly, the pipes in the wall groaned hard, which made her jump. She got up, opened the door, and went out into the landing.

The bathroom door was ajar, and steam was sifting softly out. She went and looked inside. She saw her mom kneeling beside the tub. Water was thundering out of the hot tap.

'Just running your dad a bath,' she said. 'Might perk him up a bit.'

'How is he now?'

'Go and ask him yourself. He'll appreciate that.'

Becca walked along the landing. As she passed Brody's bedroom, she paused and glanced inside. The door was wide open, and he sat cross-legged on the floor, bolting together two metallic components with a spanner.

His bedroom walls were lined with Junkyard Rescue posters – his current TV obsession. A couple of the posters were even signed. They'd gone and met the presenter Milton at a convention in the city. Milton had once been an engineer at NASA. Now, once a week on TV, he'd build some cool weapon out of scrap parts in a junkyard and would show them off in some incredibly destructive demonstration.

Dan Sampson was a mechanic. So when he noticed Brody was taking an interest in engineering, he started to build things with his son. They even constructed a little lean-to in the back yard that they called 'the workshop'. Dan filled it with old parts he would bring home from work, along with spare tools from whenever he'd replace ones in the garage.

Dan loved being out there with Brody. He'd always found it challenging to connect with him, on account of the autism. He'd tried dozens of bonding activities over the years. Board games. Video games. Soccer. Baseball. Mini golf. Fishing. Camping. Hiking. But Brody hadn't taken to any of them. So it felt great to have finally found something they could do together – something they could share.

But Brody had soon learnt enough to work solo. So while they'd still go and work in tandem in the workshop once or twice a week, Brody spent most of his time dismantling old appliances and car parts and creating new innovations, all by himself.

The shelves in his bedroom were heavily laden with all the contraptions he had built. Sling shots, crossbows, miniature trebuchets, and more. Much more.

Becca looked warily at the array of weapons he'd been amassing. She preferred when his obsession had been dinosaurs.

What Happened Next

His room had once been bustling with Jurassic goodies. Every inch of wall space was either papered with dinosaur posters or held shelving filled with velociraptor models, T-Rex toys, little clay dino eggs, or papier-mâché brachiosaurs. His bed sheets used to have fern leaves on, with glowing, yellow eyes peering through the gaps in between. Little, motorized pterodactyls had dangled from his ceiling on threads.

But now he just sat around, quietly building these little contraptions.

Dan coughed, down the landing. Becca carried on walking and pushed open the door to her parents' room. It was dark inside, but a beam of bright light bled through a crack in the curtains and painted some detail on the shape under the bed covers.

'Dad, you awake?' she asked.

He coughed. 'W-where am I?'

'You're at home, dad.'

'My stomach.' He groaned and clutched at his belly. It gurgled loudly.

'Mom!' Becca called down the landing. 'I think we should call an ambulance. He doesn't seem–.'

'Nonsense! He just needs a nice bath,' Jo called back. 'It'll freshen him right up.'

'I can taste blood,' Dan said.

Becca frowned. 'Do you want some water?'

Dan stirred. 'Who's that?'

'It's Becca.'

'Becca?' Dan asked.

'Yeah. Yeah, it's me.'

'Who's Becca?'

She gave a little gasp.

Jo shouted as she came down the landing, 'Right, it's nearly ready! Let's get him down there.'

She came in, swung Dan's legs out of bed, and lowered them to the floor. Then she sat him up, wrapped his arm over her shoulder, and hoisted him up. He was wearing nothing but his boxers.

'Well, don't just stand there!' Jo snapped. 'Help me. He's heavy, you know.'

Becca rushed to her dad's other side, took his arm, and wrapped it around her shoulders. Together the two Sampson women walked him out of the room, along the landing, and into the bathroom. He stepped weakly and murmured groggily as they went.

Jo left Dan leaning on Becca as she turned the taps off. She poured some Relaxo Salts into the water and stirred it with her bony little arm. Then, without warning, she turned and pulled her husband's boxers down. Becca looked away sharply.

'Let's get him in,' Jo said.

Slowly and with great difficulty, they maneuvered him into the tub. He slid down into the warm water, eyes closed.

'Right,' Jo said. 'We'll leave him to soak. I'll get started on lunch.'

Becca followed her out. Jo went down the stairs. Before Becca could step back inside her room to crash onto her bed and listen to Courting Armageddon, she heard splashing coming from the bathroom.

Quickly, she rushed back down the landing.

She tapped on the door. 'Dad?'

No answer. She tapped again. Nothing. Silence now. She pushed the door open and stepped inside.

The water was so red, it was like there was no water in it - like it was *all* blood. It was pouring out onto the floor and splashing up onto the blinds and the toilet, and the sink. She could just see his nostrils poking up out of the scarlet soup.

She ran over and pulled his head up. His eyes were closed. She shook him, and she screamed, 'Wake up! Dad, wake up! Wake up!' But he wouldn't.

Jo tumbled into the bathroom. She saw Becca fighting to keep Dan's head afloat, so she plunged her arm deep into the tub and pulled the plug out. But the water wouldn't drain away. The plughole was all clogged up with fleshy, pink matter. Jo tried plucking it away with her fingers, but there was too much of it.

'Pull him out!' she said finally, desperately.

She grabbed him under his arms, and Becca grabbed at his legs, and they hoisted as hard as they could. But he was too heavy.

'Dad,' Brody said. He stood in the doorway, with his hands by his sides.

'Brody! Help us!' Becca panted. 'Help us!'

He stepped over, grabbed at his father's waist, and pulled. Dan slammed down onto the floor so hard it was like a gunshot had echoed all around the room.

If he wasn't dead already, Becca thought, *we just killed him.*

Jo rolled him over and put her ear to his mouth.

'He's breathing,' she said. 'Call an ambulance!'

Chapter 4
Old Pennies

Milo kept watch out of the kitchen window for the ambulance.

In the end, after several failed attempts to get through to the nine-one-one switchboard, he'd reached a very young dispatcher. He had to give his address at least six times and was finally told, 'Someone will be with you shortly.'

That was forty-five minutes ago.

'Anything yet?' his mom asked. She was kneeling beside Sally's high chair, with a bowl of warm water from the sink between her knees. She was cleaning the blood off her daughter's face with a cloth. She wrung it out after every wipe. The bowl water was black and had ugly, fleshy scrags floating in it.

Every minute or so, she'd crawl over to check her husband was still breathing. They'd laid him onto the floor and put him in the recovery position. He was still unconscious, and the breaths were wheezy and unsteady, but he *was* breathing.

Jill had a good mind to drag him out to the car and drive

him to the ER herself. But he was very heavy – at least three times her own weight – and she didn't want to trigger some sort of convulsion while lugging him around like a piece of furniture.

A white van crawled to a stop at the bottom of the drive. It had the outline of a fish etched onto the side, with the words 'New Hampshire Cod Company' printed below it.

Milo frowned.

'Mom, did you order some fish?'

'*Fish?*'

The van's doors flung open, and two podgy men stepped out onto the concrete. Their white overalls were covered in dark brown stains. They pulled open the doors at the back of the van and took out some plastic aprons, which they slipped over their heads and tied at the back. Next, they took out a folded, steel stretcher, expanded it, and wheeled it up the driveway on its castors.

Milo went and opened the door.

'*Hello?*'

'We're here to collect...' one of the men started, before quickly checking his clipboard, '... Dallas Winters.'

'What's with the fish van?'

'Is he here or not, son? We have a lot of collections today.'

'Come through.'

The stretcher clattered onto the kitchen tiles. It made the glasses rattle inside the cupboards.

The men gazed in horror at the breakfast table. The thick, black blood filled the plates and the spaces in between them, and it dribbled off the table's edges.

The room stank of old pennies.

Sally waved at one of the men from her high chair. He gave a half-smile and waved back.

'Oh, thank god. Thank god,' Jill said as she dropped the bloody cloth into the bowl of meaty, black soup. 'He-he's still breathing. We put him on the floor. We thought that was best.'

Her eyes were red and raw, like they'd been pepper-sprayed.

The two men stood still and stared down at Dallas blankly.

'Aren't you... gonna check his vitals?' she asked, after waiting for them to spring into action. 'Give him oxygen? Give him *anything*? Aren't you going to *do* anything?'

The men quickly exchanged a glance.

'Uh, we're just here to bring him in, ma'am,' one said.

'The doctors and nurses will take good care of him,' added the other.

Jill shook her head. 'What the fuck is going on in this country?' she muttered under her breath.

The men wheeled the stretcher beside Dallas, lowered it, hoisted him on, and then raised it again. His arm drooped over the side like a limp trouser leg hanging out of a laundry basket. They fastened straps across his legs and chest.

As one of the men stepped back, something crunched under his boot. He reached down and picked up a rattle. He handed it to Sally, who giggled and shook it fiercely.

'We're gonna take your daddy to the hospital now, sweetheart,' he told her.

Sally reached out her chubby fingers towards Dallas as they wheeled him out of the room, and she cried, 'Dadda.'

Jill picked her up from the high chair, held her to her chest, took the Mamba's keys off the side, and jerked her head for Milo to follow. They all stepped out onto the driveway and watched as the fish men lifted Dallas into the back of the van.

'You're taking him in *that*?' she asked as she read the logo.

'Ambulances are all occupied,' one of the men said. 'Our whole fleet has been roped in. Same for Deliver-It and The Parcel People.'

In every direction, they could hear a choir of sirens wailing in the distance.

'We're dropping them at the loading bay around back. They're asking that family members stay at home.'

'*Stay at home?*' Jill asked.

'We've seen the ER, ma'am. It's carnage. Honestly, your kids are better off here at home. The hospital will keep you posted with any updates. Just stay by the landline. The mobile networks are all jammed.'

The two men climbed back into the van. It took off down the street. The mask shot up out of the drain and floated around in the air like an autumn leaf.

'Get in the car,' Jill said, as she unlocked the Mamba.

'Didn't you hear what that guy said?'

'Get in the car.'

'He said to stay here. He said they want families to stay at home.'

'Get in the car.'

'Mom, he said ER is carnage.'

'Get in the fucking car, Milo! Do as your mother says for once in your life!'

'But–.'

'I don't care what a goddamn fish seller says. Something is happening, and we all need to stay together. We aren't letting them stick your father in a hallway somewhere to forget about him. We're gonna go to the hospital and scream in the faces of every doctor and every nurse until somebody helps him.'

'Why don't I stay here with Sally? It's not gonna be nice for her there, is it?'

Jill rolled her eyes. 'What did I just say?'

'You can go. I can stay here with her.'

'Everyone's getting sick. What if you get sick? What if Sally gets sick? Cell phones aren't working, Milo. How are you gonna get hold of me?'

Milo didn't have any answers.

'You're coming with me to the hospital. That's the end of it. Now get in the damn car.'

Chapter 5
Peters

I t was still known as 'the farmhouse' even though the farm hadn't operated in thirty years. The animal pens sat empty, and the field was just a dustbowl, especially on a hot day like today.

Lieutenant Peters had bought the old place with his wife twenty-five years ago. They had a good couple of decades there. Until she got the diagnosis, of course. It was a short illness. She went quickly, which was better than most people got.

She was buried over on the east side of the land, in a patch of shade under the pines. A little wooden cross marked the spot. The Lieutenant would wander over there every day just to talk. Tell her about work. Not that there was much to tell anymore. Captain Malsetti had started to wind down his duties on account of his retirement coming up next year.

A high-pitched whistle erupted from the farmhouse. It rang out across the empty pens and the old barn.

'Alright, alright, I'm coming,' Peters said, as he flushed the toilet and limped into the kitchen.

The Lieutenant was stocky and sun-reddened. He was in his late fifties and had thinning gray hair. His belly hung over his black boxer shorts, and a moth-eaten old night robe dangled from his shoulders, caked in crumbs and food stains.

He took the kettle off the stove. A scolding-hot column of steam piped from its spout, screaming like a banshee as it went. He filled his mug with bubbling water and spooned in some coffee.

The farmhouse kitchen was narrow and untidy. A stack of dirty dishes sat in the sink. Used cups and bowls lined the worktops; most of them with soiled cutlery sticking out. He'd taken to eating packet noodles straight out of the pot.

Lucy would have never let it get that way. She used to clean up after him morning and night. But Peters never was the house-proud of the pair.

He pulled open the fridge and took out the milk carton. There was a little cream on the spout. He gave it a sniff and screwed up his face. It smelled like rotten fruit, but he didn't much fancy running to the store on a Sunday, so he added a dollop to his mug and mixed it in. White lumps floated to the top.

It was a little after ten, and he'd not long climbed out of bed. He was always off-duty on Sundays. For Peters Sundays were days of sitting in his boxers, eating cereal, and watching reruns of old detective shows. The likes of Miami Murders and Hopkirk Investigates.

The shutters in the lounge were closed, and the room was dark as he stepped inside, sipping from his mug.

Something stirred on the couch as he entered the room. Bessie was an old, gray terrier. She slept there most nights when Peters retired upstairs to bed. Her aging joints couldn't handle the steepness of the staircase anymore.

She raised her head to look at her master as he came in, but quickly lowered it again. She rested her snout on her paw.

'Where's that goddamn remote?'

He rummaged around through the newspapers that lined the arms of the sofa and dug out the small, black control. The television set that sat in the corner of the room burst into color.

The TV resumed the channel he'd been dozing off to the night before – Motoring Men. Only it wasn't a motor show that came onscreen. It wasn't Banger Brothers. It wasn't Junkyard Rescue. It wasn't Gears and Guns. It wasn't any of the programming Peters had grown to love from Motoring Men. It was the Channel One news.

Peters flicked the channel over to The Great Outdoors. But again – no Wilderness Willy. No Camping Cookouts. No Duck Hunting double bill. It was the Channel One news again.

He flicked again. And again. The Channel One news was on every channel. It had taken over everything.

Harrowing clips of ER rooms up and down the country. Patients drenched in blood. Queues miles long. Angry mobs congregating outside hospitals. Smashed glass. Fire hoses blasting people into the road. Riot police shunting crowds back with their interlocking shields.

The scrolling, red banner across the bottom of the screen read '*EMERGENCY ROOMS OVERWHELMED AS MYSTERY ILLNESS SWEEPS STATES.*'

'Well, girl. Looks like the whole world's going to hell.'

Bessie looked up at him with sad eyes and let out a long breath that sounded like a sigh.

'I'm glad your mom ain't here to see this.'

Lucy was a nervous wreck at the best of times. She used

to lose sleep over saying 'you too' to waiters after they told her 'enjoy your meal'. If she saw those news reports, she'd be rocking back and forth in the corner of the room. Peters was sure of it.

Beside the sofa stood a tall, narrow, metal table. An old wired phone sat on top. After a few minutes of sipping coffee and watching the TV, the phone started to ring. The Lieutenant took it from its cradle.

'Peters.'

'It's me.'

'Oh, hi, Cap. Thought I might be hearing from you.'

'You got the news on?'

'Yes, sir,' Peters said. 'World's going to shit.'

'How are you feeling? Any stomach cramps? Wooziness?'

Peters sat and thought about it for a moment. There was a dull pain in his temples, but that was likely from the couple of bottles he'd emptied the night before.

'No more than usual,' he said. 'What about you, Cap?'

'It's too hectic here,' the Captain said. 'I don't have time to die.'

Peters smiled. 'What's going on? Any indication of what's happening from further up the line?'

'We've heard nothing from anyone. Plenty of rumors flying around in the office, though.'

'What rumors?'

'Russian nerve agents. Microchips in the water. Phone masts emitting deadly signals. Usual bollocks. As to what's actually happening, we don't know. What I *do* know is that I've got half my officers off, and every hospital in the county has a riot in its ER. So the handful of doctors and nurses that *were* able to make it into work today are spending their time under siege instead of saving lives.'

'I'll get dressed, and I'll head to City Hospital, Cap.'

'I got a ton of guys there already.'

'Then where do you need me?'

'You ever been to Masterson?'

'Masterson? Yeah, a few times. There's a junkyard there, where I get parts for my Rattler.'

'Sheriff Callow is in charge there. *Was* in charge, I should say.'

'I know Andy. Jesus, he get sick?'

'I got a call this morning. Wife woke up, and he was dead in bed next to her. Choked on his own blood.'

'Jesus.'

'As it stands, the town is entirely without police presence. So it's gonna get ugly. I've got three cadets from the academy ready to send over there. But they need a senior officer to take charge.'

'I can do that, Cap.'

'Good man. I'll tell them to meet you outside Riley's Motor House. It's a block over from the hospital, so you can get things straight before you go bursting in there.'

After they were done ironing out the details, Peters sat the phone back in its cradle and sat in silence for a few moments. Then he looked down at Bessie.

'I don't think I'll be seeing you for a while, girl. If I leave a big heap of food out, are you capable of rationing?'

She looked at him blankly.

Chapter 6
An Airport on Christmas Eve

When the Winters got to the hospital, there was nowhere to park. Cars had been untidily abandoned the whole way down the road. A couple had even smashed into each other – their noses were entangled, and steam rose up into the air. But there wasn't a person in sight. They were all inside, screaming at the reception staff.

Jill slung the Mamba up onto the curb half a mile down the street. The bumper crunched as it shunted up over the concrete. She lifted Sally out of the kiddie seat in the back and carried her hurriedly towards ER, with Milo close in tow.

When they passed through the sliding doors, the deafening chorus of shouting and crying made Sally burst into tears.

It was like an airport on Christmas Eve – a thousand people screaming, all trying to find their lost luggage. Only it wasn't suitcases and overnight bags they were looking for – it was the loved ones that had been taken away by the vans.

What Happened Next

Most of the crowd was covered in blood. They were all teary-eyed and exhausted, and desperate for updates on their family members.

Jill tried to force her way through the crowd that had congregated at the reception desk, but Sally just started to cry louder. She looked around quickly and saw a group of children sitting on the floor in a huddle, over in the corner of the waiting area.

'Take your sister,' Jill said, as she passed Sally into Milo's arms. 'Go and wait over there!'

Milo did as he was told. He stepped carefully between the folded legs of the frightened children, who sat on the floor, and found a vacant patch in the corner, where he squatted down with Sally on his lap. She nestled her teary head against his chest.

'It's okay,' he tried his best to soothe her. 'Everything's gonna be okay.'

Jill started to weave her way into the angry masses. She was so short and slight that she could pass easily between them. Milo watched her disappear into the storm cloud of flailing arms and flapping mouths.

Sally sobbed quietly on his lap, but slowly she settled, and soon he could feel her snoring against his chest. He wrapped his arms around her tightly, forming a little cocoon. He hadn't held her like that since she was a newborn.

Chapter 7
The Cadets

Riley's Motor House was a glass-fronted showroom on Benvale Street. Inside, sitting on polished white floor tiles, was a collection of classic sports cars, with pricey tags hanging from the sun visors.

The door was locked, and a man stood at the window, peering in through the glass in admiration, with his hands cupped at his temples, like blinkers, blocking out the daylight. He stood about six-foot-four and was in his mid-twenties. He was African American. His eyes were dark, and he had short, black hair. He wore all-black, and the word POLICE was printed in white across the back of his vest.

'That's a Wolfhound Seven-Seven,' Denzel said excitedly, as he turned to face the two other cadets.

Chambers sat on the hood of the squad car they'd just driven there in, from the city. She, too, was in her mid-twenties. Her dark brown hair was tied back in a ponytail, and she had pretty green eyes.

Standing between her knees, with his hands clamped onto her hips, was her boyfriend, Diaz. He was in his early thirties. Although he wasn't very tall, his muscles looked like they might burst out of his uniform at any moment. He had jet black hair and a neat, black beard that was trimmed at one tidy length.

They both glanced over at Denzel, wondering if they were supposed to know what a Wolfhound Seven-Seven was.

'I had a toy one at the home,' Denzel said, looking directly at Chambers.

'Ahhh,' she said, nodding. 'That's what that was supposed to be. You were never without that thing,' she laughed. 'Always bashing it into all the furniture. Miss Moltez confiscated it a hundred times,' she explained to Diaz.

Denzel smiled. 'Yeah, I cried every time.'

'And who was there to cheer you up?' Chambers asked.

'You were.'

'Hot chocolate and cream. Worked every time.'

'I left the car there. There was a kid there that didn't have many toys. And I was getting out. So I let him have it.'

'Moltez, huh?' Peters asked, as he stepped over to them. He'd parked up on the corner.

Miss Moltez's Home for Children sat halfway between Masterson and the city. It wasn't a big orphanage. It only had a capacity of twenty or so. Peters had been called there a few times over the years when some of the more trouble-some kids had been kicking off.

'Yes, sir,' Denzel said. 'Myself and Chambers over there are alumni. We spent years there together.'

Peters nodded. 'Good woman, Moltez.'

'She was strict when she needed to be,' Denzel laughed. 'I'm Denzel, by the way.'

'Peters,' the Lieutenant replied as he shook the cadet's hand. 'So how'd you end up there?'

'Well, my dad was never around. Took off when I was two. And when I was nine, my mom just disappeared one day.'

'Disappeared?' Peters asked.

'They found her blazer in the clubhouse of a known Klan. But never found her. No arrests made, nothing.'

Peters lowered his head. 'Jesus.'

The Lieutenant knew of Klan activity in the area. They called themselves, *The Eighty-Eight*. He'd been unlucky enough to visit a crime scene once, after a lynching. A dog walker had been wandering through the woods one day and had come across a clearing, with a burnt patch of ground. In its center, wrapped in chains, a charred skeleton. No arrests had been made following that incident, either. The Eighty-Eight were smart. And they were very well-connected.

'That's why I wanted to be a cop,' Denzel said. 'Bring justice to people like that. And when Chambers heard I'd finally enrolled, she followed.'

'And that's where she met me,' Diaz said, with a loving little smile.

'And *you* are?' Peters asked, looking uncomfortably at the way he was holding her.

'Diaz, sir,' he said.

'Mexican?'

'Half, sir.'

'And you and Chambers – you're an item?'

'It won't get in the way of our policing, sir,' Chambers said. She pulled Diaz's hands off her hips and pushed them down to his sides.

What Happened Next

'Right,' Peters said. 'As I'm sure you're aware, we might be stationed here a while. We'll set up digs in the Sheriff's office. But the first call of business is to restore some order at the hospital. Denzel, you ride with me. You two, follow in the car.'

Chapter 8
The King is Dead

The private rooms sat on the second floor of the hospital, which was far quieter than the two floors below. The RV King's room had a nice, big window overlooking Masterson, a fifty-inch TV screen, and little, potted fern plants.

The King himself lay swollen and purple under the covers, breathing raspily. His wig was askew, as it often was.

The maid had found him lying on the shower floor earlier that morning. She'd gotten through to Rex on his cell, but his nephew wasn't too interested. But once she said, 'This may be the last time you see him alive', he decided to come to the hospital, just to watch the old bastard die.

Now Rex sat in the armchair beside the bed, flicking through a nudie mag. He'd switched the TV off. All he could get was the Channel One news.

'Richard?' the King asked, croakily, from his pillow.

Rex scoffed. 'Why do you call me that?'

'It's... the name... my brother gave you,' he said quietly. 'Rex sounds... like a goddamn dog!'

Rex clenched his teeth.

The King coughed, and blood shot out and speckled the white covers.

Rex set his magazine down, stood up, and stared down at his uncle. The RV King glared back up at him. His eyes were bloodshot and full of gunk. Each breath he drew was painful and labored, and made a wheezing sound like an overstuffed vacuum bag.

Rex's face began to light up.

'You're not in the will,' the King said.

Rex's light faded. 'What?'

'I've left the house... and the money... to the Cat Sanctuary.'

'You-you hate cats.'

'I do. And still... I'd rather leave... it to those... furry little fuckers... than you.'

'What about the RV lot?'

'Left it to Reggie.'

'Reggie? The-the fucking dipshit that cleans the windows?'

The King started to laugh. More flecks of blood flung up from his lips and dotted the sheets. 'That's him.'

'Why do you hate me so much?'

'Because you're sick. And you're... not worthy... of riding on my... coat tails... any... longer.'

Puss started to drool from his left eye. It ran down his cheek. His laughter turned to a groan, and his stomach grumbled. It felt like a blade was twisting inside him.

Rex's eyes darkened.

'Look at you,' Rex said. 'I love seeing you like this.' He dug his hand into his pocket and took out his phone, and snapped a photo of his uncle. 'All bloated and purple, and pained. Like a fucking rotting blueberry. All festering on the inside. Juice seeping out.'

He snapped another photo.

'I'm gonna look at this every day. Every time I need a fucking pick-me-up.'

The King winced. His stomach rumbled louder.

'I know where you put the guns,' Rex said, happily. 'Did you really think you could hide them from me?'

The King's eyes focused on him, yellow and raw.

'You're... an... abomination. You're not... even–'

Before he could finish, a thick, black jet of blood shot through his bloated lips. It showered onto the bed and freckled Rex's face.

Then his head rolled over to the side, and one last wisp of stale breath passed through his lips, and he fell still and silent. His puffy, yellow eyes gazed blindly into nothingness.

Rex wiped the blood from his face and headed out of the room, with an erection poking into his jeans.

Chapter 9
Was it the Russians?

Milo was just about to nod off when a siren wailed outside. He jolted awake. The whole of the ER was flooded with flashing, blue light.

The reception doors slid apart, and Peters walked in. His boots clapped loudly on the floor tiles as he marched inside. A radio cackled on his belt.

The three cadets came in behind him. They had rifles strapped over their shoulders.

'Ladies and gentlemen!' the Lieutenant said.

The crowd was shouting too loudly to hear him. They continued to yell and point their fingers furiously at the exhausted staff, who were cowering behind the germ screens.

'Hey, listen up!' Denzel shouted. His low, booming voice rang through the room like a gun clap.

Everybody fell into silence and turned to face the policemen.

Sally woke in Milo's lap. He held her tight.

Chambers dragged a chair over from the waiting area.

Its feet screeched awfully as it went. The Lieutenant climbed onto it so that he towered over the many faces that were now fixed on him.

'Ladies and gentlemen,' he repeated, this time to a very attentive audience. 'My name is Lieutenant Peters. I'm sorry it took so long for you to see some police presence here today.'

'Where's Sheriff Callow?' someone called from the crowd.

Peters ran a stiff hand through his stubble. 'I'm saddened to have to inform you that your sheriff is, unfortunately, no longer with us.'

'What?' cried someone else. 'The sheriff is dead?'

'This... *illness*... has sadly claimed him. These cadets and I have been sent over from the city. We're here purely to help keep everything calm.'

'Calm? My husband just puked up about a gallon of blood!' a woman shouted.

'Mine too!' someone else added.

'So did my sister.'

Peters raised his palms high into the air to try to quiet them. 'Please, please. I know you're afraid. I know this is scary. But please rest assured that the staff here are doing their best to help your loved ones.'

'What's going on?' someone shouted. 'What's happening to everyone?'

'Is it a nerve gas?' another asked.

'Was it the Russians?'

'*We* know what *you* know,' Peters said. 'People are getting sick. And right now, the priority is to keep calm and let the medical professionals do what they do best. Now, I want everybody to get into a neat, calm, quiet line. Once they know where your loved ones are and that they are stable, the receptionists will call you out and tell you where to go.'

Slowly, as instructed, the crowd shuffled into a single-file queue. Jill looked over toward Milo and Sally to check they were okay, and then she joined the line, which snaked down the corridor and out of sight.

Peters jumped down from the chair. His knee gave way, and he started to fall, but Denzel caught him by the shoulders and helped straighten him up.

'Thanks, Denzel,' he said, with a wince.

'You alright, Lieutenant?'

'Yeah, yeah,' Peters said. 'Just old.'

'What do we do now?' Chambers asked.

'For now,' Peters started, 'we just need to stop anything from kicking off here. Spread yourselves out around the building.'

'Yes, sir,' Denzel said.

He, Chambers, and Diaz split up.

Chapter 10
Delta Ward

Two hours scraped by. Jill had been standing in the queue so long she couldn't feel her legs. She wavered weakly on the spot.

A young nurse stepped into the corridor. Her plastic apron was drenched in blood. She ripped it off and stuffed it into a yellow biohazard bin to one side of the walkway. Then she took a clipboard from the wall and read from it, 'Dallas Winters?'

'That's me!' Jill cried as she ran out of the line and towards the young woman. 'That's my husband. Is he ok? Is he alright? Where is he?'

'He's on Delta Ward.'

'Can I see him?' Jill asked.

'You can. I'll take you there now,' the nurse said.

'Wait, I need to get my kids.'

'They may not want to see him like this,' the nurse warned her.

Jill considered asking why. She thought about crying, too. But she was too exhausted to do either. She simply nodded and followed the nurse's lead down the corridor.

'It's the last door on the right, here.'

When they got to the door, the sign above it read *'Chapel'*.

'Chapel?' Jill asked.

The nurse pushed the door open, and they entered the room. A tall, concrete font stood to one side and a large, wooden crucifix was fixed to the far wall. The long wooden benches that used to line the chapel were now stacked high at its sides.

'We ran out of room,' the nurse said. 'We've had to make up new wards in the exercise room, the TV room, and the cafeteria, too.'

The room was divided into two by a white, plastic curtain that hung from a wire overhead. The curtain was lined on either side with army cots – a cheap, foldable, metal frame, with a thin foam mattress.

Each cot had a patient lying on it, barely breathing if breathing at all. Many had the bedsheets pulled right up, over their heads. Family members knelt by their sides, crying and holding their hands.

She led Jill to the back corner, where Dallas lay on a cot. His eyes were closed. His chest rose and fell with each strained breath. His skin had a purple tone. Jill crouched down at his side and clasped his hand in her own.

'His hand is so cold,' she said as she looked up at the nurse with wet, glistening eyes.

'It's the circulation,' the nurse explained. 'He's not in a good way. I'll give you some time alone with him.'

The nurse left the chapel.

'Dallas?' Jill asked, uncertainly. 'It's me.'

He didn't answer.

'Dallas, the kids are here. Milo's here. Sally's here.

They're right outside. And they're waiting on some good news. So let's give them some good news, huh?'

His lungs rattled groggily with each breath, and his breathing grew more labored as the moments ticked by.

'You know, in future, if you don't want to eat my breakfasts, you can just say,' she laughed. But the laughter soon gave way to silence.

His cold fingers were motionless in her own.

She thought for a moment.

'You know, I drove the Mamba here. Parked it in a real hurry. I caught the bumper on the curb. Heard it crunch. I think it's dented. Definitely scratched. It'll be expensive. Really expensive.'

She watched his face for any kind of reaction.

'I doubt they'll be able to match the paint. So it'll look all mismatched. And when you drive it around, all the gearheads will look over and say, *Check out that idiot, with the two different colors of bumper.*'

No reaction still.

'Come on. I know you're mad at me.'

Nothing.

'Shout at me, Dallas.'

Just more raspy breath.

'Come on, Dallas. Shout at me. Shout at me, goddamn it!'

Chapter 11
The Vending Machine

An hour passed by. Sally was sitting a couple of feet away now, rolling a ball back and forth to another toddler that had been left in the ER.

Milo leant back against the wall. His eyes didn't leave his sister; just in case she decided to bolt for the door, which she often did when Jill took her to the mall. As he sat there, watching the ball roll to and fro, he started to wonder how long it would be before his mom came and got them. She must have seen his dad by now. So why wasn't she bringing them? Was he in such a bad way that she didn't want them to see him?

Some screaming erupted in the forecourt. The ER front doors slid apart, and a trolley dashed in. Strapped to it was a boy Milo recognized from school. Carson Myers. He was a couple of years older than him. Blood down his front, like all the rest he'd seen wheeled inside. At his side, screaming and crying, hurried his mother, clutching onto her son's cold, blue fingers.

The man pushing the trolley guided it quickly down the corridor, past the sidings of queuing relatives.

Sally stood up, panicked. The screaming had disturbed her. Milo was too busy watching after the trolley to notice. She ran for the ER doors, which hadn't slid shut yet.

'Mommy?' she screamed, as she went.

At that point, Milo's head snapped around, and he locked eyes on her as she ran for the doors. He clambered to his feet quickly but fumbled, and came crashing down onto his knees. He looked up helplessly as Sally ran for the forecourt.

Peters stepped in front of her and scooped her up into his arms.

'Woah, woah, woah, slow down there, squirt,' the Lieutenant said.

Sally struggled and tried to wriggle free, but he had a good grip on her. Peters eyed Milo, who hurried over.

'This belong to you?' Peters asked, with a chuckle.

'She got spooked by that screaming,' Milo said, as Peters passed her into his arms. 'Thank you, sir.'

'Call me Peters. What's *your* name?'

'Milo.'

'Nice to meet you, Milo. And who's this?'

'Sally.'

'Hey, Sally.'

She shyly pressed her head into Milo's chest.

'Who are you here with?' Peters asked.

'My mom and dad. Well, my dad is sick. My mom is waiting for him. Or *with* him. I don't know. I haven't seen her for a while.'

'You're on babysitting duties, then?'

'Yes, sir.'

'I'll be around town for the next few days – until we can figure out what's going on,' Peters said. 'If you or your family need anything, just holler.'

'Thank you.'

Milo went back over into the corner, where the kids sat and played. He parked himself down and held Sally tightly in his lap. She'd lost her playing privileges.

'Chips,' she said.

'You're hungry?'

She nodded.

Milo looked around. A vending machine stood in the corner, over on the other side of ER. He picked up his sister and carried her over.

It was stuffed full of sodas, potato chips, cookies, and chocolate bars. He quickly scanned the selection.

'You want some puffy chips?'

She nodded.

Milo dug his hand into his pocket and took out the five-dollar bill his dad had given him earlier as payment for being his bucket holder. He fed it into the machine.

Two familiar faces appeared in the glass.

'Milo?' a voice called from behind him.

He turned. Becca and Brody stood there before him, drenched in blood.

* * *

The four of them sat in a circle on the floor, by the vending machine, with their legs folded out in front of them. Sally sat beside Milo, stuffing chips into her mouth. Her cheeks puffed out like a hamster.

Brody sat close to Becca. He was gnawing on the end of a Yorko bar that Milo had bought him. He'd asked what Becca wanted, too, but she wasn't hungry. Milo wasn't hungry, either. But his throat was dry, so he'd gotten a bottle of Turtle Cola.

'Are those good?' Milo asked Sally.

Sally nodded.

Milo looked over at Brody. 'How's that Yorko bar?' He could see that he hadn't eaten much of it – he was almost gumming the end. It was all melted and wet.

Brody locked eyes with him, but he didn't speak. He just kept on gnawing.

'He's too stressed out to talk,' Becca said. Her eyes were fixed on the floor. They were lost in thought. 'Unless you talk to him about Junkyard Rescue. That's all he's interested in these days.'

Milo smiled. 'You like Milton, Brody?'

Brody nodded.

'What's your favorite thing he's built?'

The Yorko bar came out. His lips were moist and brown. 'Trebuchet.' In went the chocolate bar again.

Milo shifted his gaze to Becca. There was blood on her shirt, and it was smeared up her arms. He tried to think of the right thing to say to her, but she spoke before he could.

'Your dad... How did it happen?' she asked. Her voice was jittery. Her eyes flitted up, towards him.

'It was quick. We finished buffing up the car, then we went inside for breakfast, and he just went downhill fast.'

'Was there blood?'

Milo nodded. 'A lot.'

Becca's eyes filled up with tears. 'I've never seen so much blood.'

Milo thought about putting his hand on her shoulder, but he knew he'd do it too awkwardly.

'Did an ambulance come?' he asked.

'It was a van,' she said. 'A butcher's van.'

Milo thought of the two men who had come to take his

father away. He drank the last of his Turtle Cola and then screwed the cap back onto the bottle.

'Can you watch Sally?' he asked Becca. 'I need to go and pee.'

Becca nodded.

Chapter 12
The Other Side

I n the chapel, Jill was kneeling beside her husband's cot. She was bent over, with her head resting on his chest. Her hand was still wrapped around his. She'd lost the feeling in her legs an hour ago from sitting on them for so long.

As she sat there, she found herself daydreaming about their wedding day.

They tied the knot two years before Milo was born. It was a beautiful event. They rented out the Hargrove Estate for a whole weekend. It cost a lot, but both sets of parents chipped in, and they got a lot for their money – the huge mansion itself, two stunning fishing lakes, a rose garden, and acres upon acres of beautiful woodland.

The ceremony itself was out on the grass. Rows of chairs faced the altar, which was tall and white, with doves and roses carved into the wood. A canopy of crisscrossing fairy lights hung overhead, dancing in the breeze. A big brass band played Motown as Jill came down the aisle in her long, frilly dress.

What Happened Next

Dallas waited anxiously beside the chaplain. When he first saw her in that dress, walking towards him with her father, his face lit up with joy. Jill knew she'd made the right choice. Anyone that looks *that* happy to see you is the person you need to spend the rest of your life with.

The ceremony went off without a hitch, and then the happy bride and groom, along with their two hundred guests, all danced drunkenly late into the night.

After a certain amount of drinks, Jill's memories of the day got a bit grainy. Sadly, there were no photos from the wedding day.

The photographer spent the whole day snapping every part of the event. Hundreds of stunning photos, chronicling the entire day beautifully.

Just after midnight, he was heading out to his car when he heard some excitable voices down by the rose garden, away from the house, where the rest of the guests were dancing the night away.

He thought maybe there was a whole pocket of guests he hadn't known about, partying away down there, and he didn't want to miss anybody out. So he started down the dark track to the rose garden.

When he got down there, he found three partygoers in their late twenties. Two men and a woman. The men had their suit jackets off and their ties undone. The three of them were gathered around a small table, with a sundial mounted to its face.

'Smile!' the photographer said as he snapped a photo.

But in the burst of light from the flash, he saw the white, powdery line that crossed the sundial and the smattering under the noses of the three guests.

'What the fuck are you doing?' one of them asked.

'Malc, don't!' the other man interjected, quickly.

'Give me that fucking camera,' Malcolm said, coming quickly towards the photographer.

'Hey, man, I'm sorry. Here, let me delete it. It's digital. I can just delete it. Here, you can watch me.' The photographer pointed the display at him and started to thumb the buttons.

Malcolm came at him, still.

'Malc, let him delete it!' the woman shouted.

'Yeah, it's your brother's wedding, Malc. Let's not have any trouble tonight.'

Malcolm grabbed the camera and tugged it fiercely so that the plastic clip on the photographer's neck strap snapped clean off. Then he threw the whole thing onto the ground as hard as he could. The lens burst into glittering shards, and microchips flew out of the housing.

The photographer wanted to stop him, but this guy looked wild. His eyes were dark and wired. So he stepped back, kept quiet, and let it happen.

'Malc, why'd you do that?' one friend asked.

'Leave it now, Malc,' the other insisted. 'Leave it.'

But Malcolm wasn't listening. He stomped his heel down onto the battered lump of black plastic with all his weight. And then again. And again, for good measure, all the while staring into the photographer's eyes.

Malcolm picked up his jacket from the garden's low stone wall, slung it over his shoulder, and then headed back up the track, towards the house.

Slowly, his two friends followed.

'Sorry,' the woman said quietly, as she passed the photographer by.

When they were gone, the photographer crouched

down and picked the camera up. He opened the flap. The storage card had snapped into three pieces. All the photos were gone.

'He's a fucking psycho!' Jill screamed at her husband the next morning when he broke the news to her. He'd had to sign a cheque for two thousand dollars to stop the photographer from calling the police.

'Look, he was off his head,' Dallas said. 'There was coke out, the guy took the photo, and he got carried away.'

Jill scoffed. 'You think it's because of the photo, Dallas? Think of the photos that fucking *'club'* he hangs out at - think of the photos they've got of him. This isn't because of the photo.'

'What are you saying?'

'He smashed that camera for the same reason he broke that guy's jaw at college, the time he ended up in jail. He smashed the camera because the photographer is–.'

'Don't say it. It's not true, alright?'

After the wedding, Jill refused to have anything to do with Malcolm. But two years later, Milo came along. And by the time he could walk and talk, Dallas was keen for him to meet Malcolm. Jill didn't have any siblings, and Dallas convinced her it was healthy to have an uncle role in a kid's life. Besides, he was off the nose powder now, by all accounts. And he hadn't come home with a black eye for months.

So, reluctantly, Jill agreed.

Eventually, Malcolm became part of their small family, regularly coming over for barbecues or the occasional fishing trip. Until all that business with the vaccinations, of course. Until the bus came to take him away.

. . .

A sudden jerk woke Jill from the daydream. She looked over at her husband. His arms were writhing at his sides. His face was purple. The veins in his neck were poking up through his skin.

'Nurse!' she screamed. She tried to get to her feet, but her dead legs buckled underneath her, and she tumbled over, onto the floor. 'Nurse!' she screamed again.

A couple of cots away, a man who had been kneeling by his wife's side quickly stood up, hearing all the commotion. He looked over at Dallas' cot.

'Oh, Jesus!' he cried, when he saw the writhing, purple body. 'I'll-I'll go and get help!'

He ran out of the chapel as fast as he could. His sneakers screeched on the parquet.

Jill got up on her knees and watched helplessly as Dallas convulsed. His eyes were swollen and red. His mouth gurgled for breath, but none came.

She didn't know what to do, so she just clamped a hand onto her husband's wrist. Tears rolled down her cheeks, and a big slug of snot shot out of her nose and trailed over her lips.

She knew what was happening. She knew it was time. She knew there was nothing that could be done now. The doctors and nurses were all too busy. She was alone. And it was time.

'It's okay, Dallas,' she said bravely, articulating the words as best as she could through the tears. 'It's okay. I'm here. If you're... *going*... I'm here.'

His arms shook at his sides. She held his hand.

'I love you,' she went on. 'I love you so much. Thank you, Dallas. Thank you for giving me the best family. The best children. And the best years. You were so loving. You were *so, so* loving. You did everything for us. Everything we ever asked for. We will all love you forever.'

The gurgling stopped. His arms stopped shaking. His head slumped on the pillow. There was silence. And there was stillness. And Dallas was gone.

Chapter 13
Stacked Up High

Denzel and Peters helped a nurse wrestle a patient into a body bag, and then they zipped it up.

'I need to find a porter to put him in the morgue,' she said.

'We can do it,' Peters insisted.

'You're sure?' she asked.

'Yeah, no problem!' Denzel said.

'Thank you!' With that, the nurse went off to the next cot to check on someone else.

Peters looked around. 'Grab that wheelchair!'

Denzel wheeled it over, and they sat the corpse in the chair, and then rolled it out of the ward.

The teary-eyed, exhausted crowds that filled the corridor backed away in horror as they saw the body wheel towards them, all bound in black plastic.

Peters manned the handles. Denzel walked along behind him.

They took a right at the end of the corridor and kept going straight, through the 'staff only' doors, and into the dimly-lit stretch of walkway beyond.

There was a private elevator there. Denzel pressed the button, and they waited for the cab to climb up the shaft. It was rickety and slow.

'You want some gum?' Denzel asked.

'Sure.'

The cadet held up the packet. Peters took a stick and stuffed it into his mouth.

Once the door slid open, they wheeled the chair inside and rode the cab down to the basement.

The door opened onto the dark underground space. The air was thick with the stench of death. The ground was littered with large objects.

'Hit the light,' Peters said.

Denzel palmed the wall until he found the switch. Some jittery, old bar lights flickered into life overhead. That's when they saw it – the pile.

A huge stack of black cocoons, just like the one they'd wheeled down there, sat against the far wall. Several had tumbled off the heap and rolled deeper into the basement.

Peters and Denzel stared at the pile in silence. They exchanged a sad look.

A loud, metallic clanging noise sounded suddenly from above, like a brick tumbling down a vent shaft. Another corpse, clad in a shimmering, black body bag, fell from an opening in the ceiling. It hit the heap, found no shoulder to lay on, and fell harshly onto the concrete.

'They're using the laundry chute,' Denzel said.

'They don't have time to wheel them down here,' Peters said. 'Too busy trying to save the lucky sons of bitches that still have a pulse.'

Chapter 14
Breaking the News

Jill was still crouching at her husband's side, clutching onto his wrist. She had no idea how long it had been since he'd passed. It might have been five minutes. It might have been three hours. Suddenly, time felt meaningless. The person she'd been traveling through time with was gone, and her future was shattered.

A tap on the shoulder shook her from these deep thoughts. She looked up. It was the nurse that had shown her into the chapel earlier that morning.

The nurse gave an apologetic expression. Behind her, two porters stood, waiting. They wore blue overalls, the fronts of which were soiled with that black, rancid blood.

'Sorry to disturb you, ma'am,' the nurse said. 'I know you're grieving right now, and I would honestly love to give you more time, but we need the cot, ma'am. There's a queue of patients out back, who are all waiting for a bed.'

Jill looked at her husband's swollen, purple face. His pained, red eyes stared at the ceiling. She let go of his hand and got to her feet.

One of the porters unrolled a body bag and flicked it,

like he was trying to get air into a trash bag. The other wrote 'Dallas Winters' onto a little white cardboard tag.

Jill walked out of the chapel. She didn't want to watch them wrestle her husband into that cheap black plastic sack.

She leant against the wall in the corridor, with her arms folded across her chest. Her cheeks were bright red from all the tears.

'Jill?' a broken voice called out from across the hallway.

Jill scanned the sad, drawn-out faces that filled the space in front of her. Then her eyes landed on a small, blonde woman.

'Jo?'

Mrs. Sampson came over. She'd been crying, too. There were purple bags under her eyes. Without any hesitation, she wrapped her arms around Jill, pulled her close, and hugged her tightly. Jill rested her palms on Jo's back.

'Who are you here with?' Jo asked, with her head resting on Jill's shoulder.

'Dallas.'

'How is he?'

Jill stammered for a moment but finally got the word out. 'Gone.'

Jo held her a little tighter. 'Dan's gone, too,' she said.

The two women pulled apart and spoke face to face.

'Where are the kids?' Jill asked.

'Out in ER.'

'Mine too,' Jill said. 'Have you told them yet?'

Jo shook her head. 'I've just been hiding out here. They needed Dan's bed, so they bagged him up and took him away. I don't know how to tell them. How do I tell them they'll never see their dad again? Brody – he isn't going to understand. They have their little workshop together, and he – he just isn't going to understand.'

'I don't know how to tell them either. Sally is only three. By the time she's five, she won't remember him at all.'

Jo wiped fresh tears from her eyes. 'What are we going to do?'

'Let's tell them together,' Jill said.

'Thank you, Jilly. Shall we tell them here? Or at home?'

'Here. Let's get it out the way.'

* * *

Milo stepped back into ER and saw Rex leaning up against the vending machine, talking to Becca.

'How many more times do I have to tell you?' she asked. 'Leave me alone!'

'You should go,' Milo said.

Rex shifted his eyes to Milo. His face darkened, and he quickly squared his shoulders and started to step towards him.

Then Jill and Jo came around the corner, and he stopped in his tracks.

'Alright, Winters. I'll leave you and your little girlfriend here alone. But I'll see you around. There won't be anyone left to protect you soon.'

With that, Rex gave a crooked smirk, and then he headed through the sliding doors at the head of ER and disappeared into the blinding daylight.

'What was he saying to you?' Jill asked, as she went over to Sally and lifted her into her arms.

'Nothing,' Milo said.

Becca stood up. 'Mom? Where's dad? Is he okay?'

Brody sat on the floor, cross-legged, humming to himself, and gently rocking back and forth.

Milo didn't have to ask. He could tell by the look in his

mom's eyes that his dad was gone. His stomach dropped to the floor, and he felt his knees weaken. He felt a sudden dizziness, and he quickly got down onto the floor to save himself from falling.

Jill crouched beside him, with Sally parked on her thigh, and she wrapped an arm around him. 'I'm so sorry,' she whispered gently in his ear.

Jo gave her daughter a quick, soft shake of the head. Becca burst into tears and brought her fingers up over her face. Mrs. Sampson took her into her arms and sobbed onto her shoulder.

Brody stared up at them, uncertain what was happening.

Chapter 15
Uncle USA

The Mamba pulled onto Oakvale Drive. Milo counted six vans as they drove down it, towards their house. A couple of stretchers were being wheeled down garden paths by exhausted van drivers – regular delivery men that had been drafted in by the government. More blood-drenched patients were strapped to the stretchers, barely clinging on to life.

Jill slung the car up onto the driveway and killed the engine. They sat in silence for a few minutes.

Just a few hours earlier, Dallas was standing out on that exact spot, sponging down the car. Now he was in a plastic body bag, in a pile of corpses in that dark expanse beneath the hospital.

Milo looked over at his mom. Her hands were still clutching the wheel. Her skin was white. She looked beyond exhausted, as if she'd just run a hundred marathons back-to-back. Her hair was slick, and thick greasy snakes clung to her face and neck.

'I'll carry Sally in,' he said.

What Happened Next

His mom didn't reply. She was staring off through the windshield, lost in twenty years of memories.

Milo unbuckled his belt and climbed out. He lifted his little sister from the kiddie seat and headed to the door. When he looked back, he saw his mum was still sitting behind the wheel, glaring forwards.

He decided to leave her out there for a while. She'd come in when she was ready. The house was throwing shade over the driveway now, so she wasn't sitting directly in the sunlight.

They'd left in such a hurry they hadn't even locked the door. Milo threw it open and carried Sally into the kitchen.

Sunlight had been blazing in through the window all morning, and it was hot and humid inside. The room smelt like a butcher's shop. The table was still black with blood that had dripped onto the floor, where a large puddle had formed.

Milo nearly puked when the smell hit him. He glared over the tabletop, at the blackened plates and festering eggs, and scrags of bacon.

He carried his sister into the living room and sat her down on the couch.

'Marnie,' she said.

'You want to watch some Marnie Moose?'

She nodded. It was an online cartoon that had come out just before the virus and was now the latest craze with every preschooler. A new episode got uploaded every Friday, but Sally generally liked to watch the same two or three episodes over and over.

Milo found Sally's tablet in the drawer under the TV unit. Luckily, it had charge. He opened up StreamTube, searched for Marnie Moose, and clicked on the first result.

An ad came up. An ad that Milo hadn't seen in a long

time. Two years ago, it had been everywhere – in every commercial break on the TV, on every app on his smart-phone, even on the streaming sites. Some government marketing executive clearly hadn't gotten round to turning it off yet. Milo tried to skip it, but it wouldn't let him.

A cartoon of an old man, with a long, white beard and a blue top hat appeared on the screen. He had a genie's tail, which swished and flicked as he floated around the screen.

'Hello, America!' he said, in a friendly and charismatic voice, with a heavy Southern accent.

'Uncle USA here, and I'm here to tell you about our exciting new Distanced Living Centers. As you might have heard, congress has now ruled that no citizen of the United States of America can be forced into receiving the Lavitika vaccination.

'Now, that is just dandy for the three percent of the adult population who strongly oppose vaccination. However, our experts believe that, while three percent of over-sixteens go unvaccinated, this virus will be able to enter those people, mutate, outgrow our vaccinations, and bring about the end of humanity.

'But we are proud to say that we've found a solution, and it's given a boom to our construction industry like we couldn't have imagined! I give you... Distanced Living Centers!'

The cartoon floated to one side of the screen, and an animation played behind it, depicting a welcoming commu-nity, complete with white, wooden buildings and luscious grass being showered by sprinklers. Butterflies fluttered in the air; families rode merrily down the street on bikes.

Uncle USA continued, 'In every state, we have built wonderful, gated communities capable of housing fifty thousand people. Far away from the main population, anti-vaxxers can come and start a new life here, with their families, without imposing danger on anybody else.

'You have until May sixteenth to get vaccinated or to check yourself into your nearest Distanced Living Center.'

Once the ad finished, Milo sat the tablet on Sally's lap. Her favorite cartoon moose appeared, dressed up in hiking gear. The episode was called, 'Marnie Moose Goes on A Walk'.

Something creaked over by the door. Milo turned quickly to look. His mom stood in the doorway, watching them.

'Are you okay?' he asked.

'Tired.'

'I can watch Sally if you want to sleep.'

Jill half-smiled. 'I need to call your grandparents. Check they're okay.' She looked at Sally, who seemed content enough, watching cartoons on her tablet. 'Put the news on, please. See if they know what's going on.'

She went and took the kitchen phone from the wall and dialed in her parents' number.

Milo turned the TV on. The Channel One news burst onto the screen. An elderly professor was being interviewed in the studio. The banner across the bottom read, *'Latest Update from Dr. Lewison.'*

Milo recognized him from the days of the virus. He was on the TV most nights, talking about immunity and vaccination efforts.

'We're noticing that none of the detainees–,' the professor started.

'Avoidants,' the news reporter corrected him.

'Yes, sorry. None of the *Avoidants* in any of the Distanced Living Centers up and down the country have been affected by the symptoms that we're seeing heavily across all fifty states, and that are being reported overseas.'

'What does that mean?'

'It means that whatever today's casualties have been exposed to, the *Avoidants* have not been exposed to.'

The reporter pressed his finger into his ear so that he could listen more carefully to an instruction coming through his earpiece.

'Thank you, Dr. Lewison. That's all we have time for today.'

'But–.'

The screen cut back to footage of the riots outside of emergency rooms again – the same clips they'd shown all day. Smashed glass. Interlocking police shields. Riot hoses.

In the kitchen, his mom leant against the counter, staring out of the window, with the phone held to her ear, listening to the endless ringing. She set the receiver back in its cradle, then called through to Milo, 'We're going to Gran and Grandpa's!'

Chapter 16
We're On Our Own

Milo's grandfather had built the house with his bare hands. He finished it a few weeks before Jill was born. The house had been perfect. White, wooden cladding that shimmered in the sunlight. Ornate fascias. Shutters with little turtle doves carved into the wood. Rocking chairs out on the porch. Flower beds in the windowsills, bursting with color.

It was built with love. And Jill had loved growing up there. She was a master at hide and seek. She'd slip into the tightest little nooks and crannies, and her parents wouldn't find her for hours. Eventually, they'd just follow the sound of her giggling.

Now, as Jill sat behind the wheel of the Mamba, sitting in the shadow of the house, staring up at it, it didn't look like that dreamy place from her childhood at all. It looked tired. The cladding was gray, and the paint was flaking off. The flower beds in the sills had long since rotted away, and the shutters were drab and sun-faded.

'Nanna, nanna,' Sally said from the back seat, looking up at the house.

Milo watched the front door through the slats in the porch rail. It stayed shut. The Mamba was loud. Every time they'd ever driven it there, his grandparents would hear the car coming up the driveway, and they'd be out on that porch, with smiling faces, ready to welcome them inside.

He glanced at his mom, who stared glumly up at the house. She gave him a quick look.

'Stay here with your sister,' she said.

Jill unclipped her belt, got out, crossed the yard of baking-hot, cracked mud, and climbed the porch steps. As soon as she started to tread over the planks, she heard a scratching noise from inside, like a dozen rats were clawing at wood.

She tried the handle, but it was locked, so she dug her hand into her pocket and took out her keychain. It was the key with red nail polish on it. She sunk it into the lock and threw open the door.

The scratching sound amplified instantly.

'Mom? Dad?' she called inside as she stepped into the hall.

Everything looked normal downstairs. The hallway was tidy. Dark parquet flooring, and a coat stand. She glared through into the lounge. Nothing out of place there, either. Just floral sofas and a big oak coffee table.

'Mom?' she called again. 'Dad?'

The scratching sound was coming from upstairs, from the landing. When she saw nothing out of place on the ground floor, she headed over to the staircase and started to climb it.

The scratching grew louder all the while – sharp claws digging furiously into timber. When she reached the top, she saw what was causing it.

'Teddy, what are you doing?' she asked.

Her parents' golden retriever was clawing at their bedroom door, which was wedged shut into the jamb. Wood shavings lay scattered all over the floorboards.

Teddy turned to look at her. But her tail didn't wag. Not a single flick. She was panting fiercely. She'd been scratching away at that door for a long time, and there was an inch-deep butterfly of claw marks at its base, with a speck of daylight poking through here and there.

'Get out the way, girl,' Jill said, as she approached the bedroom door and reached for the handle. The dog backed away.

Jill pushed the door open. The hinges gave a long groan until it came still. She peered inside. It took a long time for her to understand what she was seeing. But when she understood, when it registered, all the strength fell out of her body. She folded to her knees. They clapped hard on the floor. Vomit poured from her lips. It was watery and biley, and it slipped through the cracks in the floorboards.

In the bedroom, against the far wall, stood her parents' bed. That's where her parents were lying - on top of the duvet. Both still in their pajamas. Bare feet.

The TV played to itself in the corner – the Channel One news, with its montage of death and destruction.

A shotgun cartridge sat on the floor by the bed like a little red cigar. Its end was charred.

The shotgun itself lay across the lap of Jill's father. His cold, gray hand still clasped the handle, with a stiff finger hovering near the trigger.

Behind the bed, two enormous, red rose heads decorated the wall, side by side. They were fleshy in the middle. The blood splattered outwards like petals.

He'd shot his wife first. Then he'd reloaded and shot himself.

Teddy barged past Jill. She jumped up onto the bed and sniffed at the bare jawbones that crowned the two cadavers.

Jill puked a little more. Her stomach was one hard, painful knot. She brought her face down onto the floor-boards, and she cried. Snot poured from her nose and taped across her mouth.

* * *

Twenty minutes passed by. Milo sat out in the Mamba, looking up at the house. He was watching the time in the small clock sunken into the dash.

'Nanna,' Sally said. She'd been saying it every couple of minutes.

Milo glanced back at her, over his shoulder. 'Some-thing's not right, Sal,' he said.

She smiled.

He turned back towards the house. 'Wait here,' he said.

He got out, crossed the yard, and went up over the porch and into the hall.

'Mom? Gran? Grandpa?' he called.

'Don't come up here!' his mom screamed.

'Wuh-why?' he asked.

'Do *not* come up here!'

'Are they here? Are they okay?'

'They're – just don't come up here.'

'Should-should I call an ambulance?'

'Dial nine-one-one. Say you need a coroner.'

'A what? What is that?'

'Just ask for a coroner.'

Milo started to climb the stairs. They creaked.

'Hey, hey, hey! What are you doing?' his mom asked.

'I was going to use the phone on the landing.'

'No. Use the one in the living room. Do not come up those stairs, Milo.'

'Okay, fine.'

Milo went down the hallway, into the lounge. The phone sat on a little, wooden nest of tables by the sofa. He picked it up and dialed.

But this time, there was no wait at all. It patched through to an automated message straight away.

'We're experiencing overwhelming levels of emergency calls right now. If you or a loved one are vomiting blood, please transport them to the nearest emergency room as soon as possible and then wait at home. If resuscitation is required, please search for "National Cross CPR Instructions" on StreamTube. If the patient has already passed away and CPR is not possible or has not been successful, please move the body to another room in the house. Clearly label the name of the deceased and then wrap the body in cellophane, paper, sheets, or blankets. Keep the door closed.'

The line cut dead.

Milo dropped the phone.

Something came clambering down the staircase. It sounded like a suitcase full of bricks. But Milo soon saw that it was Teddy. She came down the hallway, with her tail wagging slowly behind her, and her long, pink tongue hanging out in front.

'Hi, girl!' he said.

She came strolling up to him, and he crouched down on the rug and started stroking her neck and back.

Teddy sniffed his cheek. He saw the smattering of red on her snout. She was painting his face with it.

'Urgh, what's that?'

He could feel it running down his jaw. He ran his

fingers through it and sniffed at the dark red liquid. The unmistakable metallic smell. He wretched.

'What happened up there, girl?'

Jill came down the stairs. She looked down the hall at him. 'Where's Sally?'

'She's out in the car.'

'You left her–? What's that on your face?'

'It was on Teddy's nose.'

'Oh, Christ. Go in the kitchen and wash it off. Did you get through to anyone?'

'No, it's a robot.'

'A robot?'

'A machine. An automated machine answering the calls.' He splashed water into his face from the kitchen sink. 'It says to take casualties to the hospital. And dead bodies – to wrap them up in paper or sheets, or–.'

'Jesus Christ.' Jill clapped her palm to her forehead. 'We're on our own.'

Teddy bolted out of the house suddenly. She bounded over the porch and down onto the cracked mud that surrounded the house. As soon as she got out into the daylight, she started barking – not a playful bark, but the heavy, aggressive bark that she reserved for intruders, like the mailman.

Milo and his mom ran out after her. Sally was wailing in the back seat of the Mamba.

A large crow had landed on the arm of her kiddie seat, and it was pecking at the crumbs in her lap.

Teddy stood up against the car's side and barked fiercely. The crow cawed once, and then it dove upwards into the air and took off into flight. It vanished over the tree-tops, into the neighboring yards.

Jill lifted Sally into her arms. The whaling settled to a gentle whimper.

Teddy sat at Jill's feet and cocked her head to one side.

'Good girl.'

'Are they dead?' Milo asked as he stepped down off the porch, with water dripping from his chin.

Jill nodded.

Milo sat down on the porch step and put his head in his hands. No tears came. He wanted to cry, but he couldn't. He'd spent all his pennies.

Jill sat beside him, perched Sally on her lap, and wrapped an arm around her son's shoulders. Teddy came and lay on the dirt by their shoes.

They sat there in silence for more than an hour, shaded under the porch roof. The crow came back to the Mamba a few times to pluck some more crumbs from the kiddie seat. Teddy would chase it away.

Finally, Milo took his head out of his hands.

'The message said to wrap them in paper. Or sheets,' he said.

'That's in case you're in the same house with them,' his mom replied. 'So you don't get sick from the body as it starts to break down. It's only them here.'

'So you're just gonna leave them up there?'

'I don't want to. But I don't want you to see them, Milo.'

'We should bury them,' he said.

Jill frowned. That's exactly what she'd wanted to do. And it's what her parents had wanted, too. They had a plot picked out in Masterson Cemetery. But they'd never get them over there. They were too heavy. And she didn't want Milo seeing them. Not like that.

'It's too far to the cemetery, Milo. They're too heavy. We can't cart them around like that.'

'Not the Cemetery. We can bury them *here*. He built this house for her. For *you*. This is where they belong.'

Jill looked at the mud under her feet. It was so dry, it was practically white, and it was riddled with cracks.

'We'll never dig into this, My.'

'We can put them in the vegetable patch. It's compost. It's soft. Grandpa's got shovels in the shed. I used to help him dig up the potatoes, remember?'

She did remember. Milo didn't own any Wellington boots, so they used to put plastic grocery bags over his shoes and fasten them with elastic bands.

'Alright,' Jill agreed. 'I'll wrap them up in the bedroom. I'll wrap them in sheets. And I'll tape them up. And I'll drag them out into the landing. And then I'll shut the door. But you don't come up until the bedroom door is closed, okay?'

'Yes, mom.'

'Okay. Go and get the shovels.'

* * *

Together, Jill and her son pulled the thick, white cocoons down the stairs, one at a time, and then dragged them outside and around to the patch of soft, black soil at the back of the house.

Various shoots rose up out of the compost, but they had all withered and wilted under the day's intense heat.

Milo had made a start digging. A trench sank deep into one side of the vegetable patch. Jill took up the other shovel and started digging the second grave while Milo deepened the first.

Large mounds of clumpy, black dirt formed at the sides of the two openings. Once they were about three feet deep, the mother and son were too exhausted to carry on any further.

'That's deep enough,' Jill said.

Milo climbed out of the first grave, and he pulled his mom out of the second. Together, they lowered one large, white cocoon into one trench, and then they shoveled the dirt on top of it and patted it down with the spade heads. Then they sank the second cocoon into the grave beside it, and they filled, too.

'Two lovers, side by side, forever,' Milo said, as he stared down at the dirt.

'Is that Shakespeare?'

'Goblin Avenger 2,' he said.

Teddy came up slowly behind them, and she lay in the dirt between the two graves. She rested her head on the compost and let out a long whine.

They let her grieve for a while, and then finally, Jill said, 'Let's go home.'

Milo nodded. There was black soil all up his arms and jeans, and it covered his shirt.

Jill went into the lounge and got Sally. She'd fallen asleep on the sofa. She carried her out to the Mamba and strapped her into the seat in the back.

Milo headed towards the car, but then he stopped in his tracks. He turned back and called to Teddy, 'Come on, girl. You can come with us.'

Teddy stayed put, with her snout pressed into the dirt.

'Come on, girl!' he insisted.

Jill looked over from the Mamba.

Milo walked up to Teddy, grabbed hold of her collar, and tried to pull her. But she wouldn't budge.

'She doesn't want to leave them,' Jill said softly.

Milo started to cry. 'Come on, girl. You can come live with us now. We'll take care of you.'

Teddy looked up into his eyes, with her head still resting on the ground.

'Teddy!' Sally called from the kiddie seat.

Teddy got up and dashed over to the car – her paws throwing up soil as she ran.

Milo laughed and followed her. He lifted her into the back of the Mamba. She plastered Sally in licks all over her face and neck.

Sally giggled.

Jill looked at Milo. 'Ready to go home?'

He glared over at the vegetable patch one last time. He saw himself standing out there, six years old, with plastic bags banded around his ankles. Shovel in hand. His grandfather standing beside him, showing him how to dig out the potatoes. His grandmother bringing them lemonade and cookies on a tray.

Milo looked back at his mother and nodded. 'Ready.'

Chapter 17
The First Night

The Mamba crawled back into its spot on the drive, and Jill clunked the handbrake into place. The mother and son sat in the front, covered in soil from the vegetable patch. Teddy lay in the back, with her head resting on Sally's lap. Sally tickled her snout softly.

Jill stared down Oakvale Drive. The street was empty now, but sirens still echoed in the distance. The sun was starting to sink below the houses now, and the road was mostly in shadow, but great strafes of warm, orange light burst through the gaps between each residence.

'It doesn't feel real,' Milo said.

'I know,' his mom replied.

They sat in the shadow of the house until the last of the light fell out of the sky. Then the spotlight above the front door came on, and they found themselves sitting in the white orb that it cast on the driveway.

'Come on, mom,' Milo said. 'Let's go in.'

Sally had fallen asleep by the time they vacated the Mamba. Milo carried her inside.

Teddy jumped down onto the concrete and tottered along behind them, wagging her tail.

The rancid metallic smell in the kitchen was even more pungent now. The table was crawling with flies. They were skittering over the breakfast leftovers and sucking at the black blood. Some flew in circles overhead, buzzing merrily.

Jill threw open the double doors that overlooked the backyard. She grabbed hold of one side of the table and started to drag it across the floor tiles. Milo set Sally down in the lounge and then came back and grabbed the other side of the table. Together, they lifted it out into the back yard. Next, they took out the high chair. The lap-tray was still filled with Dallas' blood.

When they came back inside, the kitchen felt bare. But at least they weren't faced with that constant reminder of that awful morning.

A small, black puddle sat on the floor, where the blood had dripped from the table's edge. Jill stared at it hauntedly.

'I'll mop that up,' Milo said.

'Thanks, My.'

She watched, exhausted, as her son got the Floor Hero out of the kitchen cupboard, squirted a little detergent into its bucket, and then mopped away the last of her husband's blood.

Teddy came into the kitchen. Her nails clicked on the floor. She looked up at them, panting.

Jill took a bowl down from the cupboard, filled it with water, and then set it down on the tiles. The old retriever lowered her head and started to lap it up.

Milo poured the bloody swill from the bucket into the sink and then packed the Floor Hero away.

'I'll take Sally up to bed,' Jill said.

She carried the sleeping toddler upstairs and into her room.

The walls of Sally's bedroom were coated in pink glitter paint. It shimmered as you stepped around the room. The small bed in the corner had tall sides to stop her from falling out in the dead of night. It was her first 'big girl bed' after being promoted from the crib. The sheets were dotted in Marnie Moose.

The house was still warm from the blistering heat of the day, so Jill lay Sally on top of the sheets rather than tucking her underneath.

She turned on the unicorn night light that was mounted to the wall above the bed. The plastic unicorn bust glowed warmly.

Sally snoozed soundly. Often, she would wake somewhere between the sofa and her bed during the nightly carry-up. But today she was too tuckered out by all the events of the day, and she snored softly.

Jill stood and watched her for a long time. She'd often do that when she was a baby. Dallas would stand by her side, and they'd just sit and watch her little chest rise and fall with each breath. They'd done the same with Milo when he was little.

After a while, she went into the bathroom and twisted the shower taps. She ran it hot and stepped under the spray to try to wash away some of the memory of that horrible day – the black, dried-up blood and the soil, and the puke, and the tears that had crusted down her cheeks like craft glue.

Shortly later, Jill found herself standing in the doorway of her and Dallas' bedroom, staring in at the bed.

They'd bought that bed maybe a decade ago, from the furniture store down on Main, and they'd slept in it together almost every night since. Not always in each other's arms.

Sometimes, if they'd had an argument, they would both lay at the very edges, as far apart from each other as humanly possible. But still in that same bed.

She never realized how vast that mattress was. And how empty it would doubtlessly seem without her husband by her side.

Jill considered climbing into bed, just to try it. But she couldn't face that. Not today. Maybe tomorrow.

The frantic tapping of buttons and the clashing of swords sounded from down the landing. She followed the sounds and pushed Milo's door open to find him lying on his bed, blanketed in the glow from his TV, with his console controller clutched in his hands. Teddy lay at the foot of his bed, with her head resting on his legs.

Milo paused his game and shifted his eyes to his mother. He'd been crying. His cheeks were red, and his eyes were twinkly-wet.

'I thought it would take my mind off it,' he said. 'But it hasn't.'

'Can I sleep in here with you tonight?' Jill asked.

It seemed odd that way around, she thought. For years, a smaller Milo had tottered into her and Dallas' room and had asked if he could climb into bed with them.

Milo nodded. 'Of course.' He shifted over to one side of his mattress. His mom came over and laid beside him.

'So this is Goblin Avenger, huh?'

Milo unpaused the game. His character – a muscular, green-skinned being in furs and chainmail – resumed running around a stone-walled cottage, smashing wooden chests apart with his sword, and pocketing the coins and potion bottles that flew out of each one.

'Yeah.'

'Is it two-player?' she asked.

What Happened Next

She hadn't played a video game since her dad had taken her into the Neon Gallery when she was eight years old. And even then, she'd only made a yellow circle eat some pips.

Milo smiled. He took a second controller out of the drawer in his bedside table, fired it up and sat it on his mom's lap.

They played together late into the night, sobbing gently all the while.

Chapter 18
The Sheriff's House

Peters pulled up outside Masterson's small police station. It was a one-story, wooden building just a stone's throw away from the hospital.

ER had quietened down, and a couple of bouncers from the local night club came over to offer assistance in keeping things calm. Peters wasn't sure at first, but they produced their licenses, so he allowed it.

He knew he had to give the cadets a break soon. They'd had a hell of a first day on the job. The hospital had been a blood bath, so he wanted to check out the sleeping arrangements to make sure they had a decent place to recharge.

He killed the engine and headed inside.

The station was basic. There was an office at the front, with one desk and a coffee pot. In the back, there was a cell, with a small sponge mattress laying on the floor. And off to the right, there was a toilet cubicle with a broken flusher.

'Jesus Christ,' Peters sighed. He slammed himself down in the chair at the desk and put his head into his hands.

Something creaked at the front of the building. He

looked up and watched a woman climb the steps to the door and then come inside. The little bell above the jamb dinged.

The woman had wavy blonde hair and blue eyes. She was short and slim and wore all-black. A navy-blue handbag dangled from a strap over her shoulder.

'Good evening,' Peters greeted her.

'Are you Peters?'

'Yes, ma'am, I am. How can I help?'

'I'm Cathy Callow. The Sheriff was my husband.'

'Oh.' Peters' friendly expression dropped. 'I'm so sorry.'

'Thank you.'

'I knew your husband.'

'I know, he speaks – he *spoke* highly of you.'

Peters smiled. 'That's nice to hear, thank you.'

'I'm staying right across the road there. I was waiting for a car to turn up.'

'What can I help you with?'

'Where are you and your men planning on staying?'

'Well, here. It's the only law-owned building in Masterson.'

'That's what I was worried about,' she said. 'Well, Andy just wouldn't have that. He was Mr. Hospitality. We have a bungalow over on Washington Street. I'm living with my sister now 'cause I can't bear to be in the place. There are three bedrooms. Two bathrooms. A kitchen with a big dining table. Plenty of food. Plenty of towels. Plenty of everything. I would really like you and your guys to go and stay there. And Andy would've liked that, too.'

Peters gave a warm smile. 'That's a very kind offer, Mrs. Callow.'

'Please, call me Cathy.'

'It's a kind offer, Cathy. But I don't think we could impose like that.'

'You wouldn't be imposing at all. Like I say, I'm not even there. Please, Peters. For him. Let us do this for you. He wouldn't have a bunch of lawmen sharing a small cot. No washing facilities. No cooking facilities. Hell, no toilet. Please.'

Peters sighed. The station certainly wasn't suitable for all of them – especially for an extended stay. They could end up being there for weeks. Maybe even months.

'Alright, thank you, Mrs. Callow.'

She smiled and stepped over and set the key down on the desk.

An hour later, Peters threw open the bungalow door. He stepped into the entrance hall. The walls were painted in pastel shades of green and pink and blue as you stepped between the different rooms, and the floor was lined with great, shimmering walnut planks.

Denzel followed him in. Diaz and Chambers came in after, hand in hand.

'What a beautiful home!' Chambers said.

'I'm gonna get you a place like this one day,' Diaz said, squeezing her hand a little tighter. 'Just you see.'

The entrance hall opened out into the large, open kitchen area. The units wrapped around the outside wall, and an enormous oak dining table stood in the middle of the floor. On the table was a bottle of whiskey. Cathy had left a note that read, *'Peters – you probably need this!'*

'Alright, Mrs. Sheriff!' Denzel cheered as he lifted the bottle and pointed it to Peters. 'Drink, Lieutenant?'

'We can toast to all the people that died today,' Chambers said. Her eyes were still pink from all the upset the day had thrown at her.

'Alright,' Peters said. 'Just one.'

Chambers started opening up the cupboards above the worktops until she found the one with the glasses inside. She lined up four glasses on the table, and Denzel poured a healthy measure of bronze liquor into each one.

Diaz sat in one of the chairs, and Chambers parked herself on his lap. Both of them took a glass. Denzel passed one to Peters. Once the four of them held a whiskey each, they clinked them together and necked them down.

'Ugh,' Chambers blurted as she slammed her glass down onto the desk. 'That's stronger than the stuff we have at the dorms.'

'Did you live in the dorms, sir?' Denzel asked. He took his vest off, hung it over the back of a chair, and sat down. 'When you were at the academy, I mean.'

'I did.'

'Bet you have some wild stories?' Diaz poked.

'Well, on my first night there,' Peters joined them in sitting, 'me and my roomies got a little rowdy.'

'Yeah?' Denzel asked.

'Yeah. One of them got out a bottle of tequila, and we put it all away. Then I broke out some of my records.'

'Records? Like vinyl records? Jesus!'

'I'm older than I look,' Peters laughed. 'Anyway, we were pretty noisy. And the campus was right opposite the girls' block for the nursing college. One of the girls came over. Pounded on the door. Furious. Says she's got her exams the next day, and we're keeping her up. God, she was beautiful.'

'And what happened?'

'I married her,' Peters said.

He sat his empty glass down on the table. Then he studied the faces of the three young cadets that surrounded him.

'I'm sorry your first day was like this,' he told them somberly.

'We're just happy we could help out,' Denzel replied.

'My first day out of the academy, I had to break up a fight between two hotdog salesmen,' Peters chuckled softly. 'They'd parked their carts too close together, I guess. One was encroaching on the other's turf. And they started squirting mustard at each other. High octane, right?'

Chambers smiled. 'Beats our first day, Lieutenant. Give me fighting hotdog men any day.'

'So there's three rooms?' Denzel asked.

'We'll bunk up,' Chambers said. Diaz nodded.

'Alright,' Peters said. 'Starting in the morning, I want two of us to be on patrol at all times. We'll take shifts riding around town in the cars. Keep a police presence in the streets. A deterrent for any looters.'

'Yes, sir,' Denzel said. 'I'm happy to ride out on the first shift.'

'I'll take the first shift, too,' Peters said.

Chapter 19
Those Tumultuous Teenage Years

I t was the first thing in the morning, and Becca was on her knees in the small downstairs bathroom, with her head held over the toilet. Her stomach had started hurting at the hospital. Now, she'd been sick.

That's how it started with dad, she thought. *Tummy pain. Then puking. Am I next?*

She reached for the flusher, and the contents of the bowl vanished round the u-bend. Slowly, she got to her feet. She ran the tap, cupped some water into her mouth, swilled, and spat it into the sink.

The pain eased a little. She took some deep breaths. She wasn't due her period for another couple of weeks, so it couldn't be that. And *these* cramps hurt *way* more than *those* cramps.

Becca unlocked the door and stepped uneasily out into the hallway. The wall opposite was blue and lined with family photos. Right there, in the middle of every single one, was her daddy. Dan Sampson. Her rock since the day she was born.

She'd hit those rebellious, tumultuous teenage years, where it was uncool to get on with your parents, and where it was fun to make them wait up all night worrying about you while you drank down at the park. Every time he'd open her door, she'd yell at him to close it. Every time he'd cook dinner, she'd take it up to her room rather than eat it at the table with him.

And right now, as she looked at those photos, with tears rolling down her cheeks, she wished more than anything that she could take it all back. She'd give *anything* to hear him knock on her bedroom door one more time. Or to call up the stairs that the lasagna was ready.

Her mom started whistling down the hall. Becca frowned. Her mom *never* whistled. She followed the sound. It led her to the kitchen.

Jo was standing at the breakfast bar, ripping the lid off a big tub of vanilla ice cream. She sat the lid down on the counter and then ran a spoon into the soft-scoop. She dumped the great cream ball into one of two tall glasses, which she'd set out on the side. She whistled merrily.

'Mom?'

'Oh, hello, dear. How's your tummy?'

'It hurts. What are you...? Are you okay?'

'Yes, dear. Just making you and Brody a shake each. It's gonna be another hot day, so I'm making you and Brody a shake each.'

'Maybe you should come and sit down?'

'I'm fine, dear.'

She dumped another couple of balls into the glass, and then started to fill up the other.

'I don't want a shake for breakfast, mom. I don't have an appetite. And my stomach–.'

'Your father loved a peanut butter shake. On a hot day like today.'

'I know, but–.'

'So we are going to honor him, aren't we?'

Becca said nothing.

'Now go and get your brother.'

Jo started to whisk the ice cream in the glass until it went droopy. Then she lifted a jar of peanut butter down from the cupboard and spooned some of that in, too.

'Where's Brody?' Becca asked. 'His room or his workshop?'

'In his room, dear,' Jo said, as she stirred in the peanut butter.

Becca went back down the hall and climbed the staircase.

Once her daughter was out of sight, Jo reached up high into a cupboard overhead and lifted down her small medicine basket. She quickly leafed through the boxes and packages before taking out a foil pill packet. Quickly, she put the basket back into the cupboard and closed the door. Then she started to pop out the pills into a small, gray dessert bowl. There were ten or so in total. Using the back of a spoon, she ground them into a fine, white powder.

The doctor had prescribed the sleeping pills a couple of years ago, but she'd found them too strong. She'd ended up sleeping until way past noon the following day. So the remainder of the packet had sat in the kitchen cupboard, until now.

She poured the powder in two equal parts – half into one milkshake and half into the other. Then she stirred it in, into the delicious, icy-cold blend of vanilla cream and peanut butter.

Jo put the packet in the bin and set the bowl down in the sink.

* * *

Becca knocked on Brody's door.

'Okay,' he said.

She opened it and found him sitting on the floor, cross-legged, tightening the nuts on some contraption with a little spanner.

'Mom's making us a peanut butter shake.'

'Pancakes for breakfast,' Brody said.

'Yeah, I know. But it's shakes today.'

'Monday is pancakes for breakfast,' he repeated.

'Yes, usually, but it's shakes today. Don't ask me why.'

Brody started to rock back and forth gently. He didn't stop tightening the nut the whole time.

She wanted to talk to him about their dad. She wanted to know if he understood what had happened. But she didn't know how to bring it up.

'Come on,' she said. 'Let's go and get that shake.'

* * *

Becca came back up to the breakfast counter, with Brody dawdling along behind her. She took a seat on a stool. Her little brother parked himself on the stool beside her.

'Here you go,' Jo said as she slid the shakes across the countertop.

'Where's yours?' Becca asked.

Brody planted both palms on his glass and poured it down his throat as fast as he could.

'There was only enough ice cream for you two,' Jo said. 'Now, go on, drink!'

Becca lifted the glass to her lips and took a sip. 'It's good.' She forced a smile.

'It's good?' Jo asked.

Brody slammed his empty glass down on the breakfast bar.

'Yeah,' Becca replied. 'It's good.'

'Then drink it.'

'I did.'

'Drink it all. We're drinking milkshakes in honor of your father, and you take the most insulting little sip.'

'Okay, okay,' Becca said. She gulped down the whole glass and then set it down on the countertop.

'Good girl. Now, come out to the car. We're going on a little drive down to the park. I want to go to your father's favorite spot.'

'Mom, *today*?' Becca asked.

'Yes, today.'

Jo walked over to the door that opened into the garage and pulled it open.

'Come on!' she said, as she stood waiting.

Becca sighed. She got off her seat and walked slowly over to the door.

'Go on!' Jo said. 'In you go!'

She did as her mom said. It was dark inside the garage, and it smelt of oil. The far wall was lined with battered, old boxes. They were filled with her dad's old fishing gear and trophies.

In front of the boxes stood the pick-up truck. Jo had backed it in earlier, once they'd gotten back from the hospital. She never kept it in the garage. It was always parked out on the driveway, at the front of the house. When Becca had asked why she was putting it inside, she'd said, 'In case of looters.'

Brody came in next. Jo stepped inside last.

Becca went to open the passenger door, but her mom stopped her.

'No, no. Sit in the back with your brother,' she said as she pulled the back door open.

'I always sit in the front.'

'He might be scared. You can hold his hand,' Jo insisted. 'Go on – hop in the back.'

Becca swayed suddenly. Everything had gone dark for a second, like she'd blinked for way too long.

'I think I might be sick again,' she said.

'Plenty of places to be sick in the park,' Jo said. 'Go on, get in the back.'

Becca climbed into the back and then slid over onto the other side. Her brother clambered in and sat in the seat beside her. She helped him with his seatbelt.

Another heavy blink, and a moment of darkness.

'Mom, I don't feel good,' she said.

When she looked at Brody, he'd fallen asleep. He snored, with his head limp against the belt.

'Stop your whining,' Jo said. 'I know you miss your father. But mommy is fixing it.'

'Fixing it?' Becca asked. Her words were slurred and drawn out.

'That's right. I'm fixing it. We'll all be together again soon.'

Jo pressed the window button. The glass dropped down half an inch. Then she slammed the door shut.

Becca watched, sleepily, as her mother took the hose pipe from the corner of the garage and started to uncoil it. She could hear her taping it to the exhaust pipe at the back of the pickup. Then she fed its mouth into the open gap in the window above Brody's head.

Becca tried to reach for the door handle, but she couldn't. Her arms were lifeless. Numb. Another long blink, and a terrifying moment of darkness.

When her eyes came open again, she saw her mother climbing into the front seat and starting the engine.

And then darkness.

Chapter 20
A Better Way Out

When Milo woke, his bed was empty. Teddy wasn't laying across his legs anymore, and his mom wasn't sleeping at his side. He could hear her clattering around in the kitchen.

Slowly he climbed out of bed, changed into a fresh pair of boxers and a t-shirt, pulled on some clean jeans and socks, and then headed downstairs.

Sally was in her usual place on the sofa, watching Marnie Moose on her tablet. Teddy was lying lazily at her side. The old dog raised her head slightly when she saw Milo but quickly let it sink again.

He found his mom in the kitchen. She was pouring cereal into two bowls.

'Can I go check on Becca and Brody?' he asked.

'Breakfast first,' his mom said.

'I'm not hungry. Please, can I go check on her? *Them*?'

'You haven't eaten,' she said.

'I'll eat it after. I just want to go check. Just quickly.'

Jill looked through the window, out at the street. There were no vans parked up outside any of the houses from what she could see. There were no people around at all, in fact. It was quiet.

'Hmm. I don't know. It might not be safe outside. People are scared. People are dangerous when they're scared.'

'It's thirty seconds away. I'll just go, check on them, and come right back.'

'Okay. But take Teddy with you,' Jill said. 'Just in case...'

Milo smiled. 'Come on, Teddy!' he called, as he slipped on his sneakers. 'Do we have a leash for her?'

'Look in the trunk. Your father's tow rope should be in there.'

Milo went out onto the drive and popped open the Mamba's trunk. Sure enough, there was a grubby length of rope coiled up inside the spare tire. He fastened it to Teddy's collar, and the pair of them started down the street.

The Sampsons lived only ten doors down. Milo led Teddy up the garden path, and he knocked on the front door. Teddy squatted in the flowerbed and started to pee.

'Teddy, they might see!'

Teddy carried on, all the same. A yellow puddle grew around her paws, but it quickly sank into the thirsty soil. She stepped back onto the concrete and then glared off, towards the garage door.

Milo knocked again. No answer. No commotion through the frosted glass.

'They might still be in bed,' he said, looking down at Teddy. 'Yesterday was quite the day.'

He gave a final knock, waited another minute, and then said, 'Come on, then, girl.'

He started back down the path, but then the rope went taut. He turned to see Teddy standing firm, eyes fixed on the garage door.

'Come on, Teddy. Let's go home!'

He tugged the rope, but the old retriever wouldn't budge.

'What is it, girl?'

He followed her gaze and glared at the garage door, which stood over on the left-hand side of the house. Milo stepped over towards it and could hear the faint ticking of an engine inside.

'The car's running,' he said. He pressed his ear up against the aluminum for a better listen.

Teddy started to whimper and shift around uncomfortably.

Milo leant down and grabbed hold of the handle. It was locked. He quickly scanned the door, looking for any glass panes or cat flaps, or gaps around the edges – *anything* he could peer through, to get a peek at what was happening inside. But there was nothing. The door was a solid, white expanse, fixed firmly in place.

'Shit! Wait here, girl,' he said.

He tried the front door. It was locked. So then he ran up to the tall, wooden gate that stood beside the garage, and he went through into the Sampson's back yard.

From the yard, Milo could see through the kitchen window. There were a couple of empty glasses on the breakfast counter. Nothing out of place, but no signs of life at all. He tried the back door, but that was locked, too, just like the front and the garage.

Milo saw a big rock sitting on the ground, at the foot of the door.

It might have a key under it, he thought, so he reached down and picked it up. No key. Just a couple of beetles, keeping out of the sun. But he carried the rock with him, back out front, where he found Teddy staring at the big aluminum door, still trotting her paws anxiously and whining.

'Mind out, girl,' he said.

Milo smashed the rock down onto the handle of the garage door. The metallic clang rang out into the road like a gunshot. He brought it crashing down again. And again. Teddy barked fiercely.

The handle, all scuffed and battered, started to buckle. Finally, with one last blow, it came off. A plume of stenchy vapor bore through the hole and drifted up into the morning air.

Milo put his eye up to the hole and peered in. It was dark inside, but he could see the Sampson's pickup. The engine was running. He could make out a figure slumped in the front seat, but that was all.

He thought the door would open once he'd snapped the handle off. But it wouldn't. He tucked his finger into the hole and pulled. But it wouldn't budge. It was still locked. Milo started bashing the aluminum with the rock in panic. The vast door dented with each blow and made a tremendous sound, but it didn't open. It was still fixed perfectly inside its frame.

'Milo?' Peters asked as he climbed out of his Rattler, which he'd slung up on the curb.

'Peters?' Milo asked, shading his eyes with his hand. 'Peters! Thank god! Please, help me!'

'What's going on? What's with the rock?'

'My friend's family isn't answering the door. There's a car in the garage. And the door is locked. And the engine's running. And there's someone in the car.'

'*What?*'

Peters hurried up to the garage door, tucked two fingers into the hole, where the handle used to be, and pinched hold of a little metal rod, just inside. He tugged it, and a loud click sounded from either side of the door.

The door lifted up, and a thick, iridescent mist billowed out. Milo and Peters both spluttered and choked. The Lieutenant wafted his hand in front of his face.

When the chemical fog had lifted, the pickup came into view. It sat with its engine humming. Peters saw Mrs. Sampson slumped back in the driver's seat – eyes closed, mouth open.

'Milo, go wait by the road,' he said, as he stepped into the garage and pulled open the driver's door. A second cloud of silvery, toxic fog came out of the truck, and it rose to the ceiling of the garage, where it floated like a canopy of gray velvet.

The Lieutenant killed the engine and then pressed his fingers to Jo's neck. No pulse. Then he looked into the back seat.

'Oh, no!'

Milo's face appeared through the glass of Becca's window. He peered in at her, and then tore open the door.

'Becca!' he shouted.

She was leaning back in her seat. She didn't look distressed or panicked or ill. She just looked like she was sleeping. He grabbed her shoulder and shook her.

Peters took his radio from his hip. *'Denzel, I need you over on Oakvale. Now.'*

'Wake up!' Milo shouted as he rocked Becca to and fro. Fresh tears streamed down his face. 'Wake up! Please!'

Peters opened Brody's door. The stocky little guy had both his fists clenched in his lap. His eyes were shut, and his lips hung slightly apart.

The Lieutenant put his fingers on the boy's neck.

'He's got a pulse!'

He unbuckled Brody's belt, lifted him up into his arms, and carried him out of the garage. He laid him down on the driveway and then went back to the pickup.

'Excuse me,' he said.

Milo stepped out of the way. Peters took Becca's pulse. His face lit up instantly.

'She's alive, kid,' the Lieutenant said.

'She *is*?' Milo beamed.

Peters lifted her out from the truck and took her over to where her brother lay. He put her down on the concrete at Brody's side. Milo knelt beside and held her hand. He watched her face closely. He could see her nostrils flare softly with each breath.

Teddy stood over Brody. She gently prodded her nose into his chest and then waited for a reaction.

Denzel's squad car pulled up beside them, and the cadet got out. He looked down at the two sleeping children in horror.

'What happened to *them*?' he asked.

'They're alive,' Peters said. 'But there's a woman in the garage that wasn't so lucky. Got any bags in the car?'

'Yes, sir. What shall I put on the tag?' Denzel asked.

Peters looked at Milo. 'You know her name, son?'

'Jo. Jo Sampson,' he said.

Denzel opened his trunk and tore off a body bag from a roll. Then he headed into the garage.

'Looks like the hose came out from the exhaust,' Denzel called out as he stepped around the back of the truck.

'That's why your friends are still breathing,' Peters told Milo.

'Why would she do that to them? She's their mother. How could a mother do that?'

'It's a mother's job to protect her children,' Peters said.

'What's happening in the world right now – it's *terrifying*. And we don't know how it's gonna play out. So Mrs. Sampson there – she made a decision. She decided to give them a peaceful ending. No panic. No terror. No choking to death on your own blood. You just fall asleep and slip away. She was trying to give them a better way out.'

Milo looked down at Becca. She *did* look peaceful.

'Do we need to take them to the hospital?' he asked.

'There's not a bed or a doctor or a nurse free in the state,' Peters said. 'They need to sleep it off. Once they're awake, we'll be able to see if they're still themselves.'

'What's going on?' Jill cried, from the sidewalk.

Milo turned to see his mom standing there, looking down at Becca and Brody in horror. Then she saw Denzel dragging a body bag out of the garage.

Chapter 21
Sleeping Beauty

J ill stood in the doorway of her bedroom, staring in at the two children who lay sleeping on her and Dallas' bed. The Lieutenant and the officer had carried them in a few hours ago.

'Keep a close eye on them,' Peters had told her before he and Denzel left to carry on with their rounds.

She swung by the room every fifteen minutes or so to listen for the snoring, but she really didn't have to – Milo had knelt at Becca's bedside the whole time. His gaze was fixed on her, and his hand was wrapped around hers.

Jill studied him. She knew that look in his eyes. It was his father's look. The one Dallas had given her, back on their first dates.

She stepped inside and set down a bowl of chicken soup on the floorboards beside Milo's knee.

He glanced at it and then back at Becca. 'I'm not hungry,' he said.

'She's not going anywhere, My.'

'What do you mean?'

'You know what I mean.'

'Where's Sally?'

'On the sofa, watching crap on her tablet, of course. Now stop changing the subject and eat your soup!'

'I said I'm not hungry.'

'You haven't eaten since breakfast yesterday, and you barely ate anything then. I'm not going anywhere until you eat it.'

Her son rolled his eyes and picked up the bowl and began to spoon the soup into his mouth.

Jill smiled. But then she looked over at the sleeping bodies on her bed, and the smile faded.

'Poor babies,' she said.

'Lucky we found them when we did,' Milo said, with a mouth full of moist chicken. 'When do you think they'll wake up?'

Jill shrugged. 'It might be tomorrow. It might be the day after. The officer found an empty sleeping pill packet inside the house. They'd been crushed up. Put in the milkshake glasses, it seems like.'

'She drugged them?'

'Just stopped them resisting, I guess,' Jill said.

Milo looked down at the bowl of soup and then set it down on the floor. 'Are you gonna try to do that to me and Sally? Try to give us a better way out?'

Jill gave him a long, hard look as she determined her next words.

'Jo was scared for her children,' she started. 'And I'm scared for you. I don't know what's happening. And I don't know what's gonna happen. But I will never, *ever* take away your chance to survive. You *or* Sally. Whatever becomes of this world, I know you will both thrive in it.'

Brody spluttered suddenly and sat bolt upright on the bed. He made Milo and his mother jump out of their skins.

Jill ran around to the other side of the bed, where he sat, coughing and looking around the room, wide-eyed.

'Brody, it's okay, honey. It's okay,' she said.

Brody glared at her, stunned and silent, as she rested herself on the mattress beside him. She put a hand on his shoulder and looked into his eyes. They were bloodshot and yellow.

'God, you're dehydrated. Must feel like the worst hangover in the world.'

Brody didn't say anything. He just looked at her mouth as she spoke.

'My, go get him some water.'

Milo got to his feet and ran from the room.

Brody's eyes landed on his sister, who lay next to him on the bed, snoring lightly. She looked like sleeping beauty.

'She's okay,' Jill said. 'She's fine. You're both fine. She's just sleeping. They found you in, um... You had a car crash. That's all. You had a car crash, and you've both been here while you sleep it off.'

Milo came into the room with a glass of water. He didn't want to crowd Brody, so he handed it to his mom, being careful not to spill any.

'Take a sip of this, Brody.'

She slowly extended it towards the stocky young boy. He backed away at first, but then he took the glass between his hands and drank a little. Then he drank a little more. And then a lot more.

Brody rubbed at his eyes. 'Mom,' he said, shortly.

Jill exchanged an uncomfortable glance with Milo. Then, she turned back to the young boy.

'When your sister wakes up, we'll talk about your mom,' Jill said. She forced a smile to try to comfort him.

'Do you want to watch Junkyard Rescue?' Milo asked.

Brody nodded.

'Come on, we'll put it on!' Milo said.

Brody got up and followed Milo out into the landing. Then he collapsed onto the floor and looked around, dazed. Milo and Jill both rushed to him and crouched at his side. They helped him sit up.

'Dizzy,' he said.

Chapter 22
The Star-Spangled Coffin

'Morning, sir,' Diaz said as he came into the kitchen. He was wearing a loose soccer shirt and baggy boxers. His feet were bare.

Bright, early light poured in through the window.

Peters sat at the end of the table, eating oatmeal and watching the Channel One news on the vast TV that was bolted to the wall.

'Morning,' he replied, as he shoveled in another spoonful. His voice was gravelly, and there were great bags under his eyes.

Diaz opened the fridge and took out a carton of orange juice. He poured himself a glass and then came and joined the Lieutenant at the table.

'How did you sleep?' he asked, taking a sip.

'Hardly at all,' Peters said.

'Same, actually. Chambers snores.'

Peters laughed. 'My wife used to. Ear plugs are your friends. Trust me.'

'What's happening on the news?'

'There's some big, special broadcast about to come on,' Peters said.

The TV was filled with a red holding screen, with the words, 'STAND BY FOR WHITE HOUSE' printed across it.

The two lawmen watched it patiently.

Suddenly, the screen changed to some choppy aerial footage. The news helicopter was hanging in the air above the White House, like a buzzard circling a juicy scrap of roadkill.

'This morning, we bring you some shocking and deeply saddening news from Washington DC. We hope you are sitting down. I have the regretful duty to break to you the news that the president of the United States has passed away. The White House has said that he has died in the night. He has died in his sleep.'

Peters leant back in his chair and exhaled. The spindles groaned under the weight.

'We've just had confirmation that the president is now leaving the White House for the final time,' the reporter said, over the whirring of chopper blades.

The camera panned in on the front door as it came open. There was a pause, and then a stream of Secret Service agents slowly filed out. Each agent wore a black suit and tie and had a white armband clasped around their right bicep.

Eventually, a vast shape appeared through the doors. It was a coffin, with a large, star-spangled banner draped across it. The flag hung over its sides and bunched onto the shoulders of the four uniformed soldiers who stood beneath each corner. They carried it carefully down the White House steps and across the concrete forecourt. There, they fed it into the back of the long hearse that waited, with its rear door open.

The red banner across the bottom of the screen read *'PRESIDENT DIES PEACEFULLY IN SLEEP.'*

Peters could imagine the reality, though. He died retching up blood, wide-eyed and terrified, just like everyone else.

Chapter 23
Empty Houses

Becca slept for two whole days. Jill and Milo were watching the special broadcast about the death of the president when Becca finally stumbled into the room, rubbing at her eyes.

She was groggy as hell at first, and Jill let her rest and rehydrate for as long as she could before breaking the news about Jo. She sat her down on her own, out in the garden and told her. Becca broke down in hysterics, and Jill held her for an hour solid.

'I'll tell Brody,' Becca said, finally.

* * *

A week passed slowly by. Everybody in the household grieved together. Sometimes, they even laughed, recounting some silly thing one of their loved ones had done. Slowly, day by day, each person started to slip into their own habits and routines.

Sally spent the majority of her days rewatching her favorite episodes of Marnie Moose.

Becca spent most of her time either crying alone in the toilet, with the door locked, or sitting with Brody, making sure he was entertained enough not to tear the house apart.

Brody found amusement in disassembling the nearest appliance to hand. Jill took to giving him broken appliances from the garage. He even managed to get the old blender working again.

Milo never strayed far from Becca's side. She didn't seem to say much to him, but he liked to be close by, just in case she *did* say something.

Teddy loved having more people around. It meant more attention, more cuddles, more strokes, and more dinner scraps handed down to her when no one was looking.

Jill spent the days making sure everyone was eating and drinking enough while also keeping a careful eye on the food supply. The fridge and freezer were slowly emptying out, but they had plenty of canned foods in the cupboard for now.

She'd banned the kids from watching the news in the living room. So now, they could only watch on-demand episodes from the cloud, since the news had taken over every station.

To keep up with happenings, when no one was around, she'd listen quietly to the radio in the kitchen. The news service explained that local supermarkets were shut for the time being. All of the supply chains had been taken over by the government, and the army would start to deliver food parcels to each household in the coming days. The news instructed residents to mark an X on the front door if anybody was alive inside the household. No X, no food parcel.

Between each news story, an advert would come over the air. It sounded like a commercial for a movie, with a deep, dramatic voice speaking the words: '*Switch on your device at seven p.m. September twenty-eighth for a special announcement from the White House. The Vice President will give the details of Project Sandman: The future of America. Catch it on any radio station or any TV channel.*'

* * *

It was nine a.m., and a door slammed in the street outside. Jill quickly rushed to the kitchen window. This had become a habit whenever she heard vehicles coming and going out in the road.

The stream of vans and ambulances coming to take people away had slowed right down, but it hadn't completely stopped. Each day, one or two would park up in the street, and you'd see a blood-drenched Mastersonian wheeled down the garden path and loaded into the back to be driven away and never seen again.

As Jill peered through the glass, she could see an ambulance was parked up outside the Richardsons' place. It was five houses down, on the other side of the road. A couple of paramedics headed inside. A short time later, they came back out, with Lance Richardson strapped to a stretcher and blood all down his front.

His wife had died the week before, Jill had heard from a neighbor. And now there went Lance. They didn't have any children, so that house would stand empty. A lot of houses on Oakvale stood empty now. Eleven at least, to Jill's count.

Since she found herself standing alone in the kitchen, she switched the radio on to have a quick listen to the latest news stories while the kids were all semi-amused in the other room, shoveling down cereal. She twisted the dial on the old wireless that sat on the windowsill, and a reporter's voice came over the air.

'*Okay, we'll get an update on Chicago later today. But firstly, we are now joined by Professor Stovenwell from the Grosvenor Office of Statistics. Professor, what is our latest estimate of the death toll?*'

'*Hospitals were so overwhelmed in that initial period that they still haven't counted fatalities with any degree of accuracy. And as you know, most hospitals are going to be burning mass funeral pyres in the coming days. But we believe it to be in the region of seventy-five percent of the adult population.*'

'*And we've all heard these reports from inside Distanced Living Centers that there have been no fatalities of this nature at all?*'

'*That is correct.*'

'*Nor any fatalities of this nature in any individuals under the age of fourteen outside of the DLCs?*'

'*That is also correct.*'

'*So it looks as though these deaths are directly linked to the Lavitika vaccination.*'

'*The data does suggest that.*'

'*The vaccination that you stood on that TV stage every night and you implored everybody to go and get. The vaccination that I got. And my wife got. And my brother got. And my sister-in-law got. And every adult listening at home got.*'

'*Look, I'm not a scientist. I'm not a medical officer. I'm just a statistician. People were dying from the virus, and the greatest scientific minds told us, ensured us, promised us that this vaccine would stop that.*'

'*Well, what can we do? Has the vaccine taken everybody it's going to take? Are the rest of us safe? Are we supposed to* sit around and wait to die? To leave our children all alone in the world? We need some goddamn answers.'

'As you know,' the professor said, 'the government has been working night and day to deliver Project Sandman. The future of America, as they say. And the Vice President will announce the details to the nation on September twenty-eighth, seven p.m.'

'Mrs. Winters?' called a voice behind Jill.

She switched the radio off quickly and turned to face Becca. 'Please, call me Jill,' she said assuringly, as she offered a warm smile. 'What's up?'

'I want to pop home for some things.'

'What do you need? I've got plenty more tampons. Don't worry about that.'

'No, it's not that. Thank you. I just want some fresh clothes. And also, we have food at the house. We're eating all your supplies here, but there's stuff there going to waste. The food in the fridge might not be any good now. But there's frozen food. And tinned food, too. Huge bag of pasta. Huge bag of spaghetti. Might as well bring it all here.'

'Well, food would be useful. But are you sure you're ready to go back there?'

Becca nodded. 'I'll be quick.'

'Okay. But Milo will go with you. It might not be safe outside.'

'Do you think the looting will start soon?' Becca asked.

Jill had heard on the radio that all the major cities, come nightfall, were strife with looting and rioting. The police and army were reserving their numbers for whatever Project Sandman was, so they were just letting it happen. The whole of downtown Chicago was ablaze right now.

'No. No looting. You're safe here.' She forced a smile.

Chapter 24
Road Trip

Chambers came into the kitchen.

'Morning, sir.'

'Morning,' Peters said. 'Coffee's in the pot.'

'Thanks.' She dozily poured herself a cup, and then gave a big stretch. 'Denzel on patrol?'

'Yeah. Cleared some teens out of an old roller rink. They were having some sort of rave in there.'

'At least somebody's having fun.' She sipped from her mug.

'I've got an errand to run today,' Peters said. 'I'll be out of town for a little bit.'

'Want some company?'

Peters scratched his stubble. 'It's kind of a personal errand.'

'I don't mind. I'm getting cabin fever in Masterson.'

Peters chuckled. 'I know the feeling. Alright, sure. Finish that coffee and we'll roll out.'

* * *

Chambers sat in the passenger seat of Peters' Rattler. The footwell at her boots was full of scrunched-up burger wrappers and empty soda cans that rolled from one side to the other with every turn in the road.

They were heading out of town. The houses quickly thinned out and gave way to tall pines. There were no other cars on the road.

After ten minutes, Peters clunked the indicator on, and they turned into the gravel yard that sat in the shadow of a tall, metal building. It stood alone in the woods and was fronted by black glass. The sign up above read, '*Dalton's Pet Supplies*'.

'Pet supplies?' Chambers read.

Peters put the Rattler into park and got out. Gravel crunched underfoot. The lot was completely empty, and there was total silence, other than the gentle rustling of the pine branches.

'Is this place even open?' she asked, as she climbed out of the car.

'No, it's not,' Peters answered. He went to his trunk and took out a crowbar.

Chambers gave a short laugh. 'We're... breaking in?'

'The owners are dead,' Peters said. 'Everything inside is going to spoil.'

They went up to the main door. Peters slipped the crowbar's tip into the small gap beside the lock. Then he shunted the bar back as hard as he could. The door popped open.

He half expected some alarm to go off, but the silence stayed.

'Come on,' he said.

They headed inside. The aisles went right up to the ceiling, and there were tall ladders leaning against each one, fixed to little sliding runners. The shelves were bustling with every pet accessory imaginable – dog beds, cat stands, balls, chew toys, cages, fish tanks.

But Peters was only interested in one thing.

He grabbed a flatbed cart from the train by the door and wheeled it over to the far corner, where all the enormous wholesale sacks of dog food were piled high like sandbags in a war zone.

He grabbed one by its jagged, stitched ends and slammed it down onto the trolley. Then he grabbed another and slammed that down on top. He paused to picture the volume of the Rattler's trunk, then, he took a third.

'What's that sound?' Chambers whispered.

The Lieutenant stopped to listen. There was a low rustling noise. And there was squeaking.

Chambers' eyes landed on a large, white rubble bag that stood on the end of the aisle, across from the dog food. On the side of it was a sign that read, '*Horse oats. One dollar per pound*'. And a scoop hung on a little chain. But the white canvas was moving, pulsing. And the sound was coming from the bag.

Chambers stepped over to it and peered in. Only she couldn't see any oats. She could just see a writhing carpet of matted, brown fur and pink tails that flopped around like worms. Scratching, little claws and sharp, yellow teeth. Hundreds of rats were bowling over each other. Feasting. Clawing. Digging. Shunting each other out of the way.

She clapped her hand to her mouth.

'You don't like rats, then?' Peters laughed, as he pulled open the trunk and started to lift the bags inside. Each one pushed the suspension down a little further.

Chambers leant against the side of the Rattler, looking a little pale. 'What, you *do*?'

'I don't like them, necessarily. Used to them, though. Get plenty at the farmhouse. Maybe you'll see one.'

'We're going to your place?'

Peters nodded. 'Got an old dog there. Bessie. She'll be out of food by now. Just hope it isn't too late. I don't have as many neighbors as I used to. The closest house to mine was Tin Foil's.'

'Tin Foil?'

'Yeah. Old coot. Conspiracy theorist. They carted him off a couple of years back. Now, Mrs. Gleeson is the nearest. I keep trying her on the phone, but no answer.'

He slammed the trunk down.

* * *

Minutes later, they were back on the road. Blurred trees and bracken whizzed past the windows.

'Do you think more people are gonna die?' Chambers asked.

Peters exhaled. 'I hope not.'

'I hope not, too. But they're saying on the news that the people in the Distanced Living Centers aren't dying. So it's in the vaccine, right?'

Peters stayed quiet.

'And if they're not dying, can't they let them out? There are doctors and teachers and engineers inside those... *camps*. Good people. Talented people. They can help the rest of us.'

'Congress voted to put those people away. Only

congress can reverse those orders. But congress is coughing up blood like the rest of the country.'

'Hey, pull over here!' Chambers said, pointing.

'What, why?'

'Pull over, pull over!'

Peters started to brake. He peered up through the windshield and saw a tall building by the side of the road, three stories high. It was cladded from top to bottom in black shingles. The window frames had bowed with age, and the roof dipped a little in the middle. He pulled into the small, bricked yard in front of it and parked up.

Chambers hopped out and glared up at the building.

'I haven't been here for a while,' Peters said, as he got out. 'Have you been back here, since you left?'

Chambers shook her head. She walked up to the porch and ran her fingers over the golden plaque screwed into the wood by the door. The words, 'Miss Moltez's Home for Children,' were sunken into it.

She tried the handle, but it was locked.

'It closed down years back,' Peters said.

'Got that crowbar?'

Peters took it out the trunk and busted open the door.

Chambers stepped into the hall. She tried the light switch, but the power was off. Every corner was blanketed in cobwebs. The walls were dark gray, just as she remembered. Dust flitted through the beam of sunlight that bore in through the open door.

Peters followed her inside. She turned right, into a lounge filled with battered, old armchairs. A wood burner sat cold under the mantelpiece.

'We used to tell ghost stories to each other in here,' she laughed. 'Used to scare the shit out of each other.'

She went through into the kitchen, at the end of the

hall. The walls were equally dark in there. There were white sheets over the units.

'I used to help Miss Moltez cook most nights. She used to call me Chef Two. Denzel helped once, nearly burned the place down. We demoted him to 'chief taster' after that.'

She went back down the hall and climbed the staircase. Each step creaked underfoot.

Chambers went into the front bedroom. There were three beds in there. A big, pink bear sat on one of them. Peters stepped in behind her.

'This was my room,' she said, with a sad little smile. 'That was my bed there.' She pointed. 'And that was Jess's, and that was Billie's.'

She led him back down the landing and into the next room along. There were three bunk beds in that room. 'And this was Denzel's.'

'Hey, look,' Peters said. He picked up a little model car off a unit behind the door. 'Wolfhound Seven-Seven.'

'Oh, my god!' Chambers said, in disbelief. She ran over and took it from him. It was mostly orange, but most of the paint had been bashed off over the years. 'It's his! It's Denzel's. He left it here when he left. Left it for some kid that didn't have many toys.'

'How about that?' Peters chuckled.

She put it in her pocket.

'God!' Chambers looked around the room, with tears in her eyes. 'My parents died when I was eight. Car crash. And I ended up here. And I was so sad. I was so *scared*. And I really didn't think I'd have a future. I didn't think I'd have a family. But Moltez – she really was like a mother. She built this warm, little community. And I felt safe. I felt loved. I felt wanted. And I didn't feel alone.

'And we played games, and we learnt, and we told stories, and we cooked. And I felt like a normal little girl. I followed Denzel to the academy because I wanted to help people. I didn't want them to feel helpless. Like I felt. I wanted them to know that there is a day after today. That there is *hope*.'

* * *

Ten minutes later, they were back in the car, and trees were whipping past the windows again.

'We're nearly at the crossroads,' Peters said. 'One way goes to the city, one way goes towards Delby. That's where my farmhouse is.'

He started to slow down. Up ahead, he could see flashing, orange lights. As they approached the junction, they could see men standing in the road.

'Are those army uniforms?' Chambers asked.

Peters squinted. 'Yeah. Yeah, they are. What are they up to?'

One soldier broke off from the others, who all seemed to be trying to push a jeep off the road. He held up a gloved palm, ordering Peters to stop.

Peters let the Rattler crawl to a halt, and then he wound down the window and held his badge out into the warm morning air.

'Lieutenant Peters,' he said.

'Sergeant Holson,' the soldier said, as he stepped over.

He glanced at the badge and nodded. Peters pulled it back inside and tucked it away.

'Hey, is this a Rattler?' the sergeant asked.

'Yes, sir.'

'My uncle had one of these!' the sergeant patted the

roof. 'I'll need you to spin it around, Lieutenant. Highway's a parking lot.'

'What do you mean?'

'Miles of empty cars, all directions. Everyone tried to get somewhere – to hospital, or to family. And then half the drivers got ill. And the tailbacks grew and grew. Eventually, everyone had to abandon their cars.'

Peters stared ahead. In the distance, he could see a tank dragging a van off the road with a chain.

'So what are you guys doing?'

'We have the delightful task of clearing a path between Masterson and the city so we can get these food parcels out to people.'

'Are you clearing the highway to Delby?'

'Delby? Hell no. Ain't there like three houses there?'

Peters lowered his head. Chambers put her hand on his shoulder. He pictured Bessie curled up by the door, waiting for him, nothing but bones.

'I'm sorry, sir,' Chambers said.

Chapter 25
The Lie

Milo wheeled the little red cart along behind him down the street. It was made of tin, and the wheels wobbled as it went. It used to be his, as a kid. He'd haul rocks around the back yard. Now, it'd been handed down to Sally. Not that she ever used it. It just sat over in the sandpit, growing rust.

'Can't we just carry the food?' Becca laughed.

'Mom said it'll be easier using this thing,' Milo said, embarrassed to be dragging the toy cart along with him.

They veered up the garden path of the Sampson household, with Brody dawdling along behind them. Becca took the key from her pocket and twisted it in the lock. The door swung open.

'You sure you're alright going back in there? Milo asked.

Becca took a breath and then nodded. 'Come on.'

She stepped into the hallway. Milo went in after her and lifted the cart up over the step. Brody ran up the stairs.

'Bring that thing in here,' Becca said. Milo followed her into the kitchen.

Becca's eyes locked onto the two empty milkshake

glasses that sat on the breakfast bar, and she had a terrifying glimpse of that awful morning. She could picture her mom climbing behind the wheel of the pickup truck and firing up the engine.

'You okay?' Milo asked.

Becca shook the visions from her mind. 'Uh-huh.'

She pulled open the cupboards, revealing stacks of tinned vegetables and soups and jars of peanut butter and more. Next, she pulled open the freezer door, and icy-cold mist swept out across the floor.

'Load up your wagon, cowboy,' she said, with a smile.

But then she caught a glimpse of something out in the garden, under the shade of the tree, and the color dropped right out of her.

'What?' Milo asked. 'What is it?' He rushed to her side and followed her line of sight.

'What is that?' Becca asked.

Under the tree was a stuffed body bag. It sat there on the shaded grass like a fat black slug. A ginger tabby cat sat clawing at the plastic.

'Becca, that's... It's...' Milo didn't know quite how to say it.

'It's my mom, isn't it?' she asked.

'That officer Peters' guy – he bagged her up and took her out back.'

'Now the animals are getting at her.'

Milo lowered his head.

'We need to bury her, My,' she said.

Milo nodded. 'Have you got spades?'

* * *

They spent the next hour shoveling dirt. Gradually, a grave was carved into the hard, rain-starved earth. Not a deep grave, but a grave, all the same.

Between them, Milo and Becca managed to drag the body bag over from the corner of the garden. They lowered it carefully into the hole.

'Do you want to say some words?' Milo asked. He wiped his nose and left a big streak of mud across his face.

Becca thought for a moment and then shook her head.

'I think about her all the time. I don't need to say anything. Let's hurry up and get back. Your mom will be worried.'

They shoveled the loose clumps of dirt back into the hole and pressed them down, leaving a dark rectangle of earth by the lawn, which had become very orange and dry from the lack of water.

Once they were finished, they set down the shovels and headed back into the kitchen.

'Load that food up,' she said. 'I'm gonna go upstairs and get some clothes together for me and Brody.'

She ran up the stairs.

'Brody? Brody?'

Becca found him sitting on the floor of his bedroom, spannering a project he'd left unfinished.

She reached in and took a backpack off a hook on the wall and tossed it onto the floor by Brody's feet.

'Fill that up with whatever you want to bring with you to the Winters' place,' she said. 'Don't forget underwear, okay?' Then she headed into her room to get some things together.

Brody unzipped the backpack and started to fill it with various contraptions and tools from around the room and didn't waste any space on underwear.

Milo wheeled the cart out into the hallway. It was stacked high with tins and bags of frozen food, which steamed upwards into the warm morning air. While he waited for the Sampsons to come back downstairs, he started glancing over the photo frames that lined the hallway wall.

His eyes landed on a photo of Becca and her dad standing next to a rocky, orange ravine.

'That's the Grand Canyon,' Becca said.

Milo turned to see she was leaning over the stair rail, watching him. He smiled.

'His hat blew over the fence right after that,' she added. 'He was real pissed. I couldn't stop laughing.'

'When did you go there?'

'I was seven or eight, I guess. Brody was little. Have you been?'

Milo shook his head. 'I haven't been anywhere. Lake Farrington is the furthest place. Me and dad went there to fish with Uncle Malc. And that's only about thirty miles from here.'

'Brody,' Becca called up the stairs. 'Come on!'

He came bounding down the stairs, and the three of them shuffled slowly out of the house.

'You smell that?' Becca asked. She inhaled deeply through her nostrils.

Milo sniffed at the air. It was a burning smell. Like charcoal. It smelt like the bonfire his grandpa used to light after scraping together all the dead creepers.

He stepped out into the street and looked around. Off behind the houses, rising high into the sky, was a tremendous black column of smoke, dark and menacing. He thought it was a tornado at first.

'Where is that?' Becca asked.

'It's the hospital,' said an elderly voice.

Milo and Becca turned to see the Sampsons' neighbor standing out on her porch. She was a large, black woman, who wore her hair in a big bandana.

'Hi, Glendy,' Becca said.

'Hello, dear. I was sorry to hear what happened to Dan... and to your mother.'

'Thank you,' Becca managed, trying her hardest not to burst into tears right there on the doorstep.

'You staying over at the Winters' now?'

Becca nodded. 'Yeah, Milo here and his mom are taking good care of us.'

'That's good,' Glendy said. 'Jill is a good woman.'

'How're you holding up?' Becca asked.

Glendy tried to smile. 'Not too bad, dear. Looking forward to those food parcels, though. Been eating baked beans the last couple of days.'

Becca reached down into the red cart and took out some tinned vegetables, a bag of pasta, and some cookies. She went and sat them down on the foot of her neighbor's porch.

'No, dear! You need them more than me! More mouths to feed!' Glendy said.

'Please, have them,' Becca insisted. 'We have lots left in the cart.'

Glendy offered a warm smile. 'Thank you, dear.'

'So the hospital's on fire?' Milo asked.

The old woman's smile faded. She'd hoped they'd understand. Hoped they might have caught it on the news.

'No, dear,' she said, softly. 'It's the morgue – they couldn't possibly bury all those bodies. There's just too many of them. So there's a mass funeral pyre, out in the car park.'

'They're burning all the bodies?' Milo asked in horror. '*Together?*'

He and Becca stared back towards the colossal column of smoke that soared up into the sky. Somewhere among all that dark vapor drifted the last atoms of their fathers, floating up into the heavens as one.

After a while, they wandered back along Oakvale, with the smell of charcoal burnt into their nostrils.

It wasn't until they reached his driveway that Milo realized he'd left the cart on the Sampsons' front step.

'I forgot the food,' Milo said.

Becca rolled her eyes.

'You guys go inside. I'll run back and get it.'

They did as he said, and Milo headed back down the street, to the Sampsons' place. The red cart sat on the step, where he'd left it. As he reached for the handle, he heard a familiar voice.

'Hello, Winters.'

He turned to see a boy standing there, in the front garden. A boy in a black jacket, with pale skin, combed-back hair, and a pink scar running through his lip. A boy he'd hoped to never see again.

'*Rex?*'

'That's just about the gayest wagon I've ever seen,' Rex said, as he took a battered pack of Gunslinger cigarettes out of his pocket. He opened the flap, plucked one out, perched it in his lips, and brought a lighter to its tip. 'So where is she?'

At his side, Rex held an untidy cluster of rose stems. He'd ripped them off a rosebush on his walk there.

'Where's who?' Milo asked.

Rex glanced up at the house, with an unimpressed look

on his face. 'This is the Sampsons' place, Winters. So, who do you think I'm talking about?'

'Mrs. Sampson?'

'Becca, Winters. I'm talking about Becca. Where is she? I'm here to take her away. Her knight in shining armor. Got that big, old place to myself now that the old bastard is dead. She'll love it.'

'Didn't you hear?'

'Hear what?'

'About what happened in the garage?'

Rex shrugged. 'I guess not.'

Milo walked over to the garage door, which had been pulled down but wasn't locked. He pulled the shutter up. It swung upwards on its runners, revealing the pickup inside.

Rex stared into the garage, confused.

Milo went inside. 'Come on,' he said.

Rex followed him to the back of the pickup. Milo leant down and picked up the hose pipe.

Rex's stomach dropped. 'What–what happened?'

'Mrs. Sampson went all whacko. Drugged them with milkshakes. The glasses are still inside, on the countertop. Poke your head in and look.' He pointed to the door that went through into the kitchen.

Rex went up to it and threw the door open and peered inside. Sure enough, on the countertop were the two tall, empty glasses.

'Jesus,' Rex said.

'That was to get them all drowsy,' Milo went on. 'Then she told them to strap in. And she ran the engine, with the hosepipe through the window.'

Rex shook his head. 'And... what happened? Who saved her?'

'No one found them, Rex. No one knew. Not until days later.'

Tears started to pour down Rex's face. He tried to cover them with his hands.

Milo put his hand on Rex's shoulder, but Rex slapped it away. 'Get the fuck off me!'

He paced in circles around the small space behind the pickup truck. Tried to take it in.

'Where is she?' he asked. 'Where's her body? I want – I want to see her body.'

'They buried her in the garden,' he said.

Rex headed back out of the garage and took a right, through the gate that led through into the back yard. Milo followed.

Sure enough, there was a fresh grave right there by the lawn. Rex got to his knees beside it and wept hard. The tears fell onto his lap.

'She's buried here,' Milo said. 'Along with her mom and her brother. They didn't have time to dig three graves.'

Rex wiped away the tears on the sleeve of his leather jacket, but they kept coming.

'I–I loved her.' His eyes remained fixed on the grave.

Milo looked a little concerned.

'I know she was stubborn. I know she gave me the cold shoulder. But *god*...! I didn't want anybody else. I - I dream about her every night. And in the dream, we are - we are so happy. And then I wake up and - and she's not there. And I knew that if I could just... If I could just keep trying, I knew she'd change her mind. I knew we'd end up together.'

Milo's eyes shifted to the shovel that lay on the grass beside his foot. He considered picking it up while Rex's back was turned and plowing it into the back of his skull.

One sharp blow. Something told him he'd regret it later on if he didn't.

Rex laid his jagged gathering of rose branches down on the top of the grave.

'Did she feel pain?' he asked.

'No,' Milo said. 'You just – you just fall asleep.'

Rex nodded. 'That's good.'

He watched the grave a while. Then, finally, he got to his feet, and turned to face Milo.

'Don't tell anyone about this, Winters,' he said, as he wiped away the last of his tears.

Milo nodded. 'Sure.'

With that, Rex left the yard and disappeared down the street.

Milo waited for him to go, then went up to the front step, grabbed hold of his cart handle, and started to wheel it back towards home.

Chapter 26
Fireflies

Jill wrestled with a camping chair, out in the backyard. It was one Dallas had ordered online, and it folded down to the size of a beer car, but she was damned if she could unfold it. She'd just pulled five of them out of the garage. The others still lay in their little rainproof pouches at her feet.

'Milo! Milo! How do you open this goddamn thing?'

Milo appeared in the patio doors, and then he stepped out. 'What are you doing?'

'Just help me, will you?' she asked, pained, as she tugged at the thing from every angle.

Milo took it from her, swished it outwards, like he was flicking a magic wand, and a chair magically expanded into the air. The joints all clicked into place in the blink of an eye. He set it down on the dead, sun-battered grass.

'Right, now do the other four,' she said.

Becca stepped out into the yard. 'What's going on out here?' she asked.

'We're going to sit out here for a couple of hours,' Jill said.

She went into the kitchen and carried Sally out. She put her down on the grass, near the folded-up chairs. Teddy quickly followed her outside and started licking her all over.

Within a minute, Milo had unfolded all of the chairs. Jill arranged them to face the column, which loomed up over the houses.

'Sit, dear,' Jill said, patting one of the chairs.

Becca parked herself down in it.

'What are we doing out here?' Milo asked.

Jill nodded her head towards the column. The column was thinner now and a lighter gray, but it was freckled with embers. They floated around majestically like a gentle swarm of fireflies.

'We're going to sit, and we're going to watch the fireflies and think about them.'

There would be no wake. So this was the best she could do for Dallas – *and* for Dan. Sit their children out in the yard and watch those embers and think of them.

She had never imagined Dallas would go this way – a joint cremation with hundreds of others.

She thought he'd go before her, sure. Men tend to. And she thought she'd be there to cry at his funeral. They'd already picked out a joint plot in Masterson Cemetery, in fact. A pretty patch by the cherry tree, not so very far from the plot her own parents had bought for themselves. But they hadn't made it there either, of course.

Jill went inside and took a bottle of red down from the cupboard. She twisted off the cap and poured a glass and took a sip. It was the first drink she'd had in weeks. She and Dallas always kept a few bottles in stock, but drinking just hadn't felt like the answer up until now. But tonight, in memory of all those souls being sent off into the heavens, she decided to pour a glass.

A knock came at the front door. She set the glass down and marched down the hall.

Through the frosted glass, she could see the shape of a man. She pulled the door open and found Peters standing on the doorstep. His Rattler was parked up on the curb, with the trunk open, and there was a jumbo bag of dog food down by his feet.

'What's this?' she asked, cracking a smile.

Milo appeared behind her.

'Come on, muscles,' Peters said to him. 'There's two more in the car.'

Milo helped him bring them all inside. They stacked them up in the kitchen closet.

'Thank you so much!' Jill said. 'Where are they from? We've been feeding her our leftovers.'

'I got it for my dog, but the roads are all blocked off, so I couldn't get it to her.' He lowered his head.

'We're all out in the garden,' she said. 'Do you want to join us? I just poured a wine.'

Peters scratched his stubble. 'Uh, sure. If that's okay?'

Jill took a second glass down from the cupboard and filled it with red. Then she handed it to Peters.

'Thank you.'

He followed her out into the yard.

Sally lay on the grass, fussing Teddy and feeding her Cheese-Twists. Brody sat cross-legged nearby, sharpening pencils.

Milo sat next to Becca. Jill and Peters sank themselves into chairs, too. The four of them all stared up at the column.

A tear rolled down Jill's cheek as she watched the embers dancing and parting.

'Where did you meet him?' Peters asked. 'Your husband.'

'Middle school,' she said. 'He moved here with his folks when he was twelve. The principal appointed me as his "friendly face". When a newbie joined, they'd assign someone to look after them. Show them to classes. Eat with them at lunch. While they get settled in and make some friends. And that was that. We ended up marrying. Then Milo came along a couple of years later.'

Peters smiled. He leant back, and the canvas backing of the camping chair squeaked.

'Are you married?' Jill asked.

'Yes,' Peters said. 'My wife passed a couple of years back, but I'm still her husband.'

Jill nodded. She looked down at the ring on her wedding finger. She knew she'd still be Dallas' wife for the rest of her life.

'Do you know what Project Sandman is?' Jill asked. 'Do you know what's coming?'

Peters shook his head. 'I wish I did. I have to wait until the announcement on September twenty-eighth, like everyone else.'

'Where are you watching the announcement?' Jill asked.

'At the Sheriff's house, probably.'

'Watch it here,' Jill insisted.

Peters looked a little confused, but said 'okay', all the same.

Jill knew that whatever was coming was going to be life-changing and terrifying. Having the lawman present would help to keep the kids at ease, she was certain.

Chapter 27
Vax Kills

Peters woke to a cackle from his radio. He rolled over in bed and looked at the alarm on the bed stand. It was quarter past nine. Morning light crept in through the window.

The radio cackled again, and Diaz came over the line. *'Peters, you there?'*

He took the radio and clicked the button on the side. 'I'm still asleep, but I'm here.'

'There's an issue down at the rail bridge.'

Peters yawned. 'What kinda issue?'

'Big-ass truck thought it could fit under it.'

'Alright, I'm coming.'

* * *

The Whiston Rail Bridge was a great arch of faded, red brick and riveted steel. The words *'Vax Kills'* had been sprayed onto the side of it in yellow paint.

The cab of a huge rig had caught under the arch. The driver stood, shouting at Diaz. Diaz shouted back.

Peters parked his Rattler up on the curb, behind the squad car. He quickly got out and headed over to the two men.

'Hey, hey, what's going on?'

'This ass-wipe doesn't know when his truck is too big.'

'Hey, fuck you!' the trucker yelled.

Peters looked through the gap to the side of the cab and saw the vast trailer it was hauling. It was loaded with lengths of timber and steel. Behind it, he saw a string of trucks. Ten or more. The drivers of which had all climbed out. Some leant on their cabs. Some chatted and bantered with each other.

The flatbeds behind the cabs were laden with building materials, all strapped tightly down. Drywall, lengths of thick, plastic piping, pallets of bricks, huge spools of electrical cabling, metal canisters.

'What are you doing here?' Peters asked the driver who had tried to get under the bridge. 'What's all this stuff for?'

'Project Sandman,' the driver said.

'Where are you taking it?'

'The library,' he said.

'What are you doing with all this at the library?' Peters asked.

'I can't tell you,' the driver said.

Peters took his badge out.

'I still can't tell you,' the driver insisted.

'Want me to teach this smart-ass some manners?' Diaz asked.

'Cool your engines, Diaz,' Peters said. He looked at the driver. 'If you're heading to the library, you sure as shit aren't gonna fit under this bridge. So I suggest you go and talk to the guy at the back of the line and get him turned around. Head down Benvale and then Hughes.

153

You'll know you're at the library when you see the plinths.'

'Thanks,' the driver said. He slipped through the gap beside his cab and headed down the road.

'What is all that stuff?' Diaz asked.

'I don't know,' Peters said. 'But I don't like it.'

Chapter 28
The Eighty-Eight

Another week crawled slowly by. And then another. And then two more.

Chambers woke. She stretched out her arms and let out a yawn. Diaz had slipped out in the middle of the night to swap patrol with Denzel, so Chambers was sprawled out across the whole bed. She loved sleeping beside him, but she also loved getting that extra bit of room to spread herself out.

She looked around the bedroom. Morning light came in through the crack in the shutters. She glanced at the alarm clock on the bedside table. It was just gone eight. There was noise coming from down the hallway. Bashing. Rummaging.

'*Ugh.*'

She climbed off the mattress, pulled on some clothes, and headed out into the hallway, scratching her head, and letting out another great yawn. She followed the noise down the corridor. It was coming from Sheriff Callow's study. She peered inside.

Denzel was sitting at the desk. He was thumbing through papers. The desk drawers were all open beside him and a number of reports and photographs lay scattered across the worktop.

'Morning, kiddo,' Denzel greeted her, as he glanced up from the papers. 'How'd you sleep?'

'Better,' Chambers said. 'Why're you up so early?'

'Couldn't sleep.'

'What *is* all that?'

'Something very familiar,' Denzel said. He gave a grave look.

'Are those Callow's files?'

'Yeah.'

She picked up the cardboard folder from which all the reports and photos and clippings had come. The words, '*The Eighty-Eight*' were written across the cover in black pen.

'The Eighty-Eight?' Chambers asked. She'd heard that somewhere before.

'It's a white supremacist group,' Denzel said. 'They have clubhouses all over the state. Maine, too. Maybe other states. My mom's blazer was found in one. And nobody ever saw her again.'

He took a photo off the desk and handed it to Chambers.

It showed a terrified black woman holding her hands up in mercy. She appeared to be kneeling in a clearing surrounded by ferns and brambles. The camera flash burst off her eyes, hot and white. A trail of blood ran from her nose, down across her lips and vanished around the curve of her chin.

Chambers swallowed hard and then set the photo down on the desk.

'Is that your mom?' she asked.

'No,' Denzel said.

He pulled out an old front page of the Sunday Gazette from the papers on the desk. The headline was '*MOTHER OF THREE MISSING IN WOODS*'. Beneath it was a family photo of the woman, with her husband and their three children.

'A woman named Evie Utanga went missing from town ten years ago. Apparently, she went out for a walk in the woods and never came home. Left behind a husband and three young kids. They never found a body.' He tapped the photo on the desk of the bleeding woman kneeling in the woods. 'Looks a lot like her, doesn't it?'

Chambers glanced between the two photos. 'It *is* her. That photo in the woods – where's it from?'

'Callow had an informant, it seems like. Caught him growing weed in some old farm building years ago. Fed him photos. Kept him updated on activity.'

'Who's the informant?' Chambers asked. 'Is there a name?'

Denzel shook his head. 'No names anywhere. Not in this folder. Not in any of these drawers.' He turned and pointed to a safe that was sunken into the wall. 'Maybe it's in there.'

Chambers went over to it and ran her fingers over the keyhole.

'Where do you figure the key is?' she asked.

Denzel shrugged. 'Couldn't find it. I looked already.'

He carried on reading through the reports on the desk in front of him.

'There have been thirty disappearances of black women in this county in the last two decades. My mom included.'

'Why aren't the feds looking into this?'

'Because they're black women,' Denzel said, coldly. 'This group – The Eighty-Eight – they have a leader.

There's no names mentioned. These reports just call him the *High Eagle*. He decides who they take. Who they kill. He calls all the shots.'

'Did Callow submit any of this to the courts?' Chambers asked. 'Did he make any arrests?'

Denzel shook his head. 'No mention of any arrests. He collected all this dirt, and then he kept it in a folder.'

'Why?'

Denzel shrugged. 'Beats me.'

He scooped together all the papers and photographs and let out a long sigh.

She saw the little model car sitting next to him on the desk.

'You carry that around with you now?' she asked, with a smile.

He looked down at it.

'I can't believe you found it.'

'It was just sitting there. Like it wanted to come back to you.'

'I know it's a just a toy,' he said, picking it up and turning it over in his hand, 'but to me, it symbolizes a lot more than that.'

'What's it symbolize?'

'Hope.'

Chapter 29
The Zephertown Massacre

By the time September twenty-eighth came around, several weekly food parcels had been delivered to the house. A military truck would roll slowly down the street in the dead of night, and a recruit would sit a cardboard box on each porch where the door was marked X.

There were no thrills inside the parcels, much to Milo's dismay. No confectionaries or desserts – just nutritional essentials. Tinned veg, bread, pasta, milk, fruit, and a small selection of meat.

Jill was just grateful she'd been given enough to keep those four mouths fed.

They'd gotten into a good routine now. Everyone kept busy in their own ways. They spent less of the day crying and more of the day enjoying their own little hobbies and interests. Becca had read most of the books in the house. Milo had recompleted all of his video games. Sally had rewatched the same handful of episodes of Marnie Moose. Brody kept on building his little contraptions. Jill filled her days making sure everyone was happy and well-fed.

But Jill understood that this was all just filler. They

were all just passing the days until September twenty-eighth. Whatever Project Sandman was, she knew it was going to shape the rest of their lives, and now, at last, the day had come.

* * *

In the morning, Jill fried up some bacon. It was the first time she'd fried anything since *that* breakfast. The kids had been making do with cereal. But today felt important. She wanted them to have something special.

Sally crawled around on the floor, following Teddy. When the old retriever lapped up some water from her bowl in the corner, Sally lowered her mouth into the bowl, too.

'Sally, don't do that!' Jill shouted. 'I told you not to do that!'

Milo came into the room, rubbing his eyes. He saw the rashers sizzling in the pan. 'That smells good,' he said.

'Can you wash your sister's mouth out, please? She's drinking from the dog bowl again.'

Milo picked Sally up and took her into the downstairs bathroom that stood by the front door.

Jill watched through the kitchen window as a van pulled up across the road. The Finch residence this time. Mr. Finch was a retired lawyer. Lived there alone. A couple of men went inside. She flipped the bacon. Out came Mr. Finch, on a stretcher. Blood down his chest, like all the others.

She slipped the bacon off the spatula and onto a plate that she'd set down beside the hob. It was already loaded up with eggs.

Her stomach gave a groan, and there was a sharp pain

deep inside her gut. Slowly, it passed. It had flared up a few times over the last couple of days, but it always subsided, in time.

'Breakfast's ready,' she called.

Milo came back into the room with Sally. He put her down on the floor. Instantly, she started crawling after the dog again.

'You okay, mom?' Milo asked.

'Uh-huh. Grab a plate and help yourself.'

Milo loaded up a couple of rashers and an egg onto a plate. When Becca came into the kitchen, he passed that to her and loaded up another for himself. They went through into the living room and sat next to each other on the sofa, with their plates on their laps.

Marnie Moose was on the TV as it had been solidly for the past few weeks.

'Sally,' Milo called through into the kitchen.

'Yeah?' Sally replied from the kitchen floor, where she lay with the dog.

'Are you watching Marnie Moose right now?'

'Yeah.'

'But you're in there. Can't I put something else on?'

'No.'

Becca smiled. Then *she* called into the kitchen herself. 'Sally, can *I* watch something else?'

'Yeah,' Sally replied.

Becca laughed. 'See? She likes me more than you.'

Milo shook his head softly and tried to hide his smile. He handed her the remote.

'I fancy a documentary,' she said. She went into the recordings section, since the only live broadcast available was still the Channel One news.

'There should be a few in here. Dad loved documentaries.'

'I like dark ones. Serial killers and cults and cannibals,' Becca said, with a glint in her eye.

'So did he.'

Becca started scrolling through the thumbnails of recorded shows. Finally, she landed on one titled, 'The Zephertown Massacre".

'Ah, no way!' she said. 'We learnt about that in school last term. Let's watch it.'

'The Z what?'

'Don't you know about the Zephertown Massacre?'

Milo shook his head. 'We didn't learn about it yet. You're a year above me.'

'It was back in the seventies. This guy – a preacher – called something Zepher. Charles, maybe. He convinced a bunch of people that God had spoken to him and had told him to get together a flock of followers and take them to their own piece of land, as the rapture was coming soon, and only those in Zepher's flock would be saved from the flames.

'So he started preaching this all over the states. And he grew quite a following. And he started insisting that all his followers sell their homes and hand over their life savings so that he could buy up this plot of land, where they could go and live, ready for God to beam down and save them all.

'And that's what they did. He got a ton of money out of his flock. All kinds of people. From wealthy widowers down to broke trailer folk. And he bought up this big patch of land in South America. And they traveled down there on buses – a thousand people or so. They built little houses, and they grew veg. They called it Zephertown. And then they waited for the rapture – for God to suck them up into heaven and burn the rest of civilization to the ground.'

Milo stared deeply into her eyes as she spoke. When she paused to check he was paying attention, it took him a couple of awkward moments to realize she'd stopped talking.

'Uh - oh, and what happened? When the rapture didn't come?'

'People woke up. Started realizing he was full of shit. Started demanding their money back. Wanted to go home and resume their lives. But he wouldn't let them leave. His men kept them there at gunpoint. A girl managed to escape, though. Made it back to the states. Reported what was going on there. And so congress contacted Zepher, with plans to send a senator for a formal visit. Zepher couldn't have that, so he hosted a grand feast. And he laced the drinks with arsenic. Come morning, everyone was dead. Bodies lying everywhere, all clutching at their stomachs.'

Chapter 30
Project Sandman

L ater that evening, Jill came down the stairs from putting Sally to bed. Brody was preoccupied in Milo's room, working on one of his contraptions.

She went through to the living room. Milo and Becca sat arched forwards on the sofa, watching the Channel One news.

It was quarter to eight, and the entire nation was tuned into that station right now, ready to hear the Vice President's announcement. Ready to hear about Project Sandman.

Before she could sit down herself, a knock came at the front door. She went and pulled the door open and was happy to see Peters standing there.

'I'm glad you could make it!' she said. 'Come in, come in!'

She brought Peters through to the lounge.

'Peters!' Milo said loudly, with a big smile.

'Hiya, kid,' Peters said, as he sat next to Milo on the sofa.

Jill sat in the armchair. Together, the four of them stared

at the TV. It showed an empty podium in the address room of the White House.

'Been getting your food parcels okay?' Peters asked.

Jill nodded. 'Yes, thankfully!'

'Not everyone has. Some punks have been cleaning the X off old folks' doors so that they don't get their parcels,' the Lieutenant said.

'Jesus, that's horrible!' Jill said. 'Who would do such a thing?'

Rex, Milo thought.

At eight, as promised, the Vice President shuffled behind the podium, cleared his throat, and straightened some papers in front of him. He looked gaunt. He must've lost forty pounds since the last time he'd appeared on TV, at the president's funeral. His suit seemed to hang off him.

'My fellow Americans,' he started, 'a short time ago, my dear friend and the man you elected as president passed away from the awful and deadly illness that has been sweeping the nation – the illness that has touched every home. Since that moment, I have been working furiously with scientists and strategists to work out the best path forwards for the American people.

'Project Sandman is what you've come to know it as – its working title. But now I can reveal its true name – The Big Sleep.'

A navy-blue banner rolled down the face of the podium, with white lettering that read, *'THE BIG SLEEP'.*

'There is now indisputable evidence that the Lavitika vaccination is the direct cause of this horrifying and merci-less wave of death. And while deaths have slowed down, there are still hundreds of thousands each day. We have now surpassed a ninety percent death rate of vaccinated persons.

'*Now, my fellow Americans, I'm afraid you must brace yourselves, as I have to deliver a very sobering fact.*'

Peters and Jill looked at each other in terror.

'*If you are able to sit down while you listen to my voice, you may wish to do so. These are not words I want to say, and they are not words you are going to want to hear.*

'*We have statistical confidence that every person administered with the C-9 vaccination is going to expire in the coming weeks.*'

Jill's stomach rumbled again. She took the cushion from beside her on the armchair and sat it over her tummy to try to muffle the sound.

'Expire?' Milo asked. 'What does he mean? Does he mean die?'

Nobody in the room answered him.

Becca started to cry. She sank her face into her hands.

Peters' face was filled with uncertainty and hopelessness.

The Vice President choked a little. He took the handkerchief from the top pocket of his suit jacket, unfolded it, and dabbed at his eyes. A woman came on-screen, put her hand on his shoulder, and whispered in his ear. He shook his head. '*It's okay,*' he whispered. '*I'll finish it. Thank you.*'

He looked up into the camera, cleared his throat, and continued his address. '*So, what is The Big Sleep?*' he went on. '*The Big Sleep is about looking ahead. It's about setting up our children for a safe shot at a future. After you're gone, your children will need a safe place to grow up. To learn. To eat. To sleep. To play.*

'*All over the country, we have been preparing Youth Stations. You might have seen some activity in local town halls or in libraries. Each Youth Station has years' worth of* food supplies. There are classrooms. Medical rooms. Hundreds of board games and video games. Exercise machines. More books than your children could read in a lifetime. There are thousands of beds, and there are washing facilities.

'So, who will be in charge of these Youth Stations? We have worked with local schools to carefully select exemplary students as Leaders for each station. We've been training these Leaders for the past few weeks. They've been given instructions for every possible scenario that might arise. They have been given strict educational curriculums. They've received intensive first aid training, culinary lessons and have attended leadership workshops from the finest minds in people management.

'In these Youth Stations, your children will be fed. They will be educated. They will be clean. They will be well-rested. They will be entertained. They will be safe, and they will have a chance at a bright future.

'For now, food parcels will be delivered as normal. As soon as you start to feel unwell, you should check your children into your nearest Youth Station and say your goodbyes. You then should go home and make yourself comfortable in preparation for The Big Sleep. Thank you for listening.'

The Vice President burst into tears, and the broadcast went black. Milo saw himself, Peters, Becca, and his mom reflected in the TV screen. Four horrified faces.

'You're going to die?' Milo asked his mom, with a teary break in his voice.

Jill didn't respond. She stared glumly into space.

Becca sobbed uncontrollably.

Peters scratched his stubble. He thought about all those poor, blood-soaked fuckers he'd seen at the hospital and how he'd soon be just like them. And so would Jill. And Chambers. And Diaz. And Denzel.

Jill's stomach rumbled again.

Chapter 31
Promises

J ill knelt by the side of Sally's big-girl bed. It was two in the morning. Moonlight shone in through the window. She watched her daughter sleep. The pink blanket rose and fell softly with each breath. Gently, she ran her fingers through Sally's long, blonde locks.

Jill didn't feel much like sleeping. Not knowing what she now knew. Knowing that the moments in which she could just sit there and watch her daughter sleep were slipping away, like grains of sand through the neck of an hourglass. How many were left?

The floorboards by the landing creaked, and Jill jumped a little. She turned to see Milo come into the doorway.

'Can't sleep,' he said, softly.

'Yeah, me neither. Come here!'

He came in and sat beside her and rested his back against the bed frame.

'I'm sorry I was quiet earlier,' she said. 'I'm just... I'm processing it all.'

'I can't even imagine how you're feeling.'

'The vans out in the street – the ones that come and

take people away – they were slowing down. And I just thought – I hoped – that they would stop one day. They'd stop. And mine would never come.'

Jill knew, in a way, she'd get her wish. The vans weren't collecting anymore. Now the advice wasn't to call the hospital – it was to stay at home and wait for The Big Sleep. Some overpaid marketeer's clever spin on death.

'I really wanted to be here for you guys,' she said.

'I wanted that, too,' Milo said. He tried not to cry, but it was useless. He lowered his head and let the tears fall into his lap.

Jill shuffled closer across the carpet and wrapped her arms around him.

'My boy,' she said. 'My beautiful boy. We did such a good job with you. You're smart. And you're caring. And you'll fight for what is right.'

Milo couldn't speak. He could only sob. Jill wiped at his tears with the sleeve of her cardigan.

'When are you taking us to the Youth Station?'

Jill put a hand on her stomach.

'I've been having pains. I hope it goes away. I hope it's something else. I'd give *anything* for another few weeks with you.'

'I don't want to go there, mom. It'll be like an orphanage. But an orphanage run by kids.'

'I don't like the sound of it either,' she said. 'But it's the best option.'

'What about–?'

'What about what?'

'Well, Uncle Malc is in the DLC, right?'

Jill let out a long sigh. 'They ain't letting them out, My. They said on the news they ain't letting them out. Congress put them in there. And now there ain't enough of Congress left to take them out again. Anyway, you're better off alone than with *him*.'

'Why do you hate him so much?'

'My, promise me...' She took him by the cheeks and looked him dead in the eyes. 'Promise me you won't go looking for Uncle Malc.'

Milo shook her hands away and rested his head on her chest. They sat there beside Sally's bed, entwined, until the dawn light burst through the window.

* * *

A little later in the morning, Jill lay sprawled across the sofa, with a hot water bottle clutched to her belly.

'Are you sure it's not your period?' Becca asked, as she placed a cup of coffee on the small table beside the sofa.

'No, I only just had it.'

'But... All this stress – all the not knowing – it can screw with it, can't it?'

'It's just a bug or something, hopefully. Thanks for the coffee.'

Becca perched herself on the sofa, at Jill's feet.

Jill's eyes landed on the girl. 'Where's Milo?' she asked.

'He's upstairs. Brody's got him helping with something. God knows what he's building now,' Becca said. 'Sally's in the kitchen with Teddy. Had to stop her drinking from the bowl again.'

Jill let out a laugh, but the pain in her stomach flared up, and her humor faded. She clenched the hot water bottle a little tighter against her gut.

'Could it be the *change*?' Becca asked.

'How old do you think I am?' she asked, playfully.

'I just don't want it to be *time*,' Becca said. 'First dad...

and Dallas... then mom. I can't lose you as well. You've been like a second mother to me and Brody. You took us in when you didn't have to. And you've kept us fed. And safe. And calm. And I love you for that. And I don't want you to go.'

'I don't want to go either.' Jill's voice quivered, and her eyes went watery. She took a moment to compose herself. 'You'll look after them, won't you?'

Becca put her hand on Jill's knee. 'I promise. I will die protecting them.'

Jill placed her hand on top of Becca's.

Chapter 32
From Higher Up the Tree

Peters woke suddenly.

He found himself lying on the mattress in the small cell inside Masterson's police station. On the concrete by his side was an empty scotch bottle. After the announcement, he got drunk. He couldn't face the worry and the questions of the three cadets – not straight away – so he'd gone to the police station to drink alone and to collect his thoughts.

Now, he lay on his back on the mattress, staring up at the grubby ceiling, with a pounding pain in his skull.

The phone in the small office next door was ringing. He groaned, clambered to his feet, staggered through, and took the phone off its cradle.

'Peters,' he answered.

'How the hell are *you*?' asked a familiar voice.

'*Cap?*'

'Yeah, I'm still alive,' Captain Malsetti laughed.

'Jesus, am I glad to hear that!'

'How're you holding out?'

'Feeling a bit hopeless over here, Cap.'

'Yeah, I hear ya. Main priority is getting all the kids into the Youth Station. Once the time is right. Don't want to snatch them away if the parents have some time left.'

'Of course.'

'After that, after they're all safely inside and with the Leaders, then you and your men can stand down. Go off and prepare.'

'Prepare for what, sir?'

'The Big Sleep.'

'You finally got word from higher up the tree then, Cap?'

'Yes, Peters, I did. They think wording it this way will help keep people calmer. And they have the best psychiatrists and PR minds still breathing. So we'll word it this way, too.'

'Yeah, I get it.'

'Your Youth Station is Masterson Library. Take it you've probably seen trucks coming and going.'

'We saw 'em.'

'Best to base one of your guys there full time. Well, until they, you know – *clock out*. Just to keep things calm while the Leaders get into their roles.'

'I've got just the officer.'

'That's good. Say, listen, Peters. You might not hear from me again. Stomach started hurting yesterday. This might be our last chat.'

'Oh, Christ, Cap. I'm sorry.'

'So, I just want to say it was an honor working with you.'

'It was an honor working with you, too.'

The Masterson library was a vast complex of gray brick and curved glass. The front building was three stories high, but then a ground-floor corridor fed into a secondary two-story building, where they held conferences and events. The library had been funded by a local horror writer, who was lucky enough to make it into the big league and wanted to give something back.

Peters parked his Rattler in the small parking lot out front, next to the plinths that listed all the names of the townsfolk that had died from the virus. The memorials made him laugh as he looked up at them. The 'cure' had ended up killing a thousand times more people than the virus.

Chambers stared up at the library through the passenger window.

'There she is, then,' Peters said. 'Masterson's Youth Station.'

They both climbed out of the car, slammed their doors, and headed towards the main entrance.

Through the glass, they could see a tall boy, with a bowl cut and thick specs, pottering around inside, talking to himself. He caught sight of them and came to the door to let them in.

'Hello, officers,' he said, anxiously.

'Hi, there,' Peters said. 'You're one of the Leaders here, right?'

The boy nodded. 'Uh-huh. I'm Leader Richards. There are six Leaders here in total.'

Peters gave a short smile. 'Well, this here is Officer Chambers. She's going to help you to get everybody settled in.'

Richards blushed when her eyes met his. 'How do you do?' he asked, as held out his hand. Chambers shook it.

'Nice to meet you,' she said.

'So, has anyone checked in yet?' Peters asked.

'Forty-five children so far. Would you guys like the tour?'

'Sure,' Peters said.

'Follow me, please,' Richards said.

Chapter 33
Say Your Goodbyes

Two days went by.

Jill stood at the bathroom sink, brushing her teeth. She glanced at her reflection. Her skin was deathly white. The sockets around her eyes were deep and purple. Her hair was unwashed and wild. She couldn't remember the last time she'd brushed it.

She spat the white froth into the basin and watched the tap's flow wind it away down the plughole. Then came a quick, sharp, involuntary cough. And then there was red in the sink. A big, dark clump of blood. The spinning water tugged at its edges, and long, pink branches began to curl away from the crimson mass at the center.

Milo tapped on the door. 'Mom, you nearly done? I need to pee.'

'Try the other bathroom, My.'

'Becca's in there. She's taking ages.'

'Nuh-nearly done!'

Quickly, she broke up the bloody blotch with her finger-tips. The tiny, fleshy clumps slurped away down the plug-hole. Then she cupped a couple of handfuls of water into her mouth, swished it around, and sent that tumbling down the drain, too. She wiped her lips and checked her face in the mirror.

Once she was happy there were no leftover remnants of blood, she unlocked the door and smiled at Milo as she stepped out of the room.

'All yours, hon.'

She went downstairs into the kitchen. The radio was on. There were no reporters or presenters anymore. Those were all at home, saying goodbye to their families. Instead, The Big Sleep voiceover played on loop.

The voice actor had a deep, calming voice. Jill recognized it from the sleeping app she used to use when she had spells of insomnia. You'd choose from a bunch of stories, and this same guy would read you to sleep. Now, here he was, relaying the government's final message.

'It's time to wind down for The Big Sleep. If you have children fourteen and under in your care, you'll need to check them in to your nearest Youth Station. Each child is permitted one medium-sized suitcase. Include any medication they might need, along with clothing. For comfort, you may pack your child's favorite toy or teddy. You're also encouraged to pack photographs of your family. In time, these will become treasured memories and keepsakes for your children.

'Be honest with them about what is happening. Tell them that you are going to die, but that you may see them again one day in the afterlife. Tell them that they are going to be living in a new home, with all of their school friends, who are all experiencing the same loss and worries as they are. And that, while it might seem strange or scary at first, it will soon feel very normal to them. Drop your child or children at the Youth Station with their suitcase.

'*Once you have said your final goodbyes, return home and make yourself comfortable. Find a nesting space, where you would like to spend the last of your days. Perhaps a sofa or a bed. Keep your rations close to your nesting space, in case you are immobile in the later days.*

'*Take the time to reflect on the good things that you did with your life. Try not to dwell on any regrets. All life comes to an end, and nobody achieves all of their ambitions. So focus on your happiest memories as you drift into The Big Sleep.*'

The message looped back around to the start. '*It's time to wind down for the Big Sleep. If you have children...*'

Jill switched the radio off and wiped away the tears that had started to roll down her face. She took the phone off the wall, carried it outside onto the patio, and shut the door behind her. She dialed the number Peters had given her and waited as it rang.

'Denzel,' a voice answered.

'Oh, hello. I was wondering if Peters is there?'

'Yes, ma'am. Hang on. Let me go and get him.'

A minute later, a familiar voice came over the line, 'This is Peters.'

'It's Jill.'

'Oh, Jill, hi! What can I help you with?'

'I'm sick.'

'Sick? Like, *sick, sick*?'

'Blood in the sink this morning. Stomach pains the last few days. Getting worse each day. I was hoping it was something else. Was hoping it would pass. But I need to be realistic. Need to accept the fact that it's here.'

'Christ. I'm so sorry.'

'I think it's time the kids went into the Station. But I feel so weak. I don't think I can drive them. And I don't think I have the heart to pull up at that place and say goodbye and throw them out of the car. I don't think I can do that. But I know it has to be done.'

'You want me to take them?'

'I know it's a lot to ask.'

'I'm happy to help, however I can.'

'I just don't want to say goodbye to them. How do you do that? How do you look at your children and say that last goodbye?'

'You'll find the strength,' Peters said. 'You're a strong woman. You held it together through everything. You lost your husband. You lost your folks. And still, you took on two more kids in need *and* a dog. So I know you've got this. Just speak openly and honestly. It'll be hard. And you'll cry. And they'll cry. But this goodbye – it'll happen.'

'Thanks, Peters.'

'I'll head over in an hour.'

* * *

Peters brought the last of the four backpacks downstairs. They'd been filled with clothes, toys, and framed photos, which Jill had taken right off the walls.

'I'll take these out to the car,' Peters said. 'I'll leave you to say goodbye.'

'Thanks,' Jill said.

Peters hobbled down the garden path, like a pack donkey, with the backpacks hauled up over his shoulders.

Jill turned to see four young faces staring at her, glumly.

Becca hugged her first. Her pretty face was glistening with tears. Over the last few weeks, she felt like she'd formed a strong womanly bond with Jill. Stronger, maybe, than anything she'd ever felt with her own mom.

'Stay strong,' Jill said as she wiped away Becca's tears. She hugged her tight and kissed her on the cheek. 'Remember your promise.'

'I will,' Becca said. She gave a quivering, upset smile and then stepped back.

Brody didn't know what was going on. But he was very disturbed by all the crying. His eyes darted, and his body waved anxiously as he shifted his weight from one foot to the other.

Jill stepped forward, towards him. 'Brody, you are the most industrious little boy I have ever met. And I'm quite sure you're a genius. Your sister here – she'll look after you. And My. And Sally. You'll all look after each other.'

She kissed him on the cheek, and he didn't pull away.

Milo hugged her next. He was already bawling uncontrollably when she wrapped her arms around him and pulled him close.

'I love you, My. I love you so, so much.'

'I love you too, mom.'

His tears rolled down her neck.

Eventually, they pulled apart, and Milo stepped back in line with the others.

Jill lifted Sally up into a tight hug. One last cuddle with her little princess.

'You're so heavy now,' Jill said, through the tears. 'Such a big girl. I love you so much, baby. And I am so, so, so sorry that I won't get to see you get any bigger. Milo and Becca are going to take care of you. You don't have to be afraid. The world can seem like a scary place, but you don't have to be afraid of it. Not when you've got family and you've got friends.'

She sniffed deeply. Took in her scent. She wanted it to be embedded in her nostrils for her last little bit of time.

'Go to your brother,' Jill said.

Sally was too young to understand what was happening, but she could read the room, and she started to cry.

Jill passed her into Milo's arms. Sally clutched onto her hair and wouldn't let go. Milo pulled her away, and a clump of hair tore out and stayed clenched in Sally's little fist.

Peters reappeared in the doorway. 'Packs are all loaded up in the trunk,' he said.

Jill turned to him. She held back the tears as best she could. 'I think we're ready,' she said.

Slowly, the four youngsters shuffled out of the hallway. They went down the garden path. Peters' Rattler sat half-up on the curb. Becca and Brody climbed into the back. Milo passed Sally to Becca, who sat her down in the middle and buckled her in. Peters climbed behind the wheel.

Milo stared back at the house. His mom stood in the doorway.

Suddenly, he remembered hopping off the school bus. It was the first day he'd ridden it. He must've been six or seven. It dropped him right there, on that curb. And he looked up at the house, and there she was. Standing there in the doorway, waiting for him to come home. She'd been waiting there a long time. Couldn't wait to see him, coming up the garden path with his book bag and his little dinosaur lunchbox.

Now, standing next to Peters' Rattler, Milo raised his hand. Jill raised hers, too. And then he climbed into the passenger seat, and the car crawled slowly down Oakvale.

Chapter 34
The Informant

Denzel sat at the dining table in his boxer shorts, with his chin resting on his fist. Every cupboard door in the kitchen hung ajar, and every drawer lay open. The contents were spilled all over the worktops and the floor: cereal boxes, pasta bags, cleaning products.

Diaz came into the room, tired from his patrol. Flakes of Captain Corn crunched underfoot. He looked around the trashed room, bemused, and then his eyes landed on Denzel, who looked rather disheveled. Diaz drew up the chair opposite and sat down.

'Morning,' Diaz said.

Denzel grunted. He looked tired. His eyes were puffy and bloodshot.

'Everything good?' Diaz asked, looking around the room.

Denzel gave a small nod. 'I'll clean it up.'

'Where's Peters?' Diaz asked. 'He's meant to be switching on patrol with me.'

'Jill Winters called him,' Denzel said. 'She's sick. He's

taking her kids into the Youth Station.' He rubbed his eyes. 'So they'll be in Chambers' care.'

'Then they'll be in good hands,' Diaz said.

'How's she getting on over there? Have you heard from her?'

'She called me last night,' Diaz said. 'It's really filling up now. She seems happy. She's got a bed and everything. She's braiding hair. Reading bedtime stories. She said it's like getting to be a mom. Which, ya know, she'll never get to do now.'

'She was always maternal,' Denzel said, with a proud little smile. 'She learnt from Miss Moltez. Always taking care of the rest of us. Putting sticky-bands on our cuts. Making us hot chocolate. Cooking for us. Reading us stories.'

'She said I can sneak over there later, after the kids are asleep.'

'It's good you've got someone to be close with these last few weeks.'

'Only thing stopping me from abandoning my post,' Diaz said. 'You think I'd stay here, policing this shithole otherwise? Hell no. I'd be off looting. Drinking. Snorting. Getting my fill. But I'm fixed on her.'

'That's good.'

'What about you?' Diaz asked. 'Why aren't you heading off? Surely there's things you'd rather be doing?'

'I've found a purpose,' Denzel said.

'You've got a girl, too, huh?' Diaz laughed.

'No. It's not that.'

'What, then?'

'There's this group operating here. Or it was, at least.'

'Group? What kind of group?'

'White supremacists.'

'What? Here? In Masterson?'

Denzel nodded. 'Call themselves The Eighty-Eight. A lot of black faces have gone missing over the years. The sheriff here – Callow – he knew about it. Even got himself an informant.'

'What's this got to do with you staying here?'

'Because I want to do something good before I punch out. I want to put these fuckers to sleep myself. They don't deserve to go the same way as you or me or anyone else. They deserve to go out screaming. *Really* screaming.'

Diaz leant back in the chair. He looked to be deep in thought. Denzel started to regret telling him.

After a few moments of silence, Diaz asked, 'So have you got any names?'

'I don't,' Denzel said. 'My best guess is he kept the names in the safe in his office. But I can't find the key. Looked in every cupboard. Every drawer.'

'Hang on,' Diaz said. He quickly left the kitchen and hurried down the hall to the master bedroom. When he came back, he was holding a little golden key. 'I found this in the sock drawer the other night. Didn't think anything of it.'

Denzel's eyes widened, and suddenly, he looked more alive. He stood up, took the key from Diaz, and then both of them moved swiftly through into the sheriff's office at the end of the hall. Denzel slotted the key into the keyhole in the safe. It fitted. He turned it, and a heavy metallic clunk came from inside. Then Denzel twisted the handle, and the door came open.

There were little cardboard folders stacked inside. Denzel took them out and slammed them down on the desk.

Quickly, he waded through them, casting each aside as he read the labels on the front: Car Insurance, Home Insurance, Life Insurance, Pension, Bills. Then, finally, there was one marked 'Work'. Denzel opened the flap and pulled out the papers inside. He leafed through them and finally found a Confidential Information form. At the bottom, it was signed, *Clark Gunner, Proprietor of Club Hellfire, Long Pine Road, Masterson.*

'This is him,' Denzel said. 'This is the informant.'

Chapter 35
The Youth Station

The drive to the Youth Station was slow. Peters seemed to take just about every wrong turn that he could. They must've crawled down every street in Masterson. Maybe it was to keep them out of the Station as long as possible, or maybe it was to give them one last look around the town. Milo wasn't sure which.

Milo sat with his head slumped against the window, sobbing. Through the glass, he watched the houses roll by. Most of them sat empty now, of course, and those that didn't would soon be home only to a lonely corpse or two.

'Why couldn't we bring Teddy?' he asked. 'My mom is gonna die, and then Teddy is going to starve.'

'I know it's not fair,' Peters said. 'But the government has been clear. No pets. And can you imagine it? If every kid brought his dog or his cat or his hamster? It'd be carnage. There'd be fur and blood everywhere.'

'Where is the Youth Station?' Becca asked sniffily from the back seat.

'It's the old library,' Peters said. 'I had a tour of it a

couple of days back. It's alright, honestly. The Leaders seem nice.'

'So we can't leave? We're stuck in there? Like prison?' Milo asked.

'Well, you can leave when you're eighteen,' the Lieutenant said.

'And we get bossed around by fourteen-year-old nerds?' Becca piped in. 'I'm fourteen. My authority figure is someone my own age?'

'Well, for now,' Peters said, 'one of my officers is there. Chambers. She's nice. You'll like her.'

'I don't want to go,' Milo said.

'I know you don't. But this is the only option. It really is.'

'There might be another option,' Milo replied.

Peters looked down at him. 'Go on?'

'There's a place we could go.'

'Where?'

'My uncle lives in the New Hampshire DLC.'

'Your uncle is an Avoidant?'

'He is. So that means he's alive. And he'll take care of us. All of us. I know he will.'

'They're not opening those up, kid. They've announced it. The government is pretending they don't exist.'

'We'll get in,' Milo said. 'We just need to get there.'

'Jesus, that's eighty miles away, kid.'

'Can you drive us?' Milo asked. 'Please?'

'I *would*. Of course, I would. But I *can't*. The highway, in that direction at least, is a car park. Trust me. I tried to get home to feed my dog. But I couldn't get anywhere near.'

'Maybe we could walk?'

'The Youth Station is the best option for you. I'm sorry, kid.'

What Happened Next

* * *

When they arrived at the library, Peters struggled to find a place to stop. The parking lot was rammed full, and queues of cars filled every row, with their engines humming, and their exhaust pipes dribbling onto the tarmac.

The Lieutenant slung the car up onto a grass verge in the end. 'Come on,' he said, as he headed around to the back to open up the trunk.

A vast crowd of parents and children lined the building's glass frontage. There wasn't a dry eye anywhere.

As they crept closer to their turn at the door, the mothers and fathers hugged their children goodbye. Long, warm hugs that they never wanted to end. And they exchanged their last words. Words that would have to carry for an eternity.

'This is horrible,' Becca said as she stared over. She and Milo headed to the back of the car to help unload the backpacks.

As Peters lifted Brody's pack, a small metal contraption rolled out of the side pocket and wheeled across the carpet that lined the trunk.

'What the hell is that?' he asked, as he went to reach for it.

As Becca approached, her eyes quickly widened. 'Careful!' she shouted.

'What? What is it?'

'It's a pencil bomb.'

'A what?'

'It's okay to pick up. Just don't twist that catch at the bottom.'

Peters slowly lifted it out. It was a cluster of thin metal pipes, all welded to a thick metal base that looked to be the mechanism from an old animal trap. Into each pipe was stuffed a sharpened pencil. They all pointed upwards. The whole thing was cocooned in clear sticky food wrap.

'He made one before,' Becca said. 'It shoots pencils out, real hard and real fast. He threw one into my gran's greenhouse, a couple of years back, before the virus got her. Never seen anything like it.'

'He made this?'

Becca nodded. 'Yeah. He's good at that stuff.'

Peters tried to hide the impressed look on his face, and he put on a disapproving tone. 'Well, it's totally unsafe. He can't take this inside there. I'll have to confiscate it.' He slipped it into an empty pouch on his belt, and then passed Brody's pack to Becca, along with her own. Then he handed Milo the remaining two packs - his and Sally's.

'Thanks, Peters,' Milo said, as he slid the backpack straps over his shoulders and then lifted Sally up into his arms from the back seat. 'We'll go and join the queue. You can take off now.'

The Lieutenant gave him an untrusting look. 'Hmm. No, I'll wait with you. Make sure you get inside okay. Don't want you getting lost on the way to the door.'

Becca helped Brody get his backpack on. Then, she hoisted hers up onto her back, too.

The five of them joined the crowd. Through the mass of people, Peters could just about see Chambers standing in the doorway, booking children in on her clipboard. Richards stood beside her, with all the other Leaders, welcoming the kids inside.

Slowly, the teary-eyed parents at the front of the crowd filtered away. New ones joined behind in their dozens. Peters and the kids shuffled gradually closer to the door until, finally, they were first in line.

'Peters?' Chambers was surprised to see him.

'Got some new arrivals for you!' he said.

She smiled at Milo, Becca, and their younger siblings. 'Well, hello there! What are your names and ages, please?'

Milo relayed his and Sally's names and ages. Becca did the same for her and Brody. Chambers jotted it all down on the sheet clamped to her clipboard.

'Okay, great! Come in, come in! Welcome to Masterson Youth Station. The Leaders here will show you where to go.'

Becca stepped inside, and Brody followed.

Milo hung back. He looked up at Peters.

'Thanks,' he said to the Lieutenant. 'You know, for everything, over the last few weeks.'

'Just doing my job, kid,' Peters said. 'Look after them, won't you?'

Milo nodded. 'I will.'

'And look after yourself, too.'

'You too.'

Milo carried Sally inside.

Chapter 36
Club Hellfire

C lub Hellfire had once been a thriving biker bar on the edge of town. It was a one-story building, clad in timber, with a corrugated tin roof. The long windows of darkened glass overlooked the bike bays out front.

Back in the day, you could expect anything up to fifty choppers to be lined up out there. Now, it sat quiet. The bays were all empty, and litter swept across the parking lot on the breeze.

Denzel parked the squad car out front and climbed out cautiously; his eyes fixed on the club's windows for any sign of motion inside. But the glass was almost black. He couldn't see a thing inside.

Slowly, he reached down and unbuckled his holster. He lifted out his handgun, and held it down by his side.

Denzel approached the club's door. It was dark wood, with a long metal handle that stretched from the top to the floor.

A rat scurried quickly out of the mound of litter that had accumulated in the corner of the doorway. It made him shudder, and he almost shot at it. The rat was well-fed, and its tail was long and fat. It vanished quickly out of sight around the side of the building.

Denzel reached for the door, and to his surprise, it swung clear of the jamb. It wasn't locked. Slow, haunting country music rang out from inside. As did laughter, and the chinking of glasses.

He stepped inside and raised the gun out in front of him.

The clubhouse was dimly lit. A few dull lamps hung out from the walls, but they gave out very little light. The booth tables lining the room were littered with crumpled peanut packets and cigarette butts.

The bar stood at the back of the room. It was painted gold, and the liquor stand behind it was all lit up like a Christmas tree. And that's where Denzel spotted the source of the laughter and the clanging of glassware.

Three teenagers were over at the bar, smoking cigarettes and drinking whiskey. Two sat on stools like punters while the third stood behind it, pouring from the selection of bottles.

'Hands up!' Denzel shouted.

Rex looked over his shoulder at the cop. He knocked back his shot of whiskey and then set the glass down on the counter.

'Chill out,' Rex said. 'We're just having a drink.'

'Who the fuck are you guys?' Denzel asked.

'We're regulars these days,' Rex remarked, with a grin.

'Names,' Denzel said. 'Give me your names.'

'I'm Rex. This is Dean, and this is Brandon.'

His cohorts nodded in turn.

'Where's Gunner?'

'Gunner?' Rex cocked an eyebrow.

'Clark Gunner. Where is he?'

Brandon knew who he meant. 'Gunner used to own this place, I think. But it closed down in the virus. Never reopened. Been empty since. Till we claimed it, a couple of weeks back.'

'Can you believe no one thought to rob this ridiculous stash?' Rex asked. His eyes glowed as he glanced over the impressive display of liquor bottles behind the bar.

'Alright, so where's Gunner now?' Denzel asked.

'Lives in a farmhouse over by the old trailer park. That's if he ain't dead,' Rex said. 'You look like you could do with one of these.'

He turned over a fresh shot glass and filled it to the top from the bottle. Then he slid it across the granite bar top.

Denzel hesitated for a few moments. Then he slipped his gun back into the holster on his hip. He wiped the sweat off his forehead and then drew up a stool, and swallowed the whiskey down.

Rex filled the glasses again.

'My old man used to drink in here, apparently,' Rex said. 'That's his photo behind the bar.'

Denzel looked up and saw a framed photo of a handsome young man with short blonde hair.

'He doesn't look much like you,' Denzel said.

'Lucky him,' Rex said.

'He must've been popular here to have his picture up,' Denzel said.

'Fuck knows. He died, years back. Crashed his truck into a tree on the way home one night. Pissed out of his skull.'

'I'm sorry,' Denzel said.

'Were you close to *your* old man?'

Denzel shook his head. 'He took off when I was two. My mom died when I was a kid, too.'

'My mum died not long after I was born,' Rex said.

'How old are you guys?' he asked.

'Fourteen all round,' Dean said.

'Jesus. Fourteen? So you're not – *vaccinated*?' Denzel asked.

'Nope,' Brandon said.

'Then you need to head over to the Youth Station.'

'The what?' Dean asked.

'Didn't you hear the announcement? Project Sandman? The Big Sleep?'

'Look around,' Rex said. 'We've been too busy drowning our sorrows.'

Denzel shook his head. 'The library. Head to the library. Everyone, fourteen years or under, is gonna live there now - since anyone older than that will be dead soon.'

'Live there? For how long?'

'Till you're eighteen.'

'What's to stop us walking out?'

'It's like Fort Knox. Once you're in, you're in. Not even the Leaders can open the doors once they're locked.'

'So all those fuckers from school will be there?' Rex asked.

'Yep. Matter of fact, my boss is taking the Winters and the Sampsons over there right now.'

'Sampsons?' Rex asked.

Dean and Brandon exchanged an uncomfortable look.

Denzel nodded. 'Yeah. Pretty girl and a dippy boy. My boss pulled them out of a gassed-up car a few weeks back. He just drove them and the Winters kids to the Youth Station.'

Denzel knocked back the second shot of whiskey and then slammed it down on the counter with a wince.

'Right,' Denzel said. 'I'm gonna go and pay Gunner a visit. Thanks for the drink.'

He got down off the bar stool and headed out of the clubhouse.

Rex looked up at Dean and Brandon. A neon-red Viper Beer sign that hung above the bar painted his face in menacing crimson.

'Becca's alive,' he said. Then he pounded his fist on the counter.

Chapter 37
The Tour

Milo knew Richards from school. He was the leader of the chess club. He'd once seen Rex flush his head down the toilet. He thought about that as Richards led him, Becca, Brody, and Sally through the Youth Station. They started the tour at the top, on the third floor.

Milo had been to that library hundreds of times. He'd been a big reader when he was younger, before video games had taken over his life. Now, he almost didn't recognize it. They'd done away with every bookcase and every book, and they'd installed partition walls left, right, and center.

'So up the ladder, on the roof, are the solar panels and all the vegetable beds. We just got soil in them yesterday, and nothing's been planted yet, so I won't take you up there today. Moving onwards, this here is the rec room. Short for recreation,' Richards said, as they passed through a large area, with five TV screens bolted to the wall. The screens were hooked up to various different consoles, and giant beanie bags lined the wall. The rest of the space was filled with short, wooden tables, each surrounded by stools.

Beneath each table, a shelf was laden with card games and board games.

'This is the CCTV room.' Richards slapped the locked door of a small, boxed-off office room in the corner of the Rec room. 'Officer Chambers has taken up residence in there for now. Until she... well, you know.

'And through here is the medical room.' They passed through a door, into a room with four hospital beds. One wall was lined with tall metal cabinets. Each door had its own little padlock. 'We've got all sorts of medicines in good supply here. Leader Singh has been on back-to-back first aid courses and medicinal courses the last couple of weeks, and they're leaving him with big cheat books to help him diagnose endless ailments.'

He took them down another flight of stairs. Then turned and gestured with his arm to the large space behind them. 'And this is the schooling area!' It was filled with rows upon rows of little gray desks. They all faced a long stretch of wall that was lined with whiteboards. 'We've been given a curriculum for each age group.'

'Do we still have to do homework if we don't have a home?' Milo asked.

Richards laughed. 'I'll show you the kitchen next.'

He led them down another flight of stairs, across the glass-fronted lobby, where Chambers was still checking in crying children, and through a pair of metal double doors. They arrived in an industrial-styled kitchen that wouldn't look out of place in any of the fancy restaurants downtown. The smell of wood glue still hung in the air from all the fresh cabinetry, and the ovens still had foggy plastic stuck to the glass.

'Leader Hayward is the head chef. He's been away the last few weeks on all manner of crash cookery courses and nutritional seminars. Tried one of his risottos last night. You're in for a treat!'

After that, Richards showed them the gym. That, too, was on the ground floor. 'This is the workout space,' he said. It was a long, gray-walled room, lined with treadmills, rowing machines, and dumbbell racks. 'We only have a small courtyard for fresh air, and there's not much room to run around out there, so if you really want to let off some steam, this'll be the place.'

They came to the corridor that led from the main building across to the two-story building that stood behind it.

'If you look out there, that's the courtyard,' Richards said, as he tapped on the window.

Becca and Milo looked through the glass and saw a bleak asphalt square, penned in by a tall chain-link fence.

'That's the only place we'll get fresh air?' Becca asked. 'We can't go out the front?'

'Government thinks if we let you off the property, you won't come back,' Richards said.

And they're probably right, Becca thought.

'Right, washrooms and sleeping quarters,' he said, as he carried on into the two-story building ahead. 'Girls are upstairs – just up that stairwell there.' He pointed to their left, where a glass staircase ascended to the floor above. 'Boys are downstairs. I'll show you the boys' for now. They're identical to the girls', save for the urinals, of course.'

In front of them was a heavy glass door. To the right of it, fixed to the wall, was a small black plastic plate.

'The sleeping quarters lock at night,' he said, as he lifted a keycard from his pocket. It had a lanyard tied through a hole in its top; the other end of which was fastened to the belt loop of his jeans. 'Only way of getting in or out after lights-out is with one of these suckers, and only the Leaders carry these. Unless there's a fire, of course - then, the doors open right up.'

'Where do we go if there's a fire?' Becca asked.

'The courtyard. Then we wait for the sprinklers to do their magic.'

He pushed open the door to the boys' sleeping quarters. They walked through it, into a vast space filled with bunk beds. Each bunk had a tall, red, two-door locker standing beside it. Some of the doors had little keys sticking out of them. The rest had already been claimed. 'Top door is for the top bunk. Bottom door is for the bottom bunk,' he said. 'You can keep all your clothes and little bits in there. You get a key each, to stop any thieving.'

As they walked between two rows of bunks, they could see that several had already become inhabited. Boys lay silently atop every other bunk, listening to music or playing on handheld consoles. The top bunks seemed to be going first.

At the end of the room, they came to a wall with an open doorway. Behind it were urinals, toilet cubicles, and shower cubicles.

'And that concludes the tour,' Richards said. 'Now, Milo and Brody, if you want to find a bunk down here, then Becca and Sally, you can find yourselves one upstairs.'

Milo looked sadly at Sally. Becca looked sadly at Brody. Then they both locked eyes with each other and seemed to speak without opening their mouths. *You look after her. I'll look after him.* Milo handed Sally into Becca's arms, and she followed Richards out of the room.

'So, which bunk shall we choose?' Milo asked Brody.

Brody stared up at him in silence.

Chapter 38
Frontier Justice

Denzel was back behind the wheel of his car, driving quickly through the town, hoping to avoid any traffic from folk dropping their kids at the Youth Station. He'd had to look up the trailer park Rex had told him about on the old coffee-stained map he'd taken from the Sheriff's office.

Slowly the buildings thinned out, and he was soon driving through woodland. Then the nice, tarmacked main road ended abruptly and transitioned into a beaten track that was full of potholes.

He passed by the sign for Dick Cooper's Trailer Paradise. He could make out the shapes of the battered old mobile homes that lay like sleeping dogs on the other side of the tree line.

Soon he came to a turning. A wooden sign stood on the corner that read, '*Gunner Eggs – Since 1932*'. He turned off the track, and the car crept down a small lane sided by tall, overgrown bushes. Great roots wormed up through the soil, creating swooping bumps that the car juddered over. The lane opened out into a large clearing.

A farmhouse stood to the left. It had once been red, but now the boards were sun-faded and weather-beaten, and what little paint still clung to them was pink. Up ahead the track led to an old barn lined with rusted, corrugated steel.

Denzel put his car on the dead grass in front of the farmhouse. Then he checked his gun was still in its holster, and he got out. He looked around and listened.

He heard the clucking of chickens and the splashing of water coming from the rusted, old barn that stood at the end of the track. He took out his gun and stalked quickly towards it. The splashing and the clucking grew louder all the while.

He headed to the tall metal door, which stood slightly open, and he peered in.

The ground was writhing with chickens. There were thousands. All pecking seed off the concrete. Small, little bursts of flight here and there. Feathers showering down. Clucking and crowing.

Over against the far wall, he could see a little man in a grubby shirt, crouching in straw, beside a trough of water. He was splashing it into his face and rubbing his wet hands over the back of his neck.

'Mister Gunner?' Denzel called, as he stepped into the barn. A few chickens spilled out.

The little man turned. He had scruffy, wet stubble, and a bad combover up on top. His shirt had holes in the front of it, through which you could see the hair on his chest. He wore no trousers or jeans – just a grubby pair of boxers, and on his feet were a pair of muddy black boots. His eyes were bloodshot.

'Who the fuck are you?' he crowed.

As he turned, he knocked a couple of empty whiskey

bottles with his knee, and they rolled off into the mass of chickens.

'I'm a cop. Are you Clark Gunner?'

'I am.' His eyes shifted to the chickens that were pouring out of the door, into the sunlight. 'Close that fucking door!'

Denzel pulled it shut. It fell a little darker in the barn, which was lit by two clear panels in the dipping roof of rusted steel.

'Now, what do you want?'

'You living out here?'

'Fucking fox keeps getting in. Had twelve the night before last. So I'm camping out here, waiting for him. Didn't show last night. But when he does... And he will...,' he gestured towards the shotgun that leant up against the water trough.

Denzel hadn't noticed the gun before now.

'You must love these chickens.'

'My brother was the chicken farmer. He loved 'em. And I loved him. So I'll keep them safe. They're good to keep. Good for meat. Good for eggs. Now, what do you want?'

'I want to know where the High Eagle is,' Denzel said.

The man seemed to sober up all of a sudden.

'The what?'

Denzel smiled. 'You know who I'm talking about.'

'Look, me and the Sheriff–.'

'The Sheriff's dead. I'm the Sheriff now. And if you want to keep on living, then you'll tell me who the High Eagle is.'

Gunner's eyes shifted to the shotgun.

'Don't,' Denzel insisted.

Gunner quickly reached his hand out for his gun.

Denzel fired. The bullet went right through Gunner's

out-stretched wrist. He fell, screaming, onto his back, and he clutched at his wrist with his other hand. Blood spewed from the wound, down onto his shirt.

The chickens flapped away in terror. They piled onto each other and quickly cleared the floor all around him.

Denzel stepped over to him as he writhed and gasped, and panted on the concrete.

'I said, *don't*.'

Gunner glared up at him with hate. 'The things we would've done to you, boy,' he barked, with spit flying from his lips. 'Oh, the things we would've done to you.'

'The High Eagle. Where is he?'

'Go fuck yourself.'

'Alright.' Denzel put his gun back in its holster. Then he reached down, grabbed Gunner by his shoulders, and rolled him over. Gunner tried to crawl away, but Denzel had already clutched the back of his shirt and was dragging him over to the water trough.

'W–what the – the hell are you doing?'

Denzel pulled him up over the metal ledge of the trough so that it dug into his belly, and then he pushed with all his might onto the back of his head, plunging it deep into the water.

Gunner's bleeding arm dripped down into the trough, turning it red, as he flapped and gurgled. Bubbles bore up from his mouth and nostrils, turning the dirty trough into a jacuzzi spa.

After a minute, Denzel pulled him up. He gasped, frantically.

'The High Eagle. Where is he?'

Gunner spat at him. 'Fuck you.'

Denzel pushed him down again. More bubbles. More

struggling. More writhing. More leg kicking. But there was no breaking free from the officer's grip.

After a while, Gunner fell limp. Denzel let go, and his body slumped to the floor like an old sack of grain.

'Come on,' Denzel said, as he slapped his cheek. 'Wake up, you piece of shit.' He slapped him again. 'You ain't dead. You ain't dead yet.'

Gunner's eyes snapped open. He coughed out a jet of pinkish water and gasped for breath.

'The High Eagle. Where is he?'

Gunner didn't reply. He just lay trembling on the ground, dripping wet.

'Alright. Back in you go,' Denzel said.

As he started to lift him up again, Gunner pleaded suddenly, 'Wait, wait, wait.'

'Okay.' Denzel relaxed. 'So where is he?'

'The DLC,' he blurted.

'Anti-vaxxer.' Denzel half-laughed. 'Of course.'

'They're *all* in the DLC.'

'But not you?'

'My brother – he had asthma. I got the vax for him.'

'Ain't that nice? Now, the High Eagle. What's his name?'

'Please! I told you where he is–.'

'You want to go back in the drink?'

'No, no. Please, no!'

'So what's his name?'

'I–I can't say it.'

'Then whisper it,' Denzel said.

Gunner nodded, tearfully. Denzel lowered his ear to Gunner's lips, and the trembling little man whispered the name into it.

'Okay.' Denzel pulled away. 'That wasn't so hard, was

it?' He reached over for the shotgun, pulled back the hammers, and pointed it at Gunner's face.

'Wait. Wait! I told you! I told you what you wanted! Please. Please, don't kill me!'

'Is that how the women begged?'

Tears streamed from Gunner's reddened eyes, and his lips quivered. 'Please. *Please.*'

'Did you show them mercy?'

Gunner said nothing. He just whimpered under the barrels of the gun.

'That's what I thought,' Denzel said. 'This is for them.'

He pulled the trigger.

Chapter 39
Taking What's Mine

'Rex, wait up!' Dean called, as he stumbled drunkenly down the wooded track. The sun was starting to set, and the trees cast long shadows on the red ground.

Rex marched fiercely ahead.

Dean looked at Brandon, who was equally drunk and equally struggling to keep up with Rex.

Brandon necked the last swig of whiskey from the bottle clutched in his hand, and then he hurled it into the trees. It hit a branch and smashed. He pounded his fists into the air above his head. 'Twenty points!'

'Wait up!' Dean repeated. 'Where are we going?'

They followed at a distance for another twenty minutes before, finally, turning the corner onto Madison Drive.

Madison Drive, or *'Millionaires' Row'* as most of the locals liked to call it, only had two houses on it. One belonged to Dr Levinski, a plastic surgeon who had retired shortly before the virus. The other house belonged to the RV King. Both houses were big, and both had pools, with pool houses to match. But the RV King's had one thing Dr Castler's didn't.

As Rex approached his uncle's house, the automated gate detected the fob on the keychain in his pocket. There was a little *ding*, and then the large, black iron gate slid to the side in its little groove and vanished behind the hedgerow to the left.

Rex went up the brick-paved driveway and through the white gate that stood to the right of the house. Dean and Brandon tailed behind. They dragged their feet sleepily and only just made it through the gate before it began sliding back into place.

The white gate led through to the back of the property, where the three teens passed the pool. The navy-blue cover was still fixed tightly in place over the top of the water.

Past the pool stood the pool house. It was a brick building with a flat roof and a face of black glass doors that all folded aside.

Brandon and Dean assumed Rex was headed to the pool house, where they'd hung out many times, but to their surprise, he carried on past it. He went down a narrow walkway to the side of it that led through to a part of the garden they'd rarely entered. It was a little, triangular patch of grass, cornered in by the tall perimeter fence that ran around the property. The grass was orange now – deadened by the sun and unwatered by the gardeners, who were long gone.

Rex turned to face the back of the pool house, which overlooked the small patch of grass. There was a metallic box fixed to the brickwork. He flipped open the panel on the front, unveiling a numbered keypad, into which he tapped a code.

There was a metallic clunk from the small triangle of

dirt behind him. He, Brandon, and Dean all turned to look. A cloud of dry dirt sprayed up from the grass as a slim rectangle of dead turf lifted up from the rest. It was a meter long and half a meter wide.

Brandon and Dean exchanged confused glances.

Rex went over to the patch of grass, reached down, hooked his fingers under the edge, and lifted it up. The underside was a thick, metal door on a hinge. Below which, a jet-black shaft ran deep into the ground. A metal ladder was bolted to one side of the shaft. Rex stepped down onto the rungs and started to descend.

When he reached a certain depth, he passed through a sensor, and a light came on beneath him, illuminating the metal-walled room below.

He stepped down onto a zebra-striped rug.

The ceiling came a couple of inches above Rex's head. Two leather loungers sat facing a huge eighty-inch TV that was bracketed to the wall. In the corner was a glass-fronted fridge. All its shelves were stuffed full with Viper Beer.

'What *is* this place?' Dean asked, as he clambered down the ladder.

Brandon came down next. He skipped the last few rungs and landed heavily onto the rug.

'It was his bunker. He put it in 'in case we get nuked', but really, it's just a man cave. He used to come down here and watch porn.'

'I don't blame him,' Brandon said. 'Look at the size of that TV.'

'And look at all that beer!' Dean rushed over to the fridge. 'Rex, why have we been hanging out at that dingy bar when we could've been here? We've got the house. The pool. This porn bunker.'

Rex let out a long sigh.

'Because this house – it's got a purpose.'

Brandon rolled his eyes. 'Let me guess. It's for you and Becca?'

Without hesitation, Rex clutched his throat in a firm grip and squeezed. Brandon clawed at his fingers but couldn't pull them off. His eyes bulged out of his head, and he clucked.

'Enough,' Dean said.

Rex didn't loosen his grip.

'Enough!' Dean repeated, more firmly. 'He's drunk. He's an idiot, and he's drunk.'

Rex let go. Brandon stumbled backwards, gasping and holding his throat.

'That's right,' Rex said. 'For me and Becca. I got it ready for her. And I went over to her place to get her. But Winters was there. And he told me she was dead. And he showed me the fucking grave. And I stood there, and I–,' he hesitated. 'She's not dead.' He smiled, and tears crept down his cheeks. 'She's not dead. But she's imprisoned. And me and you, and *YOU*, you dumb piece of shit – we are all going to go and break her out. And then me and Becca will live here and be fucking happy. We'll be fucking happy. And all the other cunts that got in the way before – they'll all be dead.'

'You heard what that cop said,' Dean said. 'That place is locked down. We can't just stroll in and walk her out of there.'

'That's why we're here,' Rex said. 'Now, back up against the wall.'

Brandon and Dean looked at each other, and then they did as they were told and stepped backwards until their boots came off the rug and thudded onto the metal. Rex tore the rug off the floor. Beneath it lay a small, metal door. He pulled it open, revealing a large, shallow storage box sunken into the floor.

The base of the box was lined with gray foam, bedded into which was a small array of weapons. There were two pairs of handguns – one pair black, one pair silver. Beside them lay three semi-automatic rifles. And lining one side of the box was a row of grenades.

'He used to keep all this in the house,' Rex said, with a grin. 'But he thought I'd end up being the next high school shooter. So he hid it all down here. Then the dumb, fat fuck left the access code on a sticky note in the drawer next to his bed.'

Dean gazed down at the trove of weapons and swallowed hard.

'Now,' Rex said, as he glared up at them, 'let's go and get my girl.'

Chapter 40
If You're Up There

Peters pulled up by the Winters' place, where the driveway met the road. He killed the engine, exhaled, and eyed his reflection in the rearview. He looked old. He felt like he'd aged another decade in the last two months. *And is it any wonder?* he thought. The shit he'd seen. And it wasn't over yet. It wasn't over until every last vaxxer had dropped dead and every last kid was tucked away safely in that library.

The Lieutenant sat a while longer and pinched the ridge of his nose between his finger and thumb. He had the beginnings of a headache coming on. A dull ache right between his eyes. After a while, it dimmed a little, and he felt ready to face his dying friend.

Peters lifted the six-pack of Power-Aid from the passenger footwell, got out from behind the wheel, and headed across the driveway. He tapped his knuckles on the front door and then watched through the pane for any sign of movement.

A few moments passed, but the misty gray strip of

hallway he could see through the door panel sat still and silent. He tapped again. Stillness and silence, still.

Hesitantly, he tried the handle. It was unlocked, and so he pushed the door ajar and called inside, 'Jill?'

No answer.

'Jill, it's Peters. Just coming by to check on you.'

He stepped into the hallway and closed the door behind him.

'Jill? The kids are dropped off safe. Left them with my officer, so they're in good hands. She's one of the good ones.'

No reply. He stepped softly towards the lounge.

'Got you a case of Power-Aid. All different flavors. I heard one of the nurses say this was the one thing they gave patients that tended to give them a little boost, after the first symptoms kick in. Got their energy up.'

As he turned the corner into the living room, his stomach dropped, and the handle of the case slipped from his fingers. When it hit the laminate, the bottles shot out in every direction and rolled into the corners of the room.

'Oh, god.'

Jill sat hunched on the sofa, with her head slumped to one side. Her eyes were wide open, as if she'd seen something horrifying. Her skin was violet. Her jaw sat ajar; her lips smothered in blood. There was a fleece blanket over her legs. In her lap, resting in a black and fleshy pool of blood, sat a framed photo. Behind the glass, four smiling faces: Dallas, his loving wife, their beautiful boy, and their little princess.

Teddy lay on the sofa next to her, guarding her, with her graying snout resting gently on Jill's knee. The retriever raised her head as Peters stepped into the room.

Peters brought a hand to his mouth as he beheld the

corpse. Then, after a few stunned moments, he lowered his trembling knees to the floor, at the foot of the sofa and stared up at Jill's face.

'I'm sorry,' he said. 'I'm *so* sorry. I–I didn't think I'd been gone that long. I wanted to be here, with you at the end. I didn't want you to be alone.'

Teddy laid her head back in place. She and Peters sat there silently, keeping Jill company, as the light through the window dimmed, and the shadows in the room dragged longer across the floor. Before long, the three of them were sitting in darkness.

Eventually, after what felt like hours, Peters got to his feet. His legs had gone numb, and his knees clicked as he straightened them out. He felt like a creaking, old tree, near-ready for felling.

The Lieutenant went through to the kitchen and flicked at light switches until he found the one he was looking for. The spotlights out in the backyard burst into life, illuminating the small, paved area through the French doors.

Peters stepped out onto the patio and inhaled deeply. The early evening air helped to rinse away the coppery smell of blood that clung inside his nostrils, and it helped to dull his headache, which was flaring up again.

His eyes shifted to the slim, metal gardener's cupboard that stood bolted to the brickwork of the house. Peters stepped over to it and pulled open the doors. Jill's small trove of gardening tools hung inside on little pegs.

He took the shovel off its peg, hoisted it up over his shoulder, and stepped out onto the yellow grass. It crunched underfoot. The far reaches of the garden were pitch black now, so he stayed within the dim range of the spotlights as he paced the yard, looking for the best spot to dig a grave.

He chose a patch over by the flowerbed, and he started

to score a perimeter into the turf before breaking in. Then he got to it. The ground was hard, and the spade head refused to bite too deeply, no matter how much weight he stomped down onto it, so it was slow work. Every half hour or so, he'd go into the kitchen and drink down a glass of water. Then he'd cup some into his hands and splash it into his face, and run his wet palms down his neck.

After a while, Teddy left Jill's side to come and see what all the commotion was. She lay out on the cool patio slabs and watched him work.

After two hours, the grave was knee-deep. After three, it was waist-deep. And that's where the exhaustion told him he'd dug enough. Every muscle in his body burned. His headache was raging like a supernova now. It was time to lay her to rest.

He found some bed sheets in the closet under the stairs. He wrapped Jill in them, and then he carried the white cocoon out to the hole he'd dug in the yard. Carefully, he lowered her in. Then he patted the dirt off him as best as he could, laced his fingers together, cleared his throat, and spoke. 'Lord. I don't know if you're up there anymore. But I'd like to say a few words here today. And if you're not listening, then the dog is, at least,' he said. 'I didn't know this woman long. But she was strong. Real strong. And she was just what these kids needed in these last few weeks. They needed a mother and a guiding light, and they needed to see what true bravery was. And that's what Jill gave them. Courage. That's what she gave them. And that's what she gave me, too. Amen.'

With that, he took up the shovel and started to fill in the grave. The dirt tumbled down into the hole. Soon, the cocoon was totally hidden. And half an hour later, the enormous mound of earth and clay had been returned into the void from where it had come, and Peters was pressing flat the rectangle of chewed-up dirt.

He lay the shovel down, wiped the sweat and muck off his face onto the sleeve of his shirt, and then headed inside.

'Come on, girl,' he said, with a quick whistle, as he passed Teddy. 'You're coming with me.'

Chapter 41
A Game of Tacko

'Alright, kiddos,' Chambers said, as she stepped into the rec room, 'bedtime!'

A chorus of disappointed huffs and grunts filled the air.

Some of the older children sat half-sunken into the giant beanbags that lined one side of the room. They thumbed furiously at the console controllers while engrossed in the action on the screens in front of them.

Most of the younger kids sat gathered around the tables on stools, playing card games and board games. Some were sinking plastic ships with little, colored pegs. Others were dropping red and yellow coins into slots, trying to get four in a row.

'Chop-chop!' Chambers said, as she crossed the floor and wasn't seeing much movement. 'Plenty of time to play tomorrow!'

The officer felt a soft tugging at the belt loop on her trousers. She looked down to see a small black boy glaring up at her from his place at a card game. The boy was skinny and had a cute little afro.

'Can't we have one more game, Miss?' the little boy asked.

Chambers stared down at him, lovingly. He looked just like Denzel had looked when she first met him, back at the home.

The table in front of the boy was covered in Tacko cards. The discard pile had gotten so high it had tumbled over and had become more of an untidy dumping ground. Around it, eight kids sat, each with a fan of cards held guardedly in front of them.

'We don't want to go to bed yet,' said one of the girls at the table. 'We don't think we'll sleep.'

Chambers let out a sigh. She dragged over a stool from the next table along and slipped it into the slim gap between two of the little ones.

'Deal me in,' the officer said, as she parked herself down. 'If I beat you, you go to bed. Deal?'

The faces around the table lit up.

'Deal!' they all said, in turn.

Quickly, they worked to massage the pile back into something resembling a deck. Then they gave it a quick shuffle and redistributed the cards around the nine players. Seven each.

'You know how to play?' the little black boy asked.

'I'm the Tacko champion,' Chambers said, with a smirk.

* * *

On the other side of the room, Milo, Becca, and Sally were having a game of their own. In turn, they tossed cards into the middle of the table. Brody sat with them but wasn't taking part. Instead, he gazed fixedly at his lap.

'Is he alright?' Milo asked, quietly.

Becca looked over at Brody as she fished out a blue seven and threw it onto the pile. 'He will be,' she said. 'It's all the people. It's going to take him some getting used to. He hates strangers.'

'They're not strangers exactly,' Milo said. 'They all go to our school.'

'Can you name half of them?' Becca asked.

Milo shook his head.

'Then they're strangers.'

Sally threw down a yellow four.

'That's a yellow, Sal. Remember, you've got to match the color or the number. You need a blue or a seven.'

She picked the card back up and then laid down a pick-up-six.

'Oh, Jesus Christ,' Milo said.

Becca laughed. 'Come on, My, pick 'em up!'

Milo took six cards from the deck and went to lay them down.

'No, no, no, you can't lay straight after you pick up!' Becca said.

'Of course, you can!'

'Maybe in your household, but not in ours!' Becca laughed.

'This is bullshit.' Milo folded his arms.

'How's your bunk?' Becca asked.

'The mattress is so thin. It's like sleeping on a cattle guard.'

They continued to toss down their cards in turn as they spoke.

'Yeah, mine and Sally's are like that, too. They're sponge, I think. We had camp-out beds like that. Never slept on those, either.'

'Will you cuddle her until she sleeps?' Milo asked. 'Mom used to do that if she was unsettled.'

Becca nodded. 'Of course.'

It was Milo's turn, but he didn't throw in. He stared darkly at the table for a few moments.

Becca reached out and put her hand on his wrist. 'My?'

He looked up at her suddenly, and his focus came back. 'Sorry.'

'Don't say sorry. You *should* be thinking about her.'

'Yeah. I just... don't know how she is. She's alone.'

'She isn't alone, My. She has Teddy with her. And do you think Peters isn't gonna be over there as much as he can? Those two were friends. He'll be there, with her.'

Milo half-smiled. 'Thanks.'

'Now, come on. I want to finish kicking your ass. I've got one card left.'

He put down a green.

'Yes, My! Good choice!' Becca laughed, as she slammed down her final card. 'Tacko!'

Sally threw her cards down angrily.

Brody looked up from his lap. The others turned to look at him.

'Brody?' Becca checked softly. 'You okay?'

'Food.'

'They cooked for us already,' his sister said. 'We've just eaten. Remember? You wolfed yours down. I don't know if we get snacks.'

'I put some chips in my pack,' Milo said. 'I'll give him some when we go back to the bunk.'

Becca smiled. 'Thank you.'

What Happened Next

Chambers slammed her last card down on the table and
pumped her fists into the air. 'Tacko!'

The kids surrounding her at the table all gave out a
playful whine. Some laughed. A couple clapped.

'Right. Bedtime, all of you!' Chambers said, delightedly,
as she got to her feet. 'You video gamers, too! Consoles off!
Butts up! Bedtime!'

Begrudgingly, stools screeched back from the tables, and
the older kids climbed up out of their beanbags and set
down their controllers.

Leader Smith and Leader Singh held open the double
doors. Slowly, the crowd shuffled out of the room. Once the
last kid in the queue had gone by, the two leaders followed
on to make sure they went to their dorms.

'And make sure you brush your teeth!' Chambers called
after them, with a smile.

Then she noticed that the table over in the corner
hadn't yet cleared. Four kids still sat around it, talking.

'Milo, Becca,' she said. 'Everything alright?'

Becca looked up at her. 'We're just worried about Milo's
mom, Miss.'

Sally gave her a little wave. It made Chambers crack a
broody smile.

'Hey, sweetie. What's your name, again?'

'Sally,' Milo said.

'Hey, Sally. Do you like unicorns?'

Sally nodded.

Chambers dug her hand into her pocket and took out a
little unicorn wristband.

'This was in my room. Left behind from the library, I
guess,' she said. She slid it across the table. Sally picked it
up and slid it over her hand.

'What do you say?' Milo asked.

'Thank you,' Sally said, shyly.

Chambers glanced at Brody.

'And what's *your* name?' she asked.

'That's Brody,' Becca said.

'He's not much of a talker?'

'He's – he's on the spectrum.'

'Ah, I see. I had a cousin like that. Danny. He was real good at remembering flags.'

'Yeah, Brody here is good at engineering.'

'Yeah? Like construction blocks?'

'Like booby traps,' Becca said, as she tried to hide her smirk.

'Ah, well, I'll watch my step, then. Did you guys choose your bunks already?'

Becca nodded. 'The mattresses are hard.'

Chambers looked around to check everyone else had left.

'Becca, Brody, come with me.'

Becca stood up, and then pulled Brody to his feet, and they followed Chambers through into the small security office in the corner of the room. It was a small storage room, with a single bed pushed against one wall, an air-conditioning unit that stood beside it, and a desk opposite. On the desk, stacked high, was a grid of monitors. Camera feeds from all over the building and all over the town were displayed on that wall of screens.

Chambers reached up at some shelving overhead.

'There are some blankets up here somewhere,' she said, as she stretched and felt around with her fingertips.

Becca heard a metallic thumping sound. She turned to see Brody standing in the corner of the room, next to the air conditioning unit. He was tapping a small, greenish-gray metal canister that was welded to the main pipe.

'Brody, stop that!'

'Shouldn't be there,' Brody said. He tapped the canister harder.

'Got them!' Chambers said, as she pulled down a pile of folded, navy blue blankets.

'Brody, stop it!' Becca shouted.

'That thing is bloody noisy,' Chambers laughed. 'If he wants to kill it, I don't mind!'

Becca grabbed his arm and pulled him away. 'Sorry,' she said. 'I don't know what's got into him.'

That's okay,' Chambers said, with a little laugh. 'Here!'

She gave two blankets to Becca and two to Brody.

'Double these over and put them under the covers,' Chambers said.

'Wow, thank you! That's a good trick.'

'Yeah, worked it out on my first night here. That bed was like sleeping on gridiron. This cushions it up. Right,' she said, checking her wristwatch, 'Time for bed!'

Becca and Brody went back to the table to collect the others, and slowly, the four of them exited the rec room.

Chambers watched them go and then took a bottle of perfume off the desk, uncapped it, and gave her neck a couple of squirts.

She glanced up at the wall of screens stacked high on the desk, and her eyes shifted to one in particular. It showed the car park and the bricked forecourt at the front of the building. Right on cue, a squad crawled to a halt right outside, and Diaz climbed out.

Chapter 42
Night Caller

Diaz sat on the bed in the security office, and Chambers stood between his knees, with her hands clasped around his neck. He started to unbutton her shirt.

The radio on the desk cackled. Then Peters' voice came through.

'*Chambers?*'

'Leave it,' Diaz said, as he planted a trail of kisses that started from her lower tummy, passed up over her belly button, and headed up towards her breasts. 'You've clocked off for the evening.' He reached around to try to unclasp her bra.

'*Chambers, you there?*' The radio asked again. '*It's important.*'

'Two minutes, babe,' she said. She went over to the desk and picked up the radio.

'Chambers here.'

'*Ah, Chambers, good,*' he said. '*I– Uh, Christ.*'

'Sir? Everything okay?'

'Milo and Sally – how are they? How are they settling in?'

'The little girl's okay. The boy is worrying about his mom. As you'd expect.'

'Yeah, well, that's what I'm calling about.'

Chambers sighed. Suddenly, she knew where this was going. 'She's gone?'

'She's gone, yeah.'

'I'm sorry, sir,' Chambers said.

'It was quick. Symptoms usually go on a while. I thought there would be more time. I didn't want her to go alone.'

'I know, sir. Jesus. Those kids. They've all been through so much already.'

'I want Milo to know,' Peters said. *'Sooner rather than later. He'll be tossing and turning all night anyway, with the uncertainty. So he needs to know. He can break it to Sally when he thinks it's right, in his own way. But him – he needs to know. So I'm gonna head over.'*

Chambers looked at Diaz, who had stripped down to his boxer shorts since she'd last looked at him.

'No, sir. Don't come over. I'll tell him. Better from a woman, I think.'

'Are you sure?'

'Yes, sir. I'll tell him now. You just go and get some rest. I know you were fond of her.'

'Okay. Thank you, Chambers. I'll come by in the morning.'

'Goodnight, sir.'

'Goodnight, Chambers.'

She sat the radio back down on the counter.

'I need to go and get Milo,' she said, as she buttoned her shirt.

Diaz lay sprawled across the small single bed. There were masses of black hair downing his legs and chest.

'Wait in here,' Chambers said.

He watched her closely as she pulled on her sneakers. She was the most caring person he'd known in the years since he'd lost his parents. He was sad to have to share her with that place, but he knew there wasn't a person anywhere in New Hampshire who could better steward that Youth Station. Nobody else had that same balance of loving and strict. And he was glad that he got to spend the last of his days with her. Even if he *did* have to sneak over after dark now. To fall asleep with that girl in his arms made what was coming less scary. And it made it feel like his whole life wasn't for nothing. It had all led up to this. It had all led up to her.

'Wait in here,' she repeated. And with that, she left the small security office.

* * *

The boys' dorm was filled with a groggy chorus of snoring and sobbing. And it was only half dark. Strip-lights lined the far wall to help guide sleepy children to the bathroom, and they painted everything in a dim neon glow.

Milo lay awake in the top bunk, staring up at the ceiling tiles. He could hear Brody snoring in the bed below, but *he* just couldn't seem to nod off. And while there were many thoughts that could have raced through his mind, it was Christmas that took front and center. That snowy Christmas when he was eight years old.

Sally wasn't around yet. But Uncle Malc was there. He'd turned up almost a week early and had sat in the lounge, watching cartoons and drinking beer for days on end.

'Viper Beer. That's what you'll drink when you're older,' he told him. 'Because all other beers are for pussies.'

Sometime on the twenty-third, it started to snow. It came down heavy, and it covered everything, and it kept on coming. Come Christmas day itself, both sets of grandparents called to say they weren't gonna brave the roads that day. And so it was just the four of them. All snowed in together.

'Hasn't snowed like this since we were kids,' his dad kept saying.

The four of them opened their presents. Then they wrapped up in their winter warms and headed out into the yard.

They rolled up a couple of giant balls, mounded one on top of the other, and then beheld the colossal snowman. It towered above all of them. Then his dad hoisted him up onto his shoulders so that he could fix in place the eye-stones and the carrot.

Then Uncle Malc lifted him off and raced him around the garden, making airplane noises. They bowled into Dallas, and they all tumbled over and lay on their backs in the snow, laughing and staring up at the white sky.

As he lay there in the bunk, surrounded by the crying and the snoring, he realized that was probably his happiest memory. That perfect day in the snow with his parents and Uncle Malc.

'Can't sleep?' a soft voice asked.

Milo turned his head. On the top bunk beside his, a little black boy with a cute, little afro lay awake. His eyes glittered in the dark. It was the boy Chambers had played Tacko with earlier that night.

'I can't,' Milo said.

'Me either.'

'What's your name?'

'Neo.'

'Cool name.'

'It's from my mom's favorite film. What's your name?'

'Milo.'

'Is that from a film?'

'No.' Milo smiled. 'I was named after my dad's barber. They needed a boy's name, and that's a name he liked.'

Neo laughed softly. 'That's dumb.'

'It is dumb.' Milo laughed, too. 'So why can't you sleep?'

'I just hate to see everybody so sad,' Neo said. 'My mom says I'm an empath. I just suck it all up. I just want everybody to be okay.'

Milo nodded. 'Everybody *will* be okay. We'll all get through these next weeks together.'

'Milo?' Chambers interrupted. She was suddenly standing between the two bunks.

'Is everything okay?' Milo asked. 'Is Sally okay?'

'Sally's fine. But I need you to come with me, please.'

'Where?'

'We'll go up to the rec room.'

'Uh... Okay, yeah, okay.'

He jumped down from the bunk.

'Put your shoes on, too. The floor is icy cold.'

He slid on his shoes and a jacket, too. Then he followed Chambers out of the dorm and up into the rec room.

Chambers sat on one of the tables and kicked a stool out towards Milo.

'You'll want to sit down.'

He parked himself on the stool. He already knew where this was going. He felt his heart break in his chest.

'Now, I have some bad news. Lieutenant Peters went by to check on your mom. To make sure she was doing okay. And I'm really sorry, Milo...'

Milo put his face into his hands, and he sobbed. Tears slipped through his fingers.

Chambers quickly clambered down from the table and wrapped her arms around him.

'I'm so sorry,' she whispered softly as she cradled him.

In the security room, Diaz stood in front of the stack of monitors, still wearing nothing but his boxer shorts. His eyes were fixed on the screen that showed the rec room, just outside the door. He reached for the little joystick that sat mounted to the desk and used it to zoom in on Chambers and Milo. He grunted. Then he went and laid down on the bed. The frame groaned under his weight.

Then they came. Four deafening gunshots that echoed through the building. They sounded like fireworks erupting in the lobby.

Diaz shot up from the bed and peered up at the screens again. His eyes darted between the monitors. Most of them had switched to night vision now and showed grainy, grayscale imagery that was harder to decipher.

But then he found the motion. The lobby screen. The glass frontage had a gaping hole in it, and three tall, dark figures were stepping into the building.

'What the fuck?'

He clambered around quickly to pull on his clothes.

Outside, in the rec room, Chambers stood up and stared at the door. She pulled Milo to his feet and put him behind her.

'What was that noise?' he asked, teary-eyed.

Diaz burst out of the security office, which startled Milo.

'It's okay!' Chambers assured him. 'He's a cop. He's with me.'

'Intruders,' Diaz said, as he clicked a clip into his gun. 'Heavily armed.' He passed Chambers her own handgun, which he'd grabbed from the holster she'd slung over the bed end.

'Milo, get in the security office,' she ordered. 'Stay in there until we deal with this. Don't leave no matter what.'

Milo nodded and hurried into the small office.

Chambers raised her radio. *'Live shooters at the Youth Station. I repeat – live shooters!'*

She and Diaz rushed out of the rec room and headed down the corridor, with their guns raised out in front.

'You head to the dorms and keep the kids safe,' Diaz said. 'I'll clear this side.'

Chapter 43
The Siege

The glass had given more easily than Rex had expected. Four quick shots from his uncle's pistol – one loosely in each corner – and a couple of kicks, and now the frontage lay all over the foyer.

He stepped into the lobby. Brandon and Dean followed him in. The glass crunched like fresh snow underfoot.

Each of them had a semi-automatic rifle hanging from a strap over their shoulder, a handgun in hand, and another tucked away in case of emergencies.

'She's in here somewhere,' Rex said. 'And it's big. So let's split up. You two take this building. Floor by floor. Work your way up. I'll head through to the back. If you find her, you bring her outside.'

With that, Rex stormed off towards the dorms.

Dean and Brandon headed towards the metal double doors that led through into the kitchen.

* * *

Milo sat on the edge of the small bed in the security office. Tears dripped down onto his pajama pants.

He couldn't shake the thought of his mom dying in that house alone, with nothing but Teddy for company.

If they'd waited just another couple of hours, they could have been with her when she went. He wouldn't have wanted to watch that. It would have haunted him forever. Yet, somehow, he was sure it would have been less haunting than the thought of her slipping away on her own – scared, pained, and longing for her family.

He wiped the tears away on the back of his hand. Then he saw movement on one of the monitors out of the corner of his eye, and he stared up at the stack of screens. He got to his feet and stepped closer.

Two figures were heading towards the kitchen. The night vision was grainy and indistinct. A third figure was heading towards the dorms. This one, he recognized instantly.

'Rex?'

He ran for the door.

* * *

Dean peered into the kitchen. No signs of movement. The kitchen sat empty. It was lit only by the bulb of an extractor hood that hadn't been turned off after dinner.

He stepped inside, cautiously. Brandon followed slowly and silently.

They passed a long island, which was crowned by a great granite worktop. They stepped softly, trying to make as little noise as possible.

'Shh!' Brandon said.

Dean stopped walking and turned his head. 'What?'

'Do you hear that?'

'Hear what?'

'Footsteps.'

Dean listened hard. 'I can't hear anything.'

Brandon turned to his left and saw a man staring right at him. In a fraction of a heartbeat, he pointed the gun and fired. Five loud shots.

Brandon's gunfire had been so unexpected that Dean had jolted hard. His gun clambered out of his hand, hit the floor, and slid off under the cabinets. His ears were ringing like school bells. He gave Brandon a harsh glance, then turned to see what he'd shot at.

It wasn't an assailant. Instead, it was the face of the tall, metallic fridge, which was so smooth and so polished that it was almost mirrored. Only now, it had five bullet holes sunken into it, and milk and OJ gushed from the punctured cartons inside.

Once his pulse had settled, Brandon lowered the gun. 'Oh, it was me.' He let out a laugh. 'It was my reflection.'

Dean shook his head. He still had sirens wailing in his ears from those gun blasts. But after a few moments, he caught the funny side, too, and he laughed as well. 'You fucking idiot!'

Then Dean's eyeball blew clean out of his head. Brandon was showered in his blood. It dripped from his brow and his nose, and it freckled his face.

The cadaver dropped to the tiles like a sack of potatoes. Before Brandon could even react – before he could even register what had just happened – a bullet tore through his head, too. And his body slumped to the ground, next to his friend's. Slowly, blood pooled around them.

Diaz stepped over to the two fresh corpses, with smoke seeping gently from the tip of his gun. He jabbed the toe of his boot into Brandon's belly to check he was dead. Then he jabbed Dean.

Quietly, he headed out into the lobby – gun still held out in front.

* * *

'Momma! Momma!' Sally cried.

She lay sobbing in bed, cradled in Becca's arms, with the sheets draped over the both of them.

'Shh! Shh!' Becca whispered gently into her ear.

The gunshots had woken everyone in the girls' dorm. Many of them were crying. A couple were hyperventilating. Most had climbed into bed with their bunk buddies. The pairs clung to each other like frightened little tarsiers.

Becca heard footsteps out in the corridor. Someone was running towards the door. A boy appeared suddenly behind the glass. It made her jump, which made Sally cry harder. Then she recognized it to be Leader Riley. He fumbled around with his key card. The door opened. He rushed inside and then closed it quickly behind him.

'Everybody, stay calm!' he ordered.

'What's going on?' Tasha Levinski asked.

'Were those gunshots?' asked one of her cheerleader friends.

'It's all okay! There are two officers here dealing with it. I just need everybody to stay calm!'

Becca swayed Sally a little, trying to soothe her with the motion. 'Shh, shh. It's okay.'

Milo stepped out into the kitchen. He saw an orange puddle emerging from beneath the fridge. Then he spotted the bullet holes riddling its door.

Quickly, he crossed the kitchen and headed behind the great granite worktop, towards the double doors. He tripped on something, and came crashing down onto something squishy and warm.

The dim light from the extractor hood could scarcely reach behind the work island, and he sat, shrouded in shade. It took a few moments for his eyes to adjust. But then he realized what he was laying on top of.

Dean's dead face peered up with its one remaining eye. Blood oozed from the gaping void beside it.

'Jesus,' Milo whimpered, as he clambered off.

He stared down at Dean's corpse. Then he looked over at Brandon's body, which lay next to it.

His night pants were drenched in blood, and it was all up his arms. It was still lukewarm. He felt a sickening knot in his stomach, and he wretched. But no vomit came up.

He watched the two teens for a few moments, in horror. He'd hated those boys. He'd hated them so much. They'd made so many people's lives miserable. They'd even held him in place whilst Rex had burnt him with that cigarette. But he'd never wanted this.

He clutched onto the worktop to steady himself. He felt dizzy, and he wretched again.

Suddenly, his eyes landed on a handgun. It lay in the puddle of blood, half-hidden under the cabinet. He reached down and picked it up.

Rex wasn't dead yet. And he was there for one reason. Becca. Milo had to stop him. He had to save her.

He drew a deep breath, and then stepped carefully over

the bodies. He headed through the double doors, out into the lobby.

* * *

Chambers stepped softly but intently down the corridor that ran around the outside of the girls' dorm. As she approached the turn ahead, she brushed her shoulder up to the wall and peered around the corner as stealthily as she could.

At the end of the next run of corridor stood a young man in a leather jacket, with a pink scar running through his lip. He was using the butt of a semi-automatic rifle to hammer at the door.

'Drop the gun!' she shouted, as she stepped out into the walkway.

Unalarmed, Rex casually turned to look at her. He continued to hold the gun backwards, with its butt facing the door.

'I said, drop it!'

Rex smiled.

She fired. The patch of wall beside his head burst into a spray of brick and dust that showered down onto the floor.

'Next one goes in your cheek.'

Rex threw the gun down.

'Now slide it over.'

Rex kicked it towards her with his boot.

'Right, now get those hands up.'

Slowly, he raised his arms into the air, which brought the tail of his jacket up above his pant-line. That's when she spotted the handgun tucked into the front of his jeans.

'The gun in your crotch. Pull it out with your finger and thumb. It goes on the floor, and it comes this way, too.'

He fished it out gently and then placed it on the floor, and kicked that over, too.

'Who are you?'

'Rex, ma'am.'

'And what are you doing here, armed to the teeth?'

Gun shots went off somewhere in the distance, and Chambers turned to look. Rex slowly tucked his left hand into his jacket pocket.

She looked back at him. 'Hey! Get that hand up!'

Quickly, he dug something from his pocket and tossed it in her direction. Then he collapsed onto the ground and clasped his hands over the back of his head.

Something metallic bounced along the corridor, like a tennis ball, and hit Chambers' boot. She glanced down at it, and her heart skipped a beat. Quickly, she kicked it towards the wall.

The grenade exploded. The lights overhead flickered and then failed, and the corridor fell into darkness. The ceiling caved downwards, burying the officer and Rex in plaster tiles and splintered, wooden battens. The wall cracked, and several great cinder blocks tumbled onto the floor.

* * *

Screaming erupted in the girls' dorm. The explosion was twice as loud as the gunshots. It was as though a jeep had crashed into the wall, and cracks stretched from ceiling to floor.

The strip-lights that lined one side of the room flickered, but they stayed on.

The fire alarm started to wail throughout the building, and the sprinklers burst into life. They showered down and quickly carpeted the entire place in puddles that shimmied and danced, and spat.

Sally howled uncontrollably in Becca's arms now as the water rained down on them. With the toddler clutched to her chest, Becca jumped down from the bunk. Her bare soles planted onto the wet floor.

All around them, girls scrambled from their beds and ran to the far wall, where the entrance to the bathroom was. Becca carried Sally to join the crowd that had amassed there.

Together, they stood, tearful and terrified - their clothes drenched and hanging heavy from the endless shower that flooded from above.

Out in the corridor, the green bulkheads that lined the wall started to glow dimly as the emergency lighting system kicked in.

Rex burst up through the debris. Chunks of plaster fell from his shoulders as he rose. His hair was white with dust, and his forehead was covered in blood. It dripped off his brow, diluted by the water that showered down from the sprinklers overhead.

Hunched over, he fished around under the layer of collapsed ceiling, tossing broken panels this way and that. Finally, he found the rifle. He lifted it up and slipped the strap over his shoulder.

Then came some confused, pained groaning a little further down the corridor. A large ceiling tile flung to one side, and from underneath it emerged a woman's hand. It was wafting around helplessly.

He walked over to it and peered down through the

small hole it had burrowed through the carpet of plaster panels, broken wood, and insulation.

Rex pointed the rifle.

'Goodbye, ma'am.'

But before he could shoot, he heard a man's voice around the corner. 'Emma?' it called. 'Emma?'

Loud boot claps approached fast.

Rex curled his lip in an ugly snarl and then slunk away like a confronted raccoon scurrying off a porch.

Diaz turned the corner and spotted the hand poking up through the debris. Without hesitation, he dove to his knees and started to bat away all the scrap, uncovering his beautiful girlfriend, who lay with her eyes closed and a cut down the side of her face.

'Emma?'

The cold droplets from the sprinklers showered onto her face. Her eyes came open, and she looked at Diaz. He was soaked through. She smiled and lifted both arms for him to pull her up.

'Are you okay?' he asked, as he lifted her into his arms.

She saw his lips moving but she couldn't hear him. She couldn't hear a thing. Not the sprinklers. Not anything. She started to panic. Quickly, her expression changed from one of love to one of fear, and she started to breathe more frantically. She massaged both ears.

'Emma? Baby? What is it? Can't you hear?'

She tucked her fingers into the canals and tried to stir them back to life. But no sound came.

'Intruder,' she said, finally, as she pointed down the corridor.

Diaz stared off down the walkway behind them. 'Okay. Okay, I'll go and deal with him. You – wait here.' He carried her over to the wall, away from the spray of the sprinklers;

then, he dug her gun out from the debris and put it in her lap. 'Stay here!' He pointed at her and then pointed down towards the ground.

She couldn't hear him, but she knew what he was saying. She nodded.

Diaz ran off through the debris, in the direction Rex had run.

* * *

Milo climbed the stairs to the top floor, where the girls' dorm was. He entered the long square corridor that circled the dorm. Both his hands were clamped around the handgun he'd taken from the kitchen. It was pointing down at the wet ground beneath his feet.

That's when he saw Rex. He stood at the door to the girls' dorm, and now that the fire alarm had been triggered, it was unlocked. He pulled the handle, and it came open.

'Hey!' Milo shouted.

Rex let the door close again. He turned and grinned at Milo. 'Oh, Winters.' He raised his rifle and fired off a rapid blast in Milo's direction. Milo dove back around the corner and sprinted down the next straight. He could hear Rex charging towards him down the corridor.

'Becca's dead, huh?' Rex's voice called after him. 'Who's grave was that, huh? Her mom's? Nice trick, Winters. But you're gonna pay.'

Quickly, Milo flung himself around the next corridor, but instantly tripped over a mound of debris on the floor, and came crashing down on top of the broken plaster and splintered wood. He let out a yell. His gun bounced away from him.

Chambers, who sat to one side, had watched as he sprinted right past her and tumbled to the floor.

'Milo?' she asked, rushing over to help him. But he couldn't hear her voice over the sloshing of the sprinklers and the drumming of his pulse in his own head.

But he *did* hear her footsteps crunching through the debris behind him. *He's right on top of me*, he thought, as he lay on his front in the debris, wincing and panting. Quickly, he scrambled forwards and reached out for his gun.

At the other end of the corridor, Diaz reappeared. He'd heard the yell, and he wanted to make sure Chambers was okay.

Milo grabbed his gun, turned, and fired at the figure that loomed over him. One shot, just below the chest. The bullet passed right through and bore into the wall behind.

Then, in the ugly dim green glow from the emergency bulkheads on the wall, the figure's face came into focus. It wasn't Rex. It was Chambers. It was the beautiful young officer who had given them blankets. Who had so delicately broken to him the news of his mother's passing. Who had told him to hide in the security office for his own safety. Who had so brilliantly mothered the entire Youth Station and had made hundreds of frightened children feel as though they had a future.

'No,' Milo said, hopelessly. His stomach dropped. His gun flopped to the floor. 'No! No! I didn't – I didn't mean–.'

Chambers' eyes grew wide. She looked shocked. Confused. Like she was trying to process what had just happened. Then her eyes started to dart. And her legs became lifeless beneath her, and her body collapsed to the ground.

'Winters?' Diaz asked from behind.

Milo turned and looked at him. 'No! I–I didn't–! I wouldn't–!'

Diaz staggered heavily forwards. His face flitted through confusion and shock, and blind rage. His gun hand twitched.

Milo glanced down at Chambers as she lay dying at his feet. Then he thought about Becca and Sally. He couldn't be gunned down here. He had to stop Rex. 'I'm so sorry,' he whispered to her, gently. Then he drew a deep breath and bolted for the safety of the corner, and disappeared around the next straight.

Diaz went to stagger blindly after him, on autopilot, but then a hand grasped his ankle. He stared down at Chambers. She lay on the bed of broken plaster boards and splintered wood, soaked in blood, shaking. Her eyes were fixed on him.

He collapsed to his knees beside her, trembling, and pulled her onto his lap, and he held her tightly.

'Don't leave me,' he said. 'I love you. You're the only one I ever loved.'

But she couldn't hear him. The pained look on her face softened. Her breathing slowed, and she fell still.

* * *

Rex waded through the water that had pooled on the dorm room floor. The sprinklers overhead had stopped now. The strip-lights along the far wall flickered, and underneath them stood a crowd of terrified girls, who all watched in horror as he approached, hunched over and grunting, with his rifle clutched in both hands.

'Becca?' he called.

Leader Riley stepped out, in front of the girls.

'Rex - you - you can't be here,' he stammered, anxiously. 'Please - please leave.'

In one quick, effortless motion, Rex jabbed the butt of the rifle into the side of Leader Riley's face. The teen slapped down onto the wet ground, unconscious, and his glasses slid off under the nearest bunk.

Tasha Levinski stepped forward, next. 'Get out of here, you – you freak!'

Rex raised the gun and pulled the trigger. The bullet went through her left cheek, just beneath her eye. Blood and brain matter blew out the back of her skull and splattered into the faces of her cheerleading buddies.

The room erupted into screams.

Becca, who still had Sally clinging to her, backed away through the writhing crowd. Once her back was against the wall, she moved along it, towards the opening to the bathroom.

'Where are you, baby?' Rex called.

Rex coughed hard. Plaster dust sprayed out of his mouth. His hair was matted with blood. He continued to advance towards the girls. He stepped unsteadily. His ankles nearly buckled on each stride.

The girls cried and shrieked. As he staggered towards them, he recognized many of them from school. They had lined the corridors that day his uncle had paid a visit. The day the RV King had taken off his belt and had given him that scar. And they had watched and laughed while he screamed and writhed on the floor. They snapped photos. And took videos. And joked and cheered. And they had lost their minds when the piss had started to pool onto the floor.

Now, as he stepped over Tasha's corpse, and he saw the terror on their faces, he felt *even*. And it felt good. Real good. He could feel warmth between his legs as his penis filled with blood.

Then he saw a figure slip through the back of the crowd and into the bathroom. A figure he'd recognize anywhere.

He shoved girls out of the way, like weightless mannikins, and followed into the bathroom. Ahead of him, Becca ran, breathing hard, with Sally's arms wrapped tightly around her neck.

Rex gave a dry laugh. 'Where do you think you're going, honey?'

Becca heard him, but she didn't look back. She ran into one of the stalls, slammed the door, and slid across the lock-bar. Then she put the toilet seat down and sat on it, with Sally whimpering against her chest.

Rex stopped beside the door.

'It's time, baby.'

'Time for what?' Becca asked.

'I'm here to save you.'

'Save me?'

'That's right. Save you from this – this fucking crèche. I've been living like a king on the outside. All the alcohol I can drink. All the junk food. All the late nights. All the nudey videos. That's freedom. But this – in here – cooped up in the fucking library. Jeez, Becca. That ain't you.'

'Go back and live like a king, then. I'm fine here, with my family.'

'You mean your dopey brother?'

'Fuck you.'

'Sorry. I don't know the right term for it.'

'He's autistic. And no. I have other people I need to look after, too.'

'Says who?'

'I made a promise.'

Rex kicked the stall door. It left a perfect boot print indented in the wood. The lock leaned forwards on its screws. Another kick, and the door swung open.

Becca and Sally stared up at him in terror.

'Come on, baby. No more running. It's time to come home, where you belong.'

He reached out his hand for her to take.

A metallic thump rang out across the bathroom. Rex's expression fell blank, and his body fell limp. It tumbled over and smacked hard onto the ground. Standing there, and looking as surprised as Becca and Sally, was Milo. He was holding a fire extinguisher in his hands. He'd jabbed its blunt end into the back of Rex's skull as hard as he could.

Rex snored groggily on the floor.

'Come on!' Milo said. 'Pack all your things. We need to go. Now.'

'Where's Brody?'

'I'll go and help him pack,' Milo said. 'Meet me in the lobby in two minutes.'

Milo reached down and picked up Rex's rifle. He put the strap over his shoulder and then ran from the bathroom.

Chapter 44
The Escape

Denzel pulled up outside The Youth Station. His face was still freckled in Gunner's blood. That shotgun had made quite the mess. After he'd pulled the trigger, he went and sat in his car, outside the farmhouse. And he thought about the night his mother was killed. How scared she would have been, staring up at all the merciless, unfeeling faces circled around her. Now, finally, he'd taken a little slice of revenge. But it wasn't enough. The rest were still out there. Tucked away in the safety of the DLC. Behind its vast walls.

He took the clip out of his gun, counted six bullets through the slot in the side, and then snapped it back in place. Quickly, he ran over the library's small, brick forecourt, where the parents had queued just hours earlier, and he went in through the missing frontage. The glass crackled like popping candy under his boots.

The building was still lit only by the emergency lights on the walls, which painted everything in an ugly green glow. The floor was wet underfoot. But the sprinklers and the siren had ceased.

He raised his radio to his lips.

'Chambers, update, please.'

Nothing came back.

He went into the kitchen and saw the corpses of Dean and Brandon beside the work island, with a great pool of blood beneath them.

'What the–?'

He backed off, back into the lobby, with a new sense of alertness. He crept quickly towards the dorms at the back of the building, where he could hear shouting and crying.

Denzel climbed the stairs up to the top floor and came out into the square corridor that circled the girls' dorm. He could hear sobbing to the left and followed it. Once he'd turned the corner, he saw the collapsed ceiling. Kneeling in the debris was Diaz, who was crying uncontrollably.

Beside him, Chambers lay on the ground. Leader Singh was administering CPR. But her lifeless, pale body just flailed with each compression. Sweat dripped off the teenager's face as he worked.

Diaz looked up at Denzel. 'She's gone,' he spluttered. Then his eyes tightened, and his face contorted, and he let out a long yell, but no sound came out.

Denzel fell back against the wall and slid down it until his ass was on the ground. He set his gun down in his lap and clasped both hands to his face.

He remembered the first time she'd come up to him, back at the home. He was so frightened, arriving at that place. But she was there for him. Always. That friendly, loving face – ready to comfort him. And he'd loved that girl. He'd loved that girl so fucking much.

'It was Winters,' Diaz said, at last.

'*What?*' Denzel asked. 'Milo?'

'I watched him do it.'

Denzel frowned. 'You're sure?'

'With my own two eyes.'

'That scrawny, little fuck?'

Diaz nodded. 'It was him, man. I promise you.'

Denzel ran his palm down his face. He sat, deep in thought. Then his eyes flitted back towards the Mexican. 'You get him?'

Diaz shook his head. 'Not yet. But when I do, it'll be slow, man. It'll be slow.'

'Alright,' Denzel said. He wiped the tears off his face. 'Let's get him.'

He got up and pulled Diaz to his feet. Diaz stared down at Chambers, one last time, as the Leader Singh continued to press into her chest in quick hard pops.

She looked beautiful. She looked at peace.

Diaz let out a long breath, and then he followed Denzel along the corridor.

'Officers!' Leader Cunningham called, as they turned the corner. He stood outside the girl's dorm. 'Officers! In here! He's in here!'

'Take us to him!' Diaz said.

They followed Cunningham into the dorms. He led them across the wet floor.

'We got him tied up,' Cunningham said.

'Nice work, kid!'

He led them over to Rex, who was tied up by one of the bunk beds. His wrists were bound behind him, his ankles were tied out in front, and a ball of socks was stuffed in his mouth. He was awake and writhed around, grunting hard.

'That ain't Milo!' Diaz said, unamused.

'Milo?' Cunningham asked. 'Aren't you looking for Rex? He just killed Tasha Levinski.' He turned and pointed at her body. 'He shot her through the head.'

Denzel squinted at Rex. He recognized him from the clubhouse.

'I'll put him in the car,' he said, as he reached down and stood Rex up. 'He ain't going anywhere for the time being.'

'Where's Milo?' Diaz asked.

'He took off,' Cunningham said. 'Him, his sister, Becca Sampson, and her brother. Backpacks and all. They slipped away before we could reset the locks.'

Diaz screamed in anger. He kicked the leg of the nearest bunk bed. It screeched a couple of feet across the floorboards. The girls, who were still huddled at one side of the room, let out a chorus of screams and gasps.

Denzel clamped a hand onto Diaz's shoulder. 'Easy, easy. We'll find him,' he said, quietly. Then he shifted his glance back to Cunningham. 'What way did he go?'

Cunningham shrugged. 'You could check the security room. It's hooked up to cameras all over town.'

* * *

A couple of minutes later, Denzel and Diaz stood in the security room, eying the monitors that were stacked high on the desk.

Peters came into the room.

'Where the hell were you?' Diaz asked.

'Where's Chambers?' Peters asked.

Diaz exhaled.

'She,' Denzel started, choking on the words. 'She didn't make it.'

Peters collapsed down onto the cot behind him. He stared hopelessly at the floor.

'How?' he asked, looking up, finally.

'Milo shot her,' Diaz said.

Peters shook his head. 'Milo? Milo wouldn't–.'

'I fucking saw him do it,' Diaz said.

Denzel used the control stick to flick between the monitors. They showed little, grayscale scenes from all over Masterson.

'You're looking for Milo?' Peters asked.

Denzel nodded. 'He took off with his buddies.'

'What are you going to–?'

Diaz shot him a dark look and then resumed looking at the screens.

Peters got back to his feet, and looked up at the monitors.

The bottom right screen showed Whiston Rail Bridge. The bridge the truck had gotten stuck under, a month earlier. He watched as four figures climbed into the metal arch, and hid away, out of sight. Diaz and Denzel kept panning through the screens. They hadn't seen it.

Slowly, Peters backed off, towards the door. Quickly, he slipped out of the small office, and ran across the rec room.

Chapter 45
The Bunking Bridge

On the inside of the Whiston Rail Bridge, there were steel overhangs that stood a couple of feet deep. Teens bunking off high school used to go and hide in those indents, and they'd smoke or make out, or both. It was known as the bunking bridge.

Becca had actually gone there once while skipping school, so she knew it was a good hiding spot. Todd Ingram had taken her there. They'd smoked, and they'd kissed, and they'd tattooed each other's arms with a Markie. He was a year older than her. So he'd gotten the vaccine. And right now, he was either winding down for the Big Sleep, or he was already sleeping.

She thought about that as she passed under the bridge with Milo and the others.

'We can hide under here,' she said.

'Shouldn't we keep moving?' Milo asked.

'We need to get off the road. That cop will be after us.'

Milo looked glumly at the ground. He could still see Chamber's stunned expression, after he'd pulled that trigger.

'Come on!' Becca said, as she climbed up behind the metal siding, with Sally held to her chest. Brody climbed up behind her.

Milo stared back down the road. It was empty, for now. He climbed inside the metalwork, after Becca.

They all rested their backs against the cold steel, and caught their breath.

'It wasn't your fault, what happened to Chambers,' Becca said, looking at Milo.

Milo didn't reply. He just stared silently at his feet.

Becca shifted her eyes to Brody.

'You okay?' she asked, patting him softly on the shoulder.

'Wet,' he said.

'Yeah. We're all wet.'

Becca looked up at the steel wall beside Milo's head. There was a big love heart, etched in marker pen with the initials, 'M.W. + E.R.' written inside it.

'M.W. - is that you?' Becca asked, with a laugh.

Milo looked at it, and then shook his head.

Sally nestled her head between Becca's collar bones and closed her eyes, and soon, she was snoozing.

The bridge fell into silence for half an hour. Becca and Milo stood with their packs at their feet, and their backs to the steel. They thought of Jill. They thought of Chambers. And they wondered what was to come next.

Suddenly, the dark void beneath the bridge filled with light, and the humming of an engine echoed off the huge steel arch above their heads.

Milo reached for the rifle, which he'd set down by his backpack.

The car wasn't simply passing by. It had stopped right

under the bridge. The ticking of the engine was amplified all around them. Then they heard a door open.

'He found us,' Becca said.

Milo took a deep breath. 'Okay,' he said. 'I'm gonna deal with it.' He raised the rifle and stepped out of the overhang.

The headlights shone in his eyes, blinding him. He pointed his gun into the light and stretched his finger towards the trigger. But then a voice came.

'Put that thing down, kid!'

'Peters?' Milo asked, shielding his eyes with his hand.

'Put that gun down and get in the car. All of you. And be quick about it!'

Teddy popped up in the passenger-side window and barked.

'It's Peters!' Milo called back to the others. 'He's got Teddy!'

Becca came out fast, with Sally still clutching to her. Brody followed.

Milo climbed into the front seat. Teddy climbed up onto his lap and licked his face. The other three bundled quickly into the back and rested their packs at their feet.

They'd hardly closed the doors before the Rattler had shot off down the road.

'Peters, I didn't mean to–,' Milo said in a flutter. 'I thought she was Rex. It just – it just went off in my hand.'

'I know you wouldn't do that on purpose, Milo.'

Milo petted Teddy, who rested her snout on his shoulder and stared at the three in the back.

'Chambers told me about my mom,' Milo said.

Peters gave a sad sigh. 'I'm sorry.'

'Were you there when it happened?'

'I wish I was with her. But no. I got there after. Teddy was with her. Didn't leave her side.'

Milo nodded.

'I buried her.'

'Thank you.'

'The very least that woman deserved.'

Milo wiped away the tears. Becca reached forward from the back seat and clasped her hand onto his shoulder. Teddy licked her fingers.

Peters' eyes kept scanning the road ahead for signs of movement, and he kept glancing in the rearview.

'You need to get out of town tonight,' he said.

'Can't we just hide somewhere?' Becca asked.

'No, they'll find you. They'll tear this place apart to find you. That cop you shot... Diaz and Denzel – they loved her. They *loved* her. She was Diaz's girlfriend, and she was practically Denzel's sister. Love outpowers everything. Logic. Reason. Duty. *Everything.* If they find you, I don't like to think what they'll do. And I can't call them off.'

'So what do we do now?' Becca asked.

'Your idea,' Peters started, glancing at Milo, 'About the DLC. Your uncle.'

'Yeah?' Milo turned to him.

'I think I know how we could make it work.'

'How?'

'The Miller-Davis Stone Line.'

'Isn't that a band?' Milo asked.

'Yeah, I think my dad has them on vinyl,' Becca added.

Peters shook his head. 'It's a railway. I remembered hearing about it on the news. Miller-Davis Stone was a quarry firm back in the early nineteen-hundreds. And the Miller-Davis Stone Line was their railway. It hauled ore from their quarry in Digger's End to the mills in Charleston.'

'Okay...?' Milo wasn't sure where this was going.

'Well, that's what was on the news. The DLC is in Charleston. And the timber yards they used to construct it were in Merle. So they used the old line and ran these little, electric carts back and forth along the line. It was quicker and cheaper than running trucks.'

'Why does that help us?' Milo asked.

Peters pulled over into a small, gritty rest area by the side of the road. It was edged by a crooked old wooden fence that had become almost completely consumed by bushes and brambles.

'Get out,' the Lieutenant said, as he climbed out of the car. He went to the trunk and took out a black duffle bag, then he slammed it shut.

Milo got out and grabbed hold of the towrope tied to Teddy's collar.

Becca lifted Sally out, and Brody came out, too. They all hauled their backpacks over their shoulders and then watched as Peters tore his way through some of the branches to the side of the rest area. He managed to unmask a small gap in the fence.

'After I buried your mom,' he said, 'I went back to the office and started looking through some of the Sheriff's old maps.'

With that, he disappeared through the gap.

'Come on!' he called from the other side.

Milo went first. He ducked under a thorny vine that dangled above the dark opening that Peters had cleared. He passed through the gap, and then, under the pale moonlight, he could see that the Lieutenant was standing on a train track. It lay perfectly hidden between two long, messy rows of bushes that stretched in either direction as far as the eye could see.

Milo tugged on the rope, and Teddy came through.

Becca followed closely, with Sally held in her arms, and
Brody wasn't far behind.

'I found that the line goes right past Masterson,' Peters
said. He stomped twice on the steel rail beneath his foot.
Then, he turned and pointed. '*That* is North. Travel that
way, and you'll reach the DLC and your uncle.'

Milo cracked a smile. Finally, he was beginning to feel
something he hadn't felt in weeks – something he thought
he may never feel again – *hope*.

'You might even come across one of the electric freight
carts if you're lucky,' Peters said. 'And you'll be even luckier
if it still has power.'

'Peters,' Milo said, 'I can't thank you enough.'

'*We* can't thank you enough,' Becca corrected.

Peters turned to Brody and held up the duffle bag.
'Think you can carry this?' he asked.

Brody grasped the handle.

'What's in it?' Becca asked.

'Food,' he said. 'As much as I could grab. There's a torch
in there, too. Try not to use it,' he said. 'You'll want to
conserve the batteries. The moon is bright tonight. Your
eyes should adjust, most of the time. But there's a tunnel en
route.'

Peters looked at the gun Milo was holding.

'That rifle will burn through its magazine in a blink,' he
said. He unclipped his holster and took out his handgun.
'Turn around,' he said. Milo did as instructed, and Peters
stuffed the gun into the pocket of Milo's backpack. 'Just in
case you need it.'

Peters stuck his hand out. Milo shook it.

'Good luck to you, Milo.'

'Thank you, Peters.'

What Happened Next

'I'll see you in the next life,' the Lieutenant said, with a sad little smile. 'Now, all of you, get on your way!'

Chapter 46
The Owl

'So why were you storming the Youth Station?' Denzel asked from the driver's seat while glancing in the rearview mirror.

Rex sat in the back. He was still tied up, but they'd taken the socks out of his mouth. His hair was stiff with dried blood.

'I came to break my girl out,' he said.

Denzel sighed. 'Then where is she?'

'Winters took her.'

Diaz, who sat in the passenger seat, reached back and looked Rex in the eye. 'Winters took my girl from me, too.'

'He does that a lot,' Rex said.

Diaz nodded. 'Fucking right. Well, we're going to kill him. But *boy*, are we gonna have some fun with him first!'

The car sped through Masterson.

'Where are we going?' Rex asked.

'Our Lieutenant seems to have forgotten that there are cameras all over town. We saw him pick up your little buddy, and he dropped them off in a rest area.'

Diaz spat into the footwell. 'Fucking traitor.'

'I don't believe it,' Denzel said. 'Look! He's still parked up there! Dumb fuck.'

They slowed to a stop next to Peters' car, which was still sitting in the gritty, overgrown rest area by the side of the road.

Peters was sitting on the hood, breathing in the cool night air and watching the tips of the bushes and trees. He'd been listening to an owl for the last twenty minutes, and he was trying to spot it.

He'd been on his way back to his car when he spotted the camera on the pole opposite the rest area. He knew it wouldn't be long until they turned up there, ready to take chase down the track.

Denzel killed the engine. Then, both he and Diaz flung open their doors and got out.

'Evening, boys,' Peters said.

'What the fuck are you doing, old man?' Diaz asked, pointing his gun. 'You helped them get away?'

'Killing children isn't going to bring her back,' he said. 'And it isn't what she'd want.'

'He's a murderer!' Diaz shouted. 'He shot her right in front of me. And I want blood. I want justice.'

'Milo didn't mean to kill her,' Peters said. 'He thought it was that vile, little dipshit in the back of your car.' He spied Rex through the glass.

'I'm going to kill him, Peters,' Diaz snarled.

'Listen to me.'

'No, you listen. I've listened plenty to you. Chambers was the love of my life. And Winters shot her. And then *you* helped him escape.'

'And killing a kid,' Peters started, 'is that what you signed up for?'

'Whatever I signed up for,' Diaz said, 'was dwarfed by

my love for that girl. Now she's dead. And we're going to get our justice.'

'Where are they?' Denzel asked. He looked past the car, at the gap in the bush.

'It doesn't matter,' Peters said. 'They're gone. And we have a smashed-up Youth Station we need to secure before we all punch our last tickets.'

'They can't have gotten far,' Diaz said.

'Come on,' Denzel said. 'Let's get after them.'

As they started to head for the gap, Peters slipped off the hood and landed on his boots in front of them. He held up his hands in a stopping gesture.

'I can't let you do that,' he said.

Denzel looked at Peters' empty holster. 'Well, you're unarmed, so you're shit out of luck.'

Peters put his hand on Denzel's chest and shoved him backwards.

'I really wouldn't do that,' Denzel warned.

'I'm not letting you hunt those kids down.'

'Peters, this is your last chance,' Denzel warned. 'Go back to the Youth Station.'

'I'm not going anywhere,' Peters said.

Denzel drew a deep breath, nodded softly to himself, and then he drew his gun. He shot Peters through the shin.

The Lieutenant tumbled to the gravel, screaming and clutching at his leg. Big chunks of splintered bones shifted under the skin, and blood showered down onto the ground. He howled until only a hiss of stale breath came out. His eyes streamed.

'Where are they headed?' Denzel asked.

The Lieutenant rolled onto his back, and let out frantic puffs of air. His eyes were clamped tightly shut, and his face was contorted in agony.

'Peters, where are they headed?' he repeated.

He fired the gun again. The bullet went into the Lieutenant's ribs, this time. A jet of blood spurted out. More agonized screaming echoed around the rest area and the track beyond. Peters opened his eyes and stared up into the night sky. He wheezed. The veins stood out in his neck. His face was purple. His cheeks were wet with sweat and tears.

'Where are they heading?' Denzel asked. He started to squeeze the trigger again.

Peters remembered something, suddenly. He reached for the pouch at the back of his belt.

Peters tried to steady his trembling hand. He pulled out a small, metallic device stuffed with sharpened pencils.

'What the fuck have you got there?' Denzel laughed.

'Looks like a pencil case,' Diaz said with a grin.

Peters twisted the bottom and tossed it towards their feet. It landed on its base, in the grit, with the sharpened pencil heads pointing up towards the night sky. The officers stared down at it in confusion as it ticked loudly. They both leant down to get a better look.

The heavy metal base of Brody's contraption snapped upwards in a thousandth of a second, and twenty pencils shot out in all directions, like the shrapnel of a nail bomb.

Two plunged into Denzel's thigh like rungs on a telephone pole. Another bore deep into the underside of his arm. His fingers shot open in pain, and his gun fell onto the ground.

A pencil pierced up into Diaz's face. It lodged itself between the flesh and his jawbone, bunching his cheek in a hump in front of his eye. Another burrowed into the fleshy pit where his groin met his leg.

'Fuck!' he whimpered. 'Fuck! Ah, fuck!'

He tried not to move. He could already feel the blood trickling down his inner thigh, and it was filling his boot.

Denzel looked down at his friend in horror. Together, they both lowered their gaze to Diaz's groin.

Diaz clutched at the pencil.

'Don't!' Denzel said.

But Diaz didn't listen. He yanked it out, unblocking the artery that it had torn straight through. A heavy waterfall of blood tumbled onto the ground. It washed away the grit, and filled the pot hole between Diaz's boots.

The Mexican dropped to his knees. The bloody puddle grew around him, fast. The rest area started to spin all around him. He looked at Peters, and then at Denzel, and then they vanished into the swirling, gray soup. Diaz slumped to the ground and slipped out of consciousness.

Denzel watched him go. Then he grunted, and tore the pencil from the underside of his arm with a quick tug. A little blood spurted out, and he winced. Then he looked down at his leg and saw the two rungs poking out. He clenched his teeth together, grabbed at one, and yanked it out. Then the other.

He looked around quickly for his gun. He spotted it lying in the grit by Peters' boots. He bent down and reached out for it. With the last of his strength, Peters kicked him hard in the face.

Denzel fell backwards, dazed, and the back of his skull clapped hard on a rock. He tried to sit up. But his body felt heavy. Too heavy to move a limb. And he felt tired. He looked across at Peters, who lay beside him, staring up at the sky, taking quick, frantic breaths.

Denzel tried to talk, but no words came. And then, he slipped out of consciousness, and into a deep, dark pool.

Peters wheezed. The pain was starting to numb now.

He could feel life beginning to get away from him. He grew more tired with each passing second. That long, good sleep was waiting for him.

He stared up at the sky. A beautiful white owl dove out of the bushes and took flight. It soared off into the night, with a long, low hoot.

As he slipped into the blackness, Peters thought about his wife, who was waiting for him at the foot of their farm. She'd been waiting a long time. And there was a dog waiting beside her.

Chapter 47
Water Unicorns

Something hooted, over to the right.

'What was that?' Milo asked.

'Just an owl,' Becca said, assuringly.

The moon was starting to sink towards the tree line now, and the sky was a pale shade of purple. Their eyes had all long adjusted. The track stretched away from them, straight and flat, and it was lined on either side by trees and bracken.

'Come on!' she said. 'It's your turn.'

Milo was carrying Sally now. She was sleeping fiercely, and her head bobbed from left to right with each clunky step.

Brody tagged along behind.

'What letter are we on?' Milo asked.

'M,' said Becca.

'Monkey,' he said.

'Brody, do you want to play yet?' Becca asked. 'An animal starting with N?'

'No,' Brody said.

'Alright. Hmm,' Becca said. 'Ah, okay. Narwhal.'

'What?' Milo laughed.

'Narwhal.'

'You can't make stuff up.'

'That's not made up. It's a – it's like a water unicorn.'

'A water unicorn?'

'It's like a big seal thing with a horn.'

Milo shook his head. 'I miss the internet. I could've looked that up.'

'That's not why you miss the internet,' Becca said, quietly.

Another hoot, off in the trees.

'What letter is it now?' Milo asked.

'Do you need to look up the alphabet, too? O.'

'O. Hmm. Octopus.'

'Penguin,' Becca replied.

'Q. There's no animal beginning with Q,' Milo said.

'There's got to be.'

'Well, there's probably a snake or something. Named after its discoverer. Qui–Quinnley Cobra.'

'Now who's making stuff up?'

Sally snorted air out of her nostrils but slept on.

Chapter 48
I'll Even Carry the Bag

T hudding. Continuous thudding.

Denzel stirred and opened his eyes. The sky above was a dull red now, and it painted everything around him in a fiery hue. Birds chirped merrily in the bushes.

The headache hit him like a shotgun blast. It felt like the worst hangover he'd had in years. He brought a shaky hand to the back of his head, where most of the pain was radiating from, and then found his fingertips coated in blood.

He looked around. Peters lay dead to one side of him. By his foot, Diaz lay dead, too. Both lay on beds of dried blood, which had sunken deep into the broken concrete beneath them.

That's when he heard the thudding. It was loud. It was what had roused him from his sleep. He got up onto his knees, steadied himself, and then stood weakly. He clung onto Peters' car to stop himself from toppling over.

He looked in the direction of the noise and saw two

boots slamming against the back window of the squad car, and he remembered his prisoner.

'Alright, alright,' he said, as he clambered over. He grabbed hold of the handle and pulled the door open.

The stench of urine hit him. He turned away in disgust.

'Jesus!' Rex shouted, 'I thought I was gonna die back here.'

'Not so loud,' Denzel said, wincing.

'Get me out of here! I've been lying here for hours!'

'Alright, alright. Keep your pissy panties on.'

Denzel grabbed Rex's ankles and pulled him most of the way out. Then he took him by the shoulders and stood him up.

Rex nearly tumbled over. His feet were completely numb, and his hands had turned purple from the bindings.

'Untie me! Please!' he pleaded.

Denzel dug a hand into his pocket and took out a pocket knife. He unfolded the blade and used it to saw through the rope that had been wound tightly around Rex's wrists. Once they were free, he moved down to his ankles and cut those loose, too.

'Thank fuck, thank fuck.' Rex groaned in pain. He marched lightly on the spot to try to get some blood back into his feet. Then he massaged his wrists in turn. 'Thought I was gonna cook alive back there once the sun comes up.'

He quickly examined the rest area and spotted the bodies that lay on the floor behind Peters' car.

'Your buddy dead?' he asked, looking down at Diaz.

'Yeah, so's the Lieutenant.'

Denzel stared off towards the gap in the hedge. He went to his trunk and opened it up. There was a backpack in there, which he quickly unzipped. He gathered up some loose cola cans that had been rolling around in the trunk for weeks, and he stuffed them inside. Then he took the torch from the emergency kit inside his spare wheel, along with some spare batteries, and he stuffed those inside, too.

'What are you doing?' Rex asked.

'I'm gonna get after them,' he said. 'They can't have gotten too far, with the little girl and the autistic.'

'I'm going with you,' Rex said.

'To hell you are! I suggest you go back to your clubhouse and stay away from the Youth Station.'

'Fuck no,' Rex said.

'Excuse me?'

'I'm going with you. I'll help you kill Winters.'

'I don't need your help, kid.'

'You don't need my help? Look at you – you're dripping blood all over the place, and you can hardly walk. And Winters – he's not as weak as he looks. He's outsmarted me before.'

That probably didn't take much, Denzel thought.

'I'll help you kill Winters. I want him dead as much as you.'

'Hmm.'

Rex snatched the backpack from Denzel's hands. 'I'll even carry the bag.'

'Fine. Whatever, kid,' Denzel gave in, with a sigh.

Rex hoisted the straps up over his shoulders. He followed Denzel over to the corpses.

Denzel picked up Diaz's gun and handed it to Rex. Then he picked up his own gun and put it back in its holster.

They passed through the gap in the hedge.

'Which way?' Denzel asked.

Rex looked left and then right.

'This way, I think,' he said.

'How do you know?'

Rex shrugged. 'A feeling.'

'Well, alright. But if you're wrong, I'll shoot you in the head.'

As they started down the line, a dark grin crept across Rex's face. Soon Milo would be dead, and Becca would be his.

Chapter 49
The Cart

The early morning light broke over the treetops that lined the track. Milo squinted into the sun. It was getting hot already, and it wasn't even seven a.m. yet.

His legs were stiff. His shoes grated harshly on the backs of his feet. He knew, when he eventually got round to peeling off his socks, that he'd find the skin would have scraped away completely.

Milo had tumbled off the track a couple of hours earlier. There was a branch that he hadn't seen in the dark. Now, his hip clicked painfully with each step.

Sally was awake now. She clung to Becca and looked around, bored.

'Walk,' she said, pointing to the ground. She was tired of being carried now, but Becca and Milo knew she'd walk too slowly, or she'd want to stop and examine rocks and twigs, and any litter that might have blown onto the track. It would just hold them up.

Teddy panted. Every so often, they'd set her bowl down

on the ground and would pour in some water. But her aging joints were sore, and her trot grew slower and lower to the ground.

Brody lumbered along at the back of the procession. He kept up the pace and didn't seem to be tiring. Becca kept making sure he had a sip of water or a bite of food every now and then.

Milo was trying to hide the pain in his hip, but Becca caught him wincing.

'Right, that's it,' she said. 'We're stopping and resting.'

'We can't,' Milo said. 'It's not safe out here. We just need to get there as fast as we can.'

'It's *days* of walking!' Becca said. 'An hour isn't going to make any difference.'

She stopped and set Sally down on the ground, much to the toddler's delight. Teddy started licking her little face, and Sally laughed.

Milo stopped, too. He looked at Becca's stern expression and realized she wasn't going to be persuaded otherwise.

'Alright,' he said. 'An hour.'

He lowered himself down onto the sleepers beneath the track and stretched his legs out in front. Becca sat beside him. Brody stood still, looking down at them.

'Brody, sit, please,' Becca said.

Brody got down onto the track next to them, and he crossed his legs.

Teddy lay down beside the track. The ballast shifted under her. Sally lay down with her and rested her head on the retriever's stomach as if she were a pillow.

Becca pulled her boots off and massaged the pads of her feet. They were numb.

Milo pretended to faint from the smell.

* * *

They sat and rested for a while. Sally made her way through a bag of cheese puffs. While she was stroking Teddy, the unicorn wristband slipped off her arm and tumbled into the ballast. She didn't notice.

The sun grew a little higher in the sky. Something shone further down the line and caught Milo's eye.

He stared down the track. There was a metal shape right ahead of them, glaring in the sun.

Quickly, he got to his feet, unzipped his pack, and pulled out the handgun that Peters had given him.

'Wait here!' he said, as he started to move down the line.

Before Becca could tell him to wait up so she could cover him with the rifle, he'd already gone.

Milo closed in quickly. The metal shape grew as he approached. He pointed the gun and watched closely for any signs of movement, but none came.

Sitting on the track in front of him was a large flat-bed cart, about the size of his father's Mamba. It had short, metal walls to the left and right, but none to the front and back, as they'd laid the timber across the cart while transporting wood to the DLC from the lumber yards. This one, thankfully, sat empty.

Milo climbed up onto the cart for a closer look. The sheet metal that formed the cart's flooring was heavily rusted, and it creaked as he stepped across it. Fixed to the right-hand wall was a little control panel. The controls looked simple enough. There was a power knob, a directional switch, and then a green button and a red button, which he presumed meant start and stop.

Milo looked up at the sky and whispered gently, 'Please, God, let there be power.'

He twisted the little knob, and there was a little whir, which Milo took to be a good sign. Then he turned the directional switch from forward to backward and hit the green button.

The rusted wheels screeched loudly. They hadn't spun in years. Slowly but surely, they started to turn. The cart crawled slowly in the direction Milo had come from. It wasn't fast, by any means, sitting at a steady seven or eight miles per hour. But it would mean they didn't have to walk, and with Milo's aching hip, that certainly felt like a godsend.

'My?' Becca called.

Milo looked towards her.

The cart was approaching her, Sally, Teddy and Brody. He hit the red button, but the cart kept on going.

'Ah, shit!'

He frantically jabbed at the button, but the cart wouldn't stop.

'My?' Becca called again.

She got to her feet. The cart trundled towards her.

'Brody, move!' she shouted, as she quickly bent down and picked Sally up, and ran down into the sidings. Teddy barked and then followed.

When Becca looked up, she saw Brody standing on the track as the cart came towards him.

Milo hit the red button again and again, but it was no use. The cart kept going forwards.

Becca set Sally down and sprinted back up onto the track. She grabbed at Brody's arm and tried to pull him away, but he was frozen, and he was unbudgeable.

Milo's eyes shifted to the power switch. He twisted it to 'Off,' and the power to the wheels cut, and the cart slowed to a halt, pressed up against Brody's chest.

Becca let out a sigh and rested her head onto Brody's shoulder.

'Brody,' she said.

'Yeah?'

'You have to do what I say, okay?'

'Yeah.'

'If I say run, you run. If I pull you, you come with me, okay?'

'Yeah.'

She wrapped her arms around his waist and held him tightly.

Milo jumped down from the cart.

'I'm sorry,' he said. 'That was stupid.'

'Yes, it was.' Becca snapped a harsh look at him. 'Put our packs on the cart! Then we'll get moving.'

'Yeah,' Milo said. 'Yeah, okay.'

He set all the packs up on the cart's rusted metal sheeting, along with the duffle bag Peters had given to Brody. Then he lifted Sally up, followed by Teddy. The two of them sat together, against the cart's short, metal wall.

Milo climbed up onto the cart next. He reached down and grabbed Brody's hand, and helped him aboard. Then he offered Becca his hand.

'I can do it myself,' she said.

She climbed up onto the cart and sat next to Brody.

'All ready?' Milo asked.

He twisted the directional switch the other way and then turned the power back on, and hit the green button. The wheels gave a screech again, and then the cart started to crawl back down the track, towards the DLC.

'Let's get some rest,' Becca said.

'I'll stay awake,' Milo said. 'Make sure we don't run into any debris.'

'Alright. Once I wake up, we'll switch.'

Becca rested her head back against the metal and closed her eyes.

Chapter 50
I Dream of Becca

enzel cracked open a soda and started to glug it
down.

'Can I have one?' Rex asked.

'Sorry, kid,' Denzel said. 'We've got to ration.'

Rex rolled his eyes. His throat was bone dry. His head
still pounded from where Milo had hit him with the fire
extinguisher, and his feet ached in his boots. They'd been
walking for hours.

The sun was high in the sky now. It was fast
approaching midday.

Denzel slurped the last of the soda out of the can,
crunched it up, and hurled it into the woods. He let out a
long belch, and then they started moving again.

Brandon would do that with his empty beer bottles, Rex
thought. He'd toss them off into the woods.

'I had two friends back there,' Rex said. 'At the Youth
Station.'

Denzel gave him an uneasy look. 'The ones you came in
with?'

'Yeah.'

'With the guns?'

'Yeah. Did you arrest them, too?'

Denzel looked glumly at the ground. 'You don't know?'

'Know what?'

'Kid, I'm sorry.'

Rex's stomach dropped. 'Sorry? Wuh–what do you mean?'

'You came into a building full of kids with guns. Diaz – he was trained for that. They didn't stand a chance against him. And if you'd come up against him, you'd be dead, too.'

The strength fell out of Rex's legs. His ass hit the track, hard. He sat on the rail, breathing unsteadily and staring absently at the ground.

'Aw, shit,' Denzel said, under his breath.

He reached into the backpack hanging from Rex's shoulders. It was still unzipped from where he'd taken out his soda. He dug out another can, popped it open, and put it into Rex's hand.

'Drink that, kid. The sugar helps with the shock.'

'I–I didn't say goodbye.'

'Drink it.'

Rex took a sip. Then another.

'They were dumb,' Rex said. 'But they were loyal. They did whatever I said.'

Denzel sat down beside him.

'Keep drinking, kid.'

Rex kept on slurping from the can. The more he drank, the less his hands shook.

'Was it quick?' Rex asked.

Denzel nodded. 'Head shots. Clean. Very quick.'

'That's... something.'

'If it helps, I'm hurting too.'

'The woman cop that Milo shot?' Rex asked. He figured

he best keep quiet about the fact he himself tossed a grenade at her just moments before that.

Denzel nodded. 'Her name was Chambers.'

'I thought she was the Mexican's girl?'

'They were together, yeah. But I knew her a hell of a lot longer. We grew up in a home together,' Denzel said. 'She was the closest thing I ever had to a sister.' A tear rolled down his cheek, and he quickly wiped it away. 'She used to take care of me. Hell, she still took care of me.'

He tucked his hand into his pocket and took out the little orange car.

'I was so scared as a kid,' Denzel said. 'And she looked after me. She made it so that I wasn't afraid anymore.'

Rex stared down the track. 'Yeah, I've got a girl like that.'

'The girl you shot up the Youth Station for?' Denzel asked.

Rex nodded. 'She's the only girl that was ever nice to me. And on my darkest day, when my uncle had just beaten the fuck out of me, and he'd given me this,' he pointed at the scar running through his lip, 'in front of the whole fucking school. And I was laying on the floor, in a puddle of my own piss. And everyone was howling with laughter or filming it – she was the only one that was nice to me. She told them to stop. She helped me up. She took me into the principal's office.

'Every single night, I relive those moments. Belt crashing down. Ripping me to shreds. Their dumb, little faces watching and laughing. And Becca swooping down, out of the haze like an angel. Saving me. Only in the dream, I say thank you. And I ask her out. And we date. And we go to the cinema. And we go to the beach. And she moves into my uncle's house. And we get married. And we have kids.

'Every night, I live this whole fucking lifetime together. And every morning, I wake up, and she's not lying there, next to me, and I feel like my heart is ripped out of my chest.'

Denzel watched him closely.

'I've got my uncle's house to myself now,' Rex said, 'back in Masterson. It's big. I've cleaned it top to bottom. Gonna bring her back there. And we'll live happily together, just like in the dream. And we'll have kids.'

This kid has lost it, Denzel thought. He half considered putting a bullet in his head. But he might come in handy once he caught up with Winters. He was outnumbered, after all.

'What's that?' Rex asked, spying something on the ground.

He leant down and picked something up from the stones between the sleepers. It was a little white wristband, with a plastic unicorn head glued to the front. A couple of feet away was an empty bag of cheesy puffs.

'They can't be too far ahead,' Denzel said, as he clambered to his feet. 'Not with the toddler. Come on! We can both grieve once this is done.'

Denzel helped Rex up. Rex finished off the soda, crushed the can, and tossed it off into the trees. It bounced off a trunk.

'Twenty points,' Rex said, under his breath.

They carried on marching down the track – the cop out in front, and Rex limping along behind.

* * *

Before long, the soda Denzel had drunk started to rumble in his gut. He tried to ignore it. He wanted to plough onwards.

279

There had been no further signs of the kids they were pursuing. He'd expected to come across a little camp site by now, with Milo sitting and toasting marshmallows over a fire. A little lamb, caught off-guard, ready for the slaughter. But the track ahead was empty as far as the eye could see.

'I gotta take a piss,' he said, defeated.

'Alright.'

Denzel stepped down off the track. He crossed the narrow strip of dead grass and walked into the woods. The ground was covered in creepers, all intercrossing and wound together. He had to pull his feet up high with each step so as not to trip.

He found a good tree to pee against – one with no stingers wrapped around the trunk. The last thing he needed out there in the middle of nowhere was a burning pecker.

As he stood, with his urine trickling down the bark face, he looked around. To his surprise, he spotted something. In a little clearing, set back from the track, covered in creepers, was an old hut.

Once he finished, he tucked himself back into his pants, pulled up his zipper, and stepped towards the hut. It was brick-walled and had a corrugated tin roof – not that you could see much of the brick *or* the tin. The whole structure was matted in ivy. It took him a moment to find the door, which was well hidden behind the shaggy hide of leaves.

He tried the handle. It was locked. He took a quick breath to prepare himself and then booted it through with one good kick. The pencil holes in his leg let out a little blood.

The door slammed hard against the inside wall, and dust shot out of the small space inside. When the mist cleared a little, Denzel peered in. A workbench sat against the far wall. It was laden with old woodworking tools, and a vice was clamped to its edge. A sign on the wall read, 'Measure twice, curse once.'

The room stank of varnish and gasoline.

Denzel's eyes sank to the enormous shape at his feet. Laying across the quarry tiles, and taking up most of the floor space in the hut, was a vast mass, covered mostly by a dust sheet. A tire poked out from under the cover. Pinned proudly at the center of the spokes was the emblem of a panther. It gazed up at the tin roof, fangs on show.

Denzel knew exactly what it was. Excitedly, he tore away the cover and stared down at the old Hellcat motorcycle that lay at his feet.

Chapter 51
Of Mountains and Tunnels

Becca found herself slouching against the wall, watching the track ahead in a bored daze. She'd switched with Milo an hour back. He slept soundly now beside Teddy and Sally.

There was no debris as of yet. The cart was passing into hillier terrain. The woods on either side rose and fell several times.

Then, to the right, the tree line pulled away from the track, and the ground fell into a steep, downward slope. Suddenly, with the pines out of the way, Becca could see it in all its glory – Mount Cheetle.

The mountain soared high over the forests that lined its foothills. It looked near-black against the bright sky, but its tip was snowy-white, and it poked into a crown of cottony clouds.

Becca was so struck by its beauty that she straightened out of her slouch. She thought about waking the others to show them, but they'd earned their rest, so she let them sleep.

A poster of Mount Cheetle hung in Mrs. Sanderson's

geography class, so she'd seen it a hundred times, but never in person. In person, it blew her away.

The cart trundled along. Soon the slope evened out again, the tree line returned to the trackside, and the pines blocked out that stunning view of the mountain as it faded into the horizon.

Becca slumped against the wall again with a sigh. She turned to face front, to watch for debris on the track ahead.

* * *

Another hour passed. Something fluttered past Becca, and it woke her from a daydream.

She looked over at the cart wall opposite to see a little robin sitting there. Belly red and full, eyes black and watchful. It looked around the cart, jerking its twitchy little head.

She smiled.

'Robins are visitors from beyond the grave,' her mom used to say, every time one landed in the garden.

'So, who are you?' Becca asked the robin softly. 'So many to choose from now.'

It looked at her and tilted its head. Then it fluttered off into the warm afternoon air.

Becca went back to looking at the track ahead.

The track turned a corner, and then suddenly, the cart passed into shadow. Looming above them was a great cliff face - near-vertical, with a few crevices and ledges high overhead. She had to crane her head right back to see the top.

Up ahead the track vanished into a black opening in the rockface - a large, hungry mouth framed with an archway of brickwork, and the cart was heading right for it. It was the tunnel Peters had told them about.

Becca reached for the duffle bag, unzipped it, and took out the flashlight. She held it close, ready to click it into life. She wasn't scared of the dark, but there could be all sorts of debris or rubble lying in that tunnel, waiting to derail the cart.

She looked down at Brody and Sally, who still slept soundly, and she prayed that it stayed that way. They would both break into panic attacks if they knew what they were about to drive through.

The cliff face grew taller above them as they approached, and the tunnel mouth grew larger and darker, and hungrier. Finally, they passed into it.

Total darkness. Becca clicked the button on the side of the torch, and a ray of white light shot out of the end. She pointed it at the track ahead of the cart.

The torch light was swallowed up by the darkness, and the glow it *did* manage to cast stopped dead a couple of meters ahead of the cart. Becca wished there was a speed setting, but there wasn't. Just 'go' and 'don't go'.

The tunnel walls arched up around her. They were made of great blocks of black stone. Water trickled down their faces and formed large, deep puddles on the ground that all bled into one another.

There was no glint of light ahead, so either the tunnel was extraordinarily long or it had become blocked off. Perhaps there had been a collapse somewhere in the middle, these last couple of years. Becca hoped not.

A heavy, stale stench lingered in the tunnel.

The cart shook as its wheels went over some rocks on the line, and a loud, crunching sound echoed down the tunnel.

Milo stirred. When he opened his eyes, he saw nothing but darkness. He sat up, panicked.

'What the–? Is it – is it nighttime... already?'

'Shh! You'll wake the others.'

Becca's eyes were fixed on the dim glow out in front. Her hand was clasped to the power dial, ready to turn it at a second's notice if some obstacle advanced quickly out of the darkness.

Milo could see the bricks now. The walls curved up around the track and met above his head.

'It stinks,' he said.

'I know. I've been breathing through my mouth.'

They both stared ahead, down the line. Finally, a small speck of bright, white light appeared in the distance.

'It's the end!' Becca said. 'It's clear!' She breathed a sigh of relief.

'What's that sound?' Milo asked.

Becca listened. She could only hear the rumbling of the cart's wheels.

'I don't hear anything.'

Milo listened hard again. He was sure he'd heard something. Some high sound. A screeching, perhaps. But it was gone now.

'Maybe it was nothing,' he said.

Slowly, the speck of light grew into a white semicircle as the cart trudged along.

'So, what do you think he'll say when we get there?' Becca asked.

'Huh?'

'Your uncle. What do you think he'll say?'

'I don't know. But he'll be happy to see us.'

'Even Brody?'

Malcolm's words, '*This mute little dipshit is good for something after all,*' rang through Becca's mind. It often rang through her mind, in fact.

285

Milo shifted uncomfortably.

'He was impressed with what Brody had built,' he said. 'He's just not very - PC. He didn't mean to upset your family. I bet he felt bad about it.'

'Uh-huh.'

'He's not a bad guy, Becca.'

'Hey, be quiet!' she said.

'No, really, he's not a bad guy.'

'Okay, okay, but be quiet! I heard something.'

They both listened. A screeching sound echoed down the tunnel. It sounded like a rodent shrieking in pain.

Becca looked up.

'Rats, you think?' Milo asked.

Becca pointed upwards, and she lifted the torch. 'It's not rats.'

Milo raised his glance. The top of the tunnel, over their heads, was filled with what looked like cocoa pods. Hundreds of them crammed in, shoulder to shoulder, hanging from their little stalks. Only when he looked a little closer, they were fleshy. And hairy. And they were starting to move.

'Oh, god.'

The bats stirred from their slumber. Their wings started to unfold. Their ears untucked. Their mouths hissed and screeched; saliva stretching in silky threads between their spiked teeth.

They started to dive down from the brickwork and beat their wings. The entire tunnel was suddenly alive. One solid, writhing, fluttering mass of fur and wing.

Becca and Milo lay flat on the cart and covered the backs of their heads with their hands.

Teddy barked and jumped up, trying to grab hold of one of the bats as they twirled and dove all around.

What Happened Next

Becca reached up and pulled her down to the cart's bed. 'Shh, girl! Shh!'

The commotion woke Sally. She looked up, saw the nightmarish storm cloud of giant, screeching creatures that churned in the air above her head, and she screamed.

Milo grabbed her and held her to his chest.

'It's okay!' he said. 'It's okay!'

She screamed and kicked, but he held on tightly.

Becca glared over at Brody. She could just about make out his shape in the dim glow from the torch, which had clattered somewhere into the bed of the cart. He lay still and seemed to still be asleep.

The white arch ahead grew, and as they approached the daylight, the mass of bats thinned out until finally, they were all behind them.

The cart exited the tunnel. The sunlight filled their eyes, and it burned like bleach. They clasped their arms over their faces to block it out, and they lay on their backs, exhausted, as the cart shunted further down the track.

Chapter 52
It Came from the Woods

Brody woke. He looked around the cart. It was stationary and empty, aside from the packs and the little, black pellets the bats had dropped. He climbed to his feet and peered over the cart's wall.

Teddy was tied to a tree down by the mouth of the forest. She wagged her tail as he looked at her.

Milo walked out of the woods, zipping up his fly.

'Hi, sleepyhead,' he said.

Brody yawned. 'Becca,' he said.

'We've stopped for a pee break. Do you need to go?'

Brody stared at him blankly.

'Do you need to pee? Urinate?'

Brody said nothing.

'Brody, go and pee!' Becca said, as she stepped out of the trees, holding Sally's hand.

Brody jumped down off the cart. He wandered slowly into the forest.

'Will he ever listen to me?' Milo asked.

'Maybe in a few years.' Becca laughed, gently. 'You've got bat crap in your hair.'

Milo ruffled it. 'Is it gone?'

Becca picked it out for him and wiped her hand on his shirt.

'How much further is it, do you think?' she asked.

Milo went to the duffle bag and took out the map. He ran his finger along the trainline.

'There's the tunnel. That was a couple of hours back. So I'd say we're about *here.*'

He pointed to a spot beside a crosshatched area marked, *'Anderson Bear Reservation'.*

'And the DLC is *there.* We're close. Just hope the battery lasts.'

He folded the map and tucked it away.

'Did she go okay?' Milo asked, shifting his eyes to Sally.

'Yeah, had to hold her up, but she went.'

Milo knelt next to his sister.

'Do you know who we're going to meet?' he asked.

Sally shook her head.

'We're going to meet your Uncle Malc. You've never met him before. That's daddy's brother. Like I'm your brother, that's daddy's brother.'

'Dadda,' she said.

Milo nodded. 'Yeah. Uncle Malc – he's gonna help us. He's gonna help all of us. We'll go find a nice, big house somewhere. And he'll keep us safe. And we'll – we'll grow veg, raise chickens, pigs, live off the land. He's a real man's man. Knows how to do all of that. And we'll all be okay.' He smiled. 'We'll all be okay.'

Brody came out of the woods, tugging at his zipper.

'Back on the cart!' Becca said, as she untied Teddy from the tree.

Milo lifted Sally and the dog aboard. Then he climbed up and helped Becca and Brody up, too.

'My turn to drive,' Milo said.

Becca sat herself down. Sally came and laid down on her. Teddy nestled down by their side. Brody sat apart from them, with his fingers laced together in his lap.

Milo started up the cart, and it began to crawl down the track.

* * *

Twenty minutes later, Milo knelt, with his arms folded over the short, metal wall that sided the cart. His chin was nestled on top of his forearms. He was staring into the trees as they slowly crawled by. Something was moving behind the tree line. It seemed to be following the cart.

Becca sat, watching him. Sally had drifted off to sleep and now lay on top of Teddy, so Becca crawled over and rested against the wall, beside Milo.

'You alright?' she asked.

He didn't acknowledge her. His eyes were fixed on the trees.

'My?' she asked. 'You with me?'

'Sorry,' he said, suddenly. 'I thought I saw... Uh, it doesn't matter.'

Becca turned her head and looked at the track.

'Stop the cart!' she shouted.

'What?'

Becca twisted the dial, and the power cut off. The cart slowed to a halt.

They both got to their feet and stared ahead.

A few meters in front of the cart, laying across the track, was an enormous branch. It was jagged at one end, where the limb had torn free from the body. It had fallen from one of the vast trees that towered over them on the left-hand side.

'Shit!' Milo said, as he jumped down onto the track.

Becca climbed down behind him.

They walked along to the branch. It was long and thick, and it looked heavy as hell.

'I think we can shift it,' Milo said. 'If we drag it, rather than lift it. Do you think Brody could help?'

'Brody, come here, please!' Becca shouted.

No answer.

'Brody, we need your help, please!' she tried again.

No movement nor response.

'Apparently not,' she said.

'Right, let's try it, the two of us. Grab this end!' Milo said, as he clutched the thick arm in his hands. Becca came over and grabbed it a little further along.

Together, they pulled as hard as they could. The branch started to move slowly. It grumbled as its rough skin scraped across the rail.

Sally screamed, suddenly. Teddy barked furiously.

Milo and Becca both unhanded the branch and stared back towards the cart. Their stomachs sank instantly.

A grizzly bear had charged out of the woods. It climbed the small rise onto the track and was now bounding towards the cart – a vast, unrelenting mound of muscle and fur. For something so large, it moved unnaturally quickly. Ballast spat up into the air with each slam of its great paws.

It was at the cart in a heartbeat. Once it was at the cart's ledge, it stood up on its hind legs. It loomed high over Sally and Brody, who stared up in horror. Teddy barked wildly. Paws planted out in front, back arched, heckles up along her spine.

The bear sniffed at the air, and its eyes quickly scanned over the cart, assessing which of the three meals in front of it would be the easiest to drag back to its cub, which waited hungrily in the forest. It pounded one paw down onto the metal bed of the cart and then reached for Sally with its other.

Teddy bowled in front of her in a flash and barked harder now. Her gums were peeled back, and her teeth were on show. Great strings of saliva flew out of her mouth with each hard, low bark.

Sally tumbled onto her back. Her jelly shoes flew off her feet and hit the cart wall. She howled in terror - face red, eyes tightly shut.

The bear retracted its paw, and then it let out an ear-piercing, bone-rattling growl.

'Ho-holy shit. What do we do?' Milo asked.

Becca's eyes were fixed on the duffle bag. The bear was attacking the cart from the other side. She was sure she could get to the bag, pull the gun out, and put one in its eye before it had snatched away Sally or her brother.

'I'm going for the gun,' she said.

She went to make a run for it, but Milo grabbed her arm.

'Are you crazy?' Milo asked. 'No sudden movements. It'll freak out.'

Teddy barked, still. The bear swiped at her. Its long, sharp claws slashed across her snout, and she let out a terrible yelp. Blood drummed down onto the metal bed below, but she stood her ground, with her paws planted firmly in front of Sally. Her guardian.

Beside them, hunched up against the wall of the cart, Brody reached for his pack. He lifted it up onto his lap, and as fast as he could, he tugged at the zip.

The bear grunted. It studied the golden retriever. Its

eyes were like two black coals. Then, it raised its paw, ready for another strike.

Brody pulled something out of his pack. It was crude and clunky and metal, and so heavy that he had to grip it in both hands. In a flash, he clambered to his feet, pointed it towards the bear, and pulled a little lever on the underside. A long metal bolt shot out of the tip of the crossbow, and it plunged deep into the bear's left eye.

Milky goo oozed down its snout, and it roared in pain. The beast stood up again, and then it moved backwards, and crashed back down onto all fours, on the ground, yelping and moving around in frantic circles.

Becca and Milo darted towards the cart. But Milo didn't make it more than five strides before he'd tripped over his own feet and had tumbled off the track. Becca didn't stop for him. She kept on running, as fast as she could. She climbed onto the cart and stood Sally up. She looked her over, quickly.

'Are you okay, baby? Are you okay?'

Sally was still crying hysterically.

Becca reached for the duffle bag, unzipped it, and rummaged around inside for the rifle.

Brody looked down at her, with a little smirk. He was holding his crossbow proudly.

'Good shot, Brody,' Becca said. She pulled the rifle strap up over her shoulder. 'I'll be back in a minute, okay? Can you watch Sally for me?'

Brody nodded.

A hundred meters down the track, a Hellcat motorcycle was tearing down the railway siding, throwing up a cloud of dust and dead grass in its wake. Denzel was manning the handlebars, whilst Rex sat on the back, grasping the saddle for dear life with fingers that had turned white.

'Woah, shit!' Denzel said, suddenly, as he caught sight of the bear up ahead. He squeezed on the brakes. The bike slowed to a stop, and he touched his boots down. From a short distance, they watched as the bear turned this way and that, stomping around heavily on its great paws, growling and snarling, and yelping all at once.

'Well, looks like that big, old grizzly is gonna do the job for us,' Denzel laughed, as he watched Becca step towards the bear, gun raised.

She brought her eye to the sight-piece, aimed at the bear's skull, and pulled the trigger. But nothing happened. No deadly spray of bullets. There was just an empty clicking sound.

Quickly, she fumbled around, looking for the safety catch. But it was too late. The bear was bounding towards her, fast and mad.

'Becca!' Rex shouted. He got off the back of the bike and ran towards the bear.

'Kid, don't!' Denzel called after him. 'You'll get yourself killed!'

Rex wasn't listening. He pulled the handgun out of the back of his pants and fired. The first couple of shots hit the ground and sent gravel spitting up into the air. But his final shot bore into the bear's rear leg.

The grizzly arched its head towards the sky and let out another long, monstrous roar. Then it turned sharply to face Rex, and it charged.

It bowled him over in an instant. Rex fell onto the ground like a ragdoll, and the vast beast ran over him – its weight bearing down. Once it had passed, it stopped, circled back, and started running back for Rex's crumpled, beaten body.

Four gunshots rang out.

Denzel had unloaded his gun. Four bullets, and then it clicked empty. Each of the shots tore into the grizzly's torso, and it stopped its charge. Blood dripped out of the wounds. It didn't drop, though. It stood, breathing deeply and whining a little. Then it turned to face Denzel, and it came at him fast. Its paws thundered across the ground.

It was on top of him in a second, clawing at his chest and face. Its claws ripped through his shirt like hot daggers through butter. Denzel screamed as they tore into his flesh.

A quick, rapid burst of gunfire rang out. Becca stood beside the bear, with smoke wafting from the barrel of the rifle. She'd found the safety catch.

The grizzly stood perfectly still for a few moments, with the metal bolt protruding from its eye socket, goo pouring off its snout, and blood oozing from the new, gaping hole in the side of its skull. Then it collapsed sideways, crashed hard onto the ballast, and was dead.

Milo climbed back up onto the track. He was winded, and he wheezed and huffed as he limped down the line.

Sally sat in the cart, crying hysterically. Milo picked her up and held her close to his chest. As he bobbed her up and down, trying to soothe her, he reached out and stroked Teddy's snout, which was still dripping blood.

'Good girl,' he said. 'Good girl!'

He shifted his gaze to Brody, who now sat with his crossbow in his lap.

'Thank you, Brody.'

Brody said nothing.

Milo stepped over to Becca, who was standing between Rex and Denzel. They both lay on the ground, groaning in pain and drifting in and out of consciousness. She still clutched the rifle tightly in both hands.

'Rex?' Milo asked, looking down at him. 'What the hell are you doing here?'

'He was coming for me,' Becca said. 'He'll *never* stop coming.'

Milo walked over to Denzel. 'And *he* was coming for me.'

'What are we gonna do with them?' Becca asked.

'There's a hospital at the DLC. According to the ad, at least,' Milo said. He'd seen it enough times between episodes of Marnie Moose. 'We should take them there.'

'Hmm.'

'*Hmm?*'

'We could just put them out of their misery out here,' Becca said, as she gripped the rifle a little tighter.

Milo frowned. 'That ain't us. You do that – you're no different to them.'

Becca looked down at Rex. His pained eyes fixed onto her, and he tried to speak, but he couldn't. His ankle was snapped, and his shoulder was out of place, and a few of his ribs had cracked too, no doubt, from where the bear had bulldozered over him.

She switched her gaze to Denzel, who lay in a puddle of blood. The bear had clawed his face and chest, and arms, and it had trampled his legs, too.

Denzel's eyes opened suddenly, and he spat out some blood. He let out an agonized groan.

'Look at him,' Milo said. 'He's no harm to us now. Let's take him to the DLC.'

'DLC?' Denzel whispered. Then he muttered some inaudible words.

'What was that?' Becca asked.

He muttered them again. Becca went and crouched beside him.

'What are you saying? I can't hear you.'

He whispered. She brought her ear closer to his mouth so she could listen clearly. Then, he passed out again.

Becca stood back up, with a worried look on her face.

'What did he say?' Milo asked.

She gave him a grave look.

'It's nothing,' she said. 'Just crazy talk, from the pain.'

She glanced up at the sky. It was beginning to turn orange. They had a couple of hours before nightfall, at most.

'Alright, we'll take them with us,' she said, decidedly. 'Let's get them on the cart. I want to get there before dark.'

Chapter 53
The DLC

The cart kept slowing to a near halt, but then it would plow forwards again at top speed. Milo put it down to the battery being almost empty. Each time it slowed, he was sure that would be the last of the juice, but to his delight, it always got going again.

Rex and Denzel sat huddled at one end of the cart. Milo had used Teddy's rope to tie their wrists together. Not that he thought he needed to - they were so injured and bent out of shape. Becca insisted on it, though, just to be doubly safe. She'd also stuffed a shirt into Rex's mouth to keep him from talking.

Denzel had been unconscious the whole time he'd been in the cart. There was a big puddle of blood underneath him now, and it seeped through the cracks in the metal sheeting and dripped down onto the track.

Rex was awake. He watched Becca with distant, broken eyes. She didn't look at him. She sat at the other end of the cart, as far away as she could get, with Sally on her lap, Teddy to one side, and Brody to the other.

Milo knelt in the center of the cart, next to the control panel. He watched the track ahead.

The sky was red now. The sun was starting to sink towards the ground.

'There it is!' Milo shouted, suddenly.

Becca looked up. Rex snapped his head around to look, too.

In the distance, a vast, metal wall grew out of the horizon. It stood twenty meters tall and one hundred across. Embedded in the wall were a pair of towering gates.

'We made it!' Becca said softly, eyes aglow. Sally clung onto her tightly.

The cart approached the end of the track. A big wooden buffer stood at the end.

Milo twisted the power dial, and the cart slowed to a stop a few feet short of the buffer. He jumped down and stared up at the gates.

'How the hell are we going to get those open?' he asked, as he stepped towards them.

Becca jumped down off the cart, and she lifted Sally down onto the ground. Teddy barked. Becca lifted the old retriever down next. She sniffed the ground with her bloodied snout, moving in little circles, with her tail wagging in tow.

'Brody, come on,' Becca said. She didn't want to leave him on the cart with those two. Not for a moment.

Brody pulled his backpack up onto his shoulders and followed them over to the gates.

Becca stared up at the top of the gates. They were truly enormous.

'They must weigh a few tons each,' Milo said. 'I thought maybe we could tie them to the cart and stick it in reverse, but there's no way. It'll never budge them.'

Brody walked up to a metal box that stood beside the gates, took off the front panel, and started to fiddle with the wiring inside. There was a great hiss from the hydraulic pipes that sat on each of the hinges the whole way up both gates, and then a series of metallic clunks sounded as the rusted, metal locking bolts slid out of their pockets. Then, with a whir, the enormous gates started to part.

Milo stepped backwards so that the vast doors didn't swipe him clean off his feet.

An alarm started, suddenly – a high-pitched beep that rose and fell every couple of seconds.

The doors slammed against their buffers and stopped, now fully ajar, and the travelers peered into the DLC for the first time.

The ground was carpeted in grass, painted orange by the sinking sun. The buildings were all wooden-clad and a uniform white. Twenty or so larger buildings stood towards the right-hand side of the site. Among them stood a chapel with a black crucifix fixed to the spire. Then, scattered along the opposing side, were a thousand or more single-story wooden chalets of varying sizes. They all had slanting, gray felt roofs and white wooden walls.

Becca smiled. She'd never seen such a beautiful, idyllic little community.

In the distance, on the far side of the site, a great lake shone red under the sunset. Beyond that, crop fields quivered gently in the evening breeze. To the right of the fields sat chicken pens and pig houses. In the furthest corner stood a tall metal barn.

This beautiful moment was spoiled, though, by the piercing alarm that had started when they'd opened the gates. It sounded from speakers pinned at the top of tall posts that were dotted around the site.

What Happened Next

'Can you kill that?' Becca asked her brother.

Brody started fiddling with the wires again. The alarm ceased, and the DLC fell into silence.

The doors to the various buildings came open, and out hurried masses of concerned faces. Some came out in families. Some came out alone.

In moments, hundreds had gathered in front of the open gates, while many more rushed over from the buildings that were further afield. They chattered excitedly among themselves as they came.

'It's open!'

'The gate! Look at the gate!'

'Who the hell are these guys?'

'Are they letting us out? Did congress overturn it?'

A tall man in a plaid shirt made his way through the crowd. The people parted for him as he came. He was in his early forties, and he had an air of authority about him. He had a thick, black beard, and his hair was thinning up on top.

'Who *are* you kids?' he asked. 'How did you get the gate open?'

'I'm here to see my uncle,' Milo said.

'Who's your uncle?'

'Malcolm Winters.'

Shocked whispers rang through the crowd.

'You're Malcolm Winters' nephew? You traveled here? From Masterson?'

'I did. *We* did. Is he – is he alive?'

The man laughed. 'Oh, he's alive.' He turned to a young man that stood behind him in the crowd. 'Go and get the High Eagle!'

The young man nodded and then disappeared through the masses.

'My name is Joey,' the tall man said. 'I'm second-in-charge here.'

'Who's first?' Becca asked.

'You're about to meet him,' Joey said.

'Out of the way!' a gruff voice shouted, from deep inside the crowd. 'Come on, out of the way!'

The people shuffled left and right quickly, creating a gap, like the sea that parted for Moses. Standing at the end of the crack was a face that Milo hadn't seen in years. A face he'd been desperate to see.

'Milo? Is that – is that really you?'

Malcolm came hurrying down the narrow parting in the crowd. He was shorter than Dallas and not so well-built. He had dark stubble, peppered with grays, and long, black hair that he slicked back with a comb. He wore dark jeans and a denim shirt, and clunky, black boots.

'It's me, Uncle Malc! It's me!'

Milo felt his knees faltering. He could barely stand. Malcolm bounded over and picked him up into a bear hug.

'I can't believe it's you!' Malcolm said. 'I can't believe it!'

Malcolm set him down.

'What are you doing here? Where's – where's your old man?'

He stared over Milo's head, through the gate, at the cart and the track.

Milo lowered his head.

'Ah, god,' Malcolm said, gently, as he held his hand up to his face. 'What happened, squirt?'

'It's the Lavitika vaccine,' Becca said. 'It killed them all.'

The crowd whispered to each other frantically. Some sobbed, thinking of their loved ones back home – the ones that hadn't listened to them. The ones that they hadn't managed to convince with their placards and their sprawling social media rants.

Malcolm crouched down and planted his ass on the ground. He sat, breathing deeply and trying to process it all. He remembered the last phone call he had with his brother. He begged him not to get the jab. Begged him.

Finally, he looked up at his nephew from his patch on the ground.

'Why aren't you in the Youth Station?' Malcolm asked.

'It's a long story,' Milo said. 'Wait, how do you know about Youth Stations?'

'Is this the lovely Becca?' Malcolm asked, quickly clambering to his feet.

Becca gave him an unimpressed look.

'Of course, it is!' he laughed. 'I'd know that scowl anywhere. You're turning into quite the young lady.' His eyes shifted to Brody. 'And look, it's the little engineer!'

'Brody got the gates open,' Milo said.

Malcolm looked up at the gates. 'Really? Jesus! Thanks, kid!'

He put his hand out for Brody to shake, but the boy just stared.

'Right, yeah, sorry, I forgot,' Malcolm said.

Next, his eyes landed on Sally, and they glittered with love.

'And this is my little niece, I'm assuming.'

'Sally,' Milo said.

Malcolm picked her up and gave her a big, toothy smile. 'Hello, darling! I'm your Uncle Malc.'

Sally started to cry.

'Hey, hey! Don't cry, darling. It's alright. I'm your uncle.'

She cried harder still. Malcolm handed her to Milo.

'Sorry, she just – she doesn't know you yet,' Milo said.

'She will,' Malcolm said. 'She will.' He looked down at Teddy, who sat by Milo's feet. 'Who's this little mutt? Jeez, he's all covered in blood.'

'You remember Teddy, don't you? My gran and grandpa's dog.'

Malcolm leant down to pet her. Teddy growled, so he recoiled.

'Sorry, she's usually friendly.'

'That's alright, kid. We'll get her cleaned up.'

Malcolm looked over at the two bodies that lay on the cart.

'And who are your guests?' he asked, stepping out, towards them. Then, in disgust, he asked, 'Is that – is that a–?'

'It's a cop, yeah,' Milo said. 'He's called Denzel.'

'He's dangerous,' Becca said. 'They both are.'

'What happened to 'em?'

'We were attacked by a bear,' Milo said. 'It got these two pretty bad.'

'A bear? Fucking hell. How'd you fight that off?'

'Brody shot it in the eye with a crossbow. Then Becca finished it off with the rifle.'

Malcolm grinned devilishly. 'Badass! What did *you* do?'

Milo shifted his feet uncomfortably. 'I, uh, I fell over.'

Malcolm laughed. 'We'll have to man you up a little, won't we?'

Milo had heard that before.

'And who is that on the cart beside him?'

'That's Rex,' Becca said.

'*Rex*? What kind of fucking name is that? He got a dinosaur fetish or something?'

'His real name is Richard,' Milo said. 'Richard Lachance.'

Malcolm let out a loud, excitable laugh. *'Richard Lachance?'*

He stepped closer to get a better look at him. Rex stared up at him – the shirt still stuffed in his mouth, puffing his cheeks out like a hamster.

'You've got the eyes,' Malcolm said, quietly, as he stared into them.

He reached forward and took out the shirt. Rex spat out some lint.

'Do I... know you?' Rex asked. Malcolm's face seemed familiar. As if he'd seen him in some distant, long-forgotten dream.

'You used to,' Malcolm said. 'And you will again.'

Malcolm looked over at Joey and yelled, 'Get these guys to the hospital! Now!'

Joey clicked his fingers, and a few young, bald-headed men ran over to the cart. They carried Rex and Denzel through the gates. The crowd opened up to let them through. A long line of blood trailed behind the cop.

Becca looked over the faces of the crowd that had amassed in front of the gates. She frowned. Something seemed odd about them. It was like something was missing, but she couldn't put her finger on it.

'Now,' Malcolm said, as he looked over the four young faces in front of the gates. 'You all look like you need to freshen up some. You've come a *long* way.'

'Thank you,' Milo said. 'I think we need that.'

'Sheila?' Malcolm called into the crowd.

A short, stocky woman in a floral dress came forwards. Her hair was knotted into a bun.

'Yes, High Eagle?' she asked. She had a gruff smoker's voice.

'This is Joey's wife,' Malcolm explained to the four young travelers. 'Sheila, find a chalet for our guests, would you?' he said.

'Yes, High Eagle!' Sheila said. 'Come on, kids!'

'Oh, and welcome to Rosewood!' Malcolm shouted at them, as they followed Sheila through the crowd.

Joey stepped over to Malcolm.

'That Rex kid,' Joey asked, quietly. 'That who I think it is?'

Malcolm nodded. He looked up at the sky, exhaled, and said, 'God has brought him home.'

Epilogue

C hambers was nine years old.

She wore a long, gray dress that danced around her ankles as she walked. Her cheeks were dotted with freckles, and her hair was tied back in a ponytail.

She stepped down the long, dark hallway of Miss Moltez's Home for Children. Warm light beamed out of the doorway at the end. It was the entrance to the kitchen.

Steam drifted softly out from the room, and she could hear the chiming of a spoon in a pot.

'Miss Moltez?' she asked, as she stepped into the kitchen.

'Hello, Chef Two,' the old woman said with a smile. 'I was wondering when you'd turn up.'

Miss Moltez wore a long, black dress. Her hair was a huge, black beehive, and she had a crook in her back.

She stood at the stove, stirring a pot of soup.

'I haven't seen you in so long,' Chambers said, tearfully.

The young girl looked around the room. The dinner table was empty. It was just the two of them.

'Where is everyone?' she asked.

As if on cue, laughter came from across the hallway. Chambers looked over at the door to the living room. It was closed, but the cracks around it glowed warmly.

She could hear Denzel's muffled voice on the other side of it, telling tall tales and cracking jokes while the other children giggled and clapped.

'Can I join the others?' Chambers asked.

'You're not ready to join them yet,' Miss Moltez said. 'There are people that need your help.'

* * *

Chambers' eyes parted, suddenly. She sat up and looked around the room in a panic.

She checked herself over. Her arms and hands were fully grown. She was an adult again. It had just been a dream.

She took in her surroundings. She lay in a hospital bed, with a drip running into her arm. A monitor beeped next to her. Her chest was wound tightly in bandages.

She felt dizzy, and her head felt heavy.

'H–hello?' she called.

Her hearing had come back, for the most part, and she could hear her own words and the beeping of the little metal box that stood by her bedside.

She tried desperately to remember what had happened.

'Hello?' she called again. 'Is anyone there?'

A Word from the Author

Dear reader,

Thank you for reading my little story.

If you enjoyed it, I'd really appreciate it if you could take a minute to leave a review.

What happens next?

If you're interested in finding out what happens to Milo and Becca next, you can keep up to date with upcoming books and new releases here:

theworldofjoncolt.com

Thank you, and I'll hopefully see you next time,

Jon